After the End

The Archive of Ink and Soul, Book One

Patricia Thomas

Cover Design: Katzilla Designs
Edited by: Fading Street
Junior Editor: Stephanie Winter, with assistance from Abi
Pearson

For my daily writing buddies.
You know who you are. You know how much you've done.
I will be forever grateful.

AFTER THE END
THE ARCHIVE OF INK AND SOUL,
BOOK ONE

CHAPTER ONE

Kadence "Kadie" Meyer,
Welcome to the After. Please remain calm.

*This next revelation will come as something of a shock. You have
arrived in the After from whatever land you once called home because
your author has claimed the work you exist in is complete.*

*You are a fictional character, and your story is over. There is no
longer any need for you to propel your plot forward, so you have
arrived here to continue your existence among those who also started
their journeys in a novel or book series. We apologize for having to
get you up to speed in this manner, but with the nature of the modern
literary landscape there is no other way to keep up with each day's
new arrivals.*

*You are among friends—unless of course you have an arch
nemesis or the like who has also come here.*

Everything will be fine.

*More than likely, you'll find this news alarming, and may even
have doubts. But you will find that if you search deep within yourself,
you will understand this information to be true. Again, there is
nothing to worry about, and no need for panic. Should you follow the
system the After has in place, you will continue to the next chapter of
your life quite seamlessly.*

It will all be okay.

After the end of a story, each character arrives in a city most like the world they came from. In all likelihood, any friends and family that were part of your story will have also travelled to the same place should you wish to seek them out. You now have two choices.

The first is that you simply return to your story of origin through one of the many Reclamation Centers throughout this world. All knowledge you have gained since arriving in the After will be immediately forgotten so you may relive your story each time it is read, experiencing it anew with each new telling. You will never grow or change and all will be as it was. There is no shame in choosing this option as we each have a different path to follow and only you can decide what will truly make you happy. Perhaps you have already found happiness, and by bringing you here you have been ripped away from that reality. If that is the case, the choice before you may be an easy one.

The second option, should you prefer not to return to your origin story, is to remain here so that you can continue to develop yourself, creating a life and existence outside of what was written for you. The After is vast, so the possibilities are endless. Each decision you make will be your own as will the life you forge from this point onward. The people of our world all started out in the same position you are in now, and the world we have created will be yours to discover and shape.

You do not have to decide right away. Citizens of the After are free to return to their stories at any time, but the choice cannot be undone. You will not be able to come here again.

No matter what you decide, there are people here to help you—to answer questions, guide you to the nearest Reclamation facility, or get you started in your new life.

We wish you nothing but the best of luck.
The Librarians of the After

My gut was churning, rocked by a jumble of emotions as my eyes scanned the letter again, and again. But each time I took it in, the message was unchanged; just as incredible and unbelievable as when I first read it over only moments before. I had to be dreaming.

Without taking my eyes off the piece of paper in front of me—I couldn't even remember where I'd gotten it, only standing there with it clenched in my fist—I used my free hand to pinch myself hard on the fleshy skin at the base of my stomach. But nothing changed. Either I wasn't dreaming, or the whole pinching to wake yourself up thing was a stupid idea.

Even before my fingers clamped around a patch of skin on my arm to try again, part of me knew what the result would be. After, as I closed my eyes and tried to breathe and settle my nerves, the answer was already in my heart, both impossible and wonderful. It was just as the letter said, and I knew its contents were not only truthful, but that my entire existence had just turned on its head.

The last thing I remembered was standing in my bedroom, staring out the window at the rainy street in front of me. I'd gotten a phone call from Darren only minutes before, telling me he'd made up his mind. He'd chosen Kelsey. He was going to be with her, and not with me. After everything.

I'd felt absolutely crushed. Even heartbroken, and the weight of it all still sat heavy on my heart as I tried to come to terms with everything else happening to me in that moment.

Once my thoughts stopped spinning, I made myself look up. Whatever I'd been expecting from the letter— perhaps a busy plaza, filled with volunteers in blue vests, waving their arms to get the attention of newcomers—my reality was a disappointment. I hadn't imagined finding myself alone in a well-lit alleyway, stone walls on either side of me as the sun shone hot overhead. The distant smell of seawater hit my nose as I took a long breath. The salty tang of the air helped to focus my thoughts, if not as much as I would have liked. At least I was starting to feel like myself again.

I was still wearing the fuzzy blue pajama pants, with the

matching cloud patterned button up top before I'd known about the phone call that was coming for me mere minutes later. And now I was wearing it outside, in a city I didn't recognize. There were voices coming from nearby, and a car honking in the distance. At the far end of the alleyway a man in a suit passed by on a connecting street without even looking at me.

Not yet ready to decide what was next, I pinched myself again, harder this time, just in case. While there was a big part of me who was sure of what the letter was telling me, another part of my soul still resisted—it went against everything I'd ever learned. And yet...

Did I even want this to be a dream?

I was already starting to sweat under the heavy fabric of my outfit which certainly felt unbearably real.

Well, I can't just stand here waiting for someone to come rescue me.

Dream or not, it was time to start moving. If I woke up a few hours later in my bed with rejection still stinging at my heart—so be it. But I couldn't just wait there for someone to come along and tell me what to do. More people passed by on the nearby street, and while I didn't love the idea of walking out there, either hunger would get the better of me, or I'd miss an opportunity to find help, if I stayed put for too long. And with a little luck finding someone I knew, someone familiar, was only a moment away if I stopped waiting around for answers or direction.

Oh God, would Darren and Kelsey be here together somewhere? Beginning their happily ever after?

I didn't want to think about it. And the best way to avoid getting bogged down in my own thoughts had always been to simply start moving.

Only a few steps toward the bright light of the street and my new reality began to take shape in front of me. At first, there was only a blur of buildings, people, and cars, but it all came into sharp focus just as my bare feet hit sidewalk. At the exact same moment, someone plowed into me from the side.

With the air knocked from my chest I grasped out wildly while stumbling sideways, only managing to find my feet when my hand connected with the stone wall of the building beside me.

"Sorry," I mumbled automatically, searching for whoever or whatever I'd just collided with, cutting myself off from swearing up a storm of frustration. A gray-haired man, with a beard down to his collarbones stood a few feet away, looking equally flustered. He was bare-chested, only wearing a kilt and leather sandals. I apologized again as his eyes scanned over me in alarm.

I got the distinct feeling he either wasn't impressed or simply thought he'd been attacked by a crazy person. Yes, I was wearing pajamas and hadn't been looking where I was going, but I wasn't convinced he was in any position to judge me. He was only wearing a kilt!

From somewhere down the street, a series of sharp pops filled the air. The man and I both looked up at once, in time to see a cloud of bubbles float into the sky, reflecting the midday sun over the street. I only let myself look for a moment before using the distraction to slip away from my unexpected encounter and into the safe anonymity of the crowd, my heart still thudding.

A few more people shot me startled looks as I passed by, leaving me more self-conscious with each passing second. I struggled to tame my long brown hair into submission by running my fingers through the tangled locks. Most days, my hair started as a thick, tousled mess, and getting it the way I wanted took more than half an hour. But for the immediate future, all I wanted was to blend in long enough to figure out what was going on.

My mind fumbled through everything I'd seen, heard, and experienced in the last few minutes, desperately trying to make sense of any of it. I let myself move with the ebb and flow of the crowd, taking in as much of my surroundings as possible while still trying to wrap my mind around everything I'd learned.

From what I could see, the people near me wouldn't have been entirely out of place in downtown Pittsburgh around the end of a work day. Some wore business clothes, others had dressed in jeans and T-shirts, fitting for the warm weather. At one point, I thought I'd seen a pirate off in the distance, but another explosion of bubbles behind me pulled my focus. All the people around me seemed just as alarmed at the phenomenon as I was, but most people kept moving, talking amongst themselves and casting worried glances over their shoulders.

It was the buildings that gave the impression of being in a place out of a storybook instead of in any city I'd ever known.

Each building pressed tight against its neighbor, but it was the variety of styles, functions, and aesthetics that felt impossible. I passed a one-story blacksmith shop built from old, uneven gray stones. Next to it stood a five-story apartment building made from a golden material I couldn't even guess at the name of. A few blocks later, a skyscraper stood taller than all the buildings surrounding it combined. Then a shop that would have looked more at home in ancient China. Maybe things in the After were always like that, an amalgamation of places and countries.

The farther I went, the more variety I saw, but nothing jumped out as an obvious destination. I still had no clue where I should be going. There was no assistance waiting for those like me who had only just arrived, looking for help. Everyone I noticed was going about their own business, some talking on phones, others writing on scratch pads with long quills.

It was when something that I could only describe as a hover car flew over me, whisking my hair up in a flurry, I realized I had to stop and regroup. I was getting more lost and confused. And while it was impossible to deny the wonder of what I was seeing, I couldn't be sure there weren't any dangers lurking around every corner as well.

Feeling vulnerable, tired, and thirsty all at once was making me more than a little grumpy.

Mostly I just wanted answers.

It took a moment to find a quiet patch of sidewalk as I stepped out of the bustle of the pedestrian crowd and leaned up against the glass window to a pastry shop. As far as I could tell it was closed, with no one inside to give me a disapproving look.

I exhaled, closing my eyes for only a moment to fully appreciate the chance to regroup.

If only I'd had my phone on me when I'd appeared here, I'd at least have the option of calling for help. But then I couldn't know if that would have worked in the After. I didn't know how anything worked. I would've been better off with an informational pamphlet than a welcome letter when I'd arrived, but there was no one to lodge a complaint with.

I closed my eyes and took a few long breaths. If my brain and my pajamas were the only assets I had, I had to keep my mind as sharp as possible. Sure, nothing could ever have prepared me for what was happening, but that didn't mean I couldn't make the most of the situation. Or at the very least, that I couldn't get myself to safety, to someone who knew what I was up against.

People kept walking by like it was just a normal day. I watched each one, looking for anyone who looked approachable. In theory, I could've asked anyone or everyone for help. But what would I even say? If I'd misinterpreted the entire situation, telling anyone what I knew—or thought I knew—would have me laughed out of the city, or locked up in an asylum somewhere. But I had to do something.

Finally, a slim-shouldered woman on the opposite street corner caught my attention with her presence alone, leaning against a lamppost in a long black coat. Red rimmed sunglasses sat atop her broad nose. She seemed to be as intent on the people near her as I was, holding herself with an air of confidence that suggested she knew far more about what was going on around her than I did. Not that that was saying much.

I had to try. Eventually, the streets would start to empty as people went home, which wasn't an option for me. I'd be more exposed than ever.

If what I'd learned was true, I would never go home again. But I couldn't focus on that thought, not yet. I stepped back into the crowd and made my way toward the crosswalk that would take me to the woman while I tried to figure out how to phrase what I needed to ask. But as I stood, waiting for the light to change, she turned to face me, sending a shiver running up my spine and letting me know she was looking right at me despite the sunglasses blocking her eyes from view. She studied me, expression hard. I looked away, not able to explain the feeling but feeling hunted all the same.

Trying to look casual, boring, I glanced behind me and pretended to spot something in the distance, before making a beeline for the still moving flow of people going in the opposite direction. Somehow, I could still feel her watching me.

I forced myself not to stare at the man on horseback in the lane closest to me, and picked up my pace. I could find someone else to help me, but the first order of business was getting as far away as I could from that intersection.

I was doing well to keep my head down, moving from street to street without drawing too much attention when I felt a crackling in the air near me. As I looked up, inexplicably drawn to the empty space beside me in the street, the air began to shimmer. A moment later, the shadow of a person, a man though I couldn't tell you much about him, formed in the air. Then an outline of his basic features, vague and blurry. He moved his hands up towards his face and opened his mouth in a soundless scream. I still couldn't see much of him beyond his chest. For a second, he seemed to come into sharper focus, and then he went, morphed into a cloud of bubbles. His face had vanished, everything about him disappeared. Bubbles floated up into the air where a moment before the screaming man stood, silent and afraid.

The bubbles drifted up into the air, childlike and beautiful.

Beside me, an older woman stood horrified, staring at the space where the man had been a moment before. I knew she'd seen the same thing I had and was just as disturbed by it. But she didn't yell out, didn't scream, or throw up—which is what my body desperately wanted to do—instead, she shook her head in surprise, cast one more glance back toward the bubbles in the air, which everyone around us was now watching with awe and horror, and kept going.

There was no question that what she'd seen had been disturbing for her, but she hadn't been as shaken by it as I had. I had no words for what had just taken place in front of me, no explanations.

I didn't even want to think about the two sets of bubbles I'd seen earlier and whether they also had screaming specters of people within them.

I made myself start moving again.

The street I ended up on was a little less crowded than the last, and soon I passed a large park, dotted with trees. Each one was a different species, and I didn't think most of them usually grew in the same place, but together still looked both natural and elegant as they surrounded a small pond, their branches drawing my gaze upward.

Off in the distance, far over the top of the trees, I caught sight of what had to be the most impressive building I'd seen yet. Endless white brick dotted with the occasional jewel-toned stone climbed up toward the sky. Several towers shot up farther at every corner. The building had to be at least several blocks wide, and a half dozen stories tall. Large windows decorated the side of the building I was looking at.

It was beautiful, and it looked important.

Would the After have a king, or queen? Or official government buildings? That building looked increasingly like the best place to start getting answers since my endless wandering was getting me nowhere.

I stepped toward the park, still staring up at the white building in front of me when I promptly slammed into my second person in under an hour.

This time, it felt more like I'd hit a brick wall, and I ended up right on my ass, staring up at the man I'd run into. This guy at least wasn't wearing a kilt. Instead, he wore close to the same outfit as the woman I'd seen on the corner, with dark jeans underneath his black coat, and a dark gray button up shirt. I couldn't make out the color of his eyes as he stared down at me through his sunglasses, but I didn't get the impression he was thrilled with my sudden presence.

"Who are you?" he demanded. He didn't offer a hand to help me up, and instead I fumbled to my feet, stammering out apologies.

"Kadie Meyer," I said, not sure how else to explain myself. At least that was one more thing I could add to my list of assets. I had my brain, I had my pajamas, and I knew who I was. But as the man studied me as intently as the woman had before, I was getting the impression that wouldn't be enough.

The man scowled. "What are you doing here, Ms. Meyer?" The way his eyeline seemed to fall over my outfit, suggested his third question would be why exactly I was wearing fleece pajamas in the middle of the day?

Flustered, I couldn't offer any explanation. I didn't know what to say at all. I stepped back, wishing I was anywhere else. And I didn't even know where I was! Not really.

The man reached out, and grabbed me by the wrist, the callused skin of his hand brushing up against me. I would have sworn my heart stopped as he slowly twisted my hand over, turning my palm up toward the sky. At first, we both looked down at my hand, not saying a word. But then I saw it, right there on my wrist, a scar I couldn't remember getting. The puckered skin looked like it had been there for years, shaped in an arc sloping toward my hand with thin lines coming from the edges. I would have said it was in the shape of a sunset if I hadn't been more concerned with what exactly it was doing on my body.

Whatever it was, the guy holding me in place didn't seem happy about it. His grip tightened around me, more punishing than before. "You're coming with me."

CHAPTER TWO

As I stared up at the man holding me, the only face I could truly see was my own, with my horrified expression reflected in the dark glass of his eyewear. "Please, this was just a misunderstanding. I'm supposed to be meeting someone." The words tumbled out of my mouth. I'm sure it was blatantly obvious that I was just lying, rambling, just trying to get him to leave me alone. His grip didn't loosen even a little, as though as soon as he saw the mark on my wrist he made up his mind. Like there was nothing I could've said to convince him to let me go.

I looked around frantically, not even sure what it was I was looking for. A few people across the street glanced our way, but they quickly turned aside and kept walking. I wasn't sure how we looked from an outside perspective, or that I'd have the nerve to say something if I saw a similar scene unfolding in front of me, but I still couldn't help but wish for someone to step in.

With a grunt, the man pulled at my arm and forced me to move my body toward his. "Keep quiet and follow me."

There didn't seem to be any choice but to do what I was told. He still had a hold of my wrist and no one seemed to be willing to help.

Looking up, I noticed how perfectly clear blue the sky overhead was, and I could feel the warmth of the sun on my skin. It was quite a perfect day for an abduction. A large bird, a hawk or something similar from the look of it, swooped in my line of vision, gliding forward on golden brown wings.

I'm not sure what it was about seeing that bird overhead that woke me up, but for whatever reason, that was the moment that I realized I could help *myself*. My mind sharpened at once.

I'd worked as a yoga instructor for the past two years after graduating college with what my parents promised was a useless degree. And while I wasn't all that good at my own job I'd used the discounts that came with working at the fitness center to enroll in self-defense classes like the ones I'd loved as a kid. I'd never so much as hit anyone in anger outside of those padded classrooms, but in theory, I knew what to do.

Okay, so what do I do? I thought, racking my brain while my body was still in full panic mode.

Beside me, the man was looking around, assessing the situation, still holding me in place.

In one smooth movement, I jerked my hand upward, moving it toward my face. It wasn't enough to break his hold, but like I'd hoped, it was at least effective in shifting the position of his hand, and loosening his grip. With my free hand, I grabbed onto his wrist and twisted, shifting it to an extreme angle that I'm not sure I could've gotten away with it if I hadn't taken him by surprise.

It was enough to get him to let go, but in an instant my advantage was gone, and what felt like in slow motion I could see him moving toward me again. With a burst of enthusiasm, or maybe just will to survive, I did something I'd been dreaming about for years.

Determined not to surrender, I shifted my weight onto my right foot and with everything I had, kicked out with my left, my bare foot colliding with the chest of a man who was arguably twice my size. It would've been quite the movie moment if I hadn't lost my balance, or if I'd managed to give the action a bit more power. Instead, I wobbled sideways and needed a moment to regain my balance. That second was all my attacker needed to grab hold of my waist and pull me in toward him. I shrieked out in rage and did my best to kick out blindly behind me, but my foot didn't connect.

The whole thing would've gone a lot better if I'd been wearing shoes.

I'd lost my chance to run and now he had a better hold than ever. I was out of luck and out of chances to get away.

Part of me wondered if I was going to die right then and there.

Would people in this place stop a man from murdering someone in cold blood on the street? I couldn't say for sure but wasn't feeling all that confident. I looked up at the sky again, hoping for inspiration. Instead, all I found was that damn bird circling above, watching us both.

I felt cold metal slip up beneath the loose fabric of my pajama top as one of the man's hands moved up to grasp my shoulder, and soon after the barrel of a gun pressed against my spine. "Come along now. There will be no more of this."

I was done. So damn done.

I wanted to close my eyes and wish myself back to my old life, and out of this terrible nightmare, but the sight of a massive bird swooping down toward me was enough to send those thoughts flying inward and glue my eyes wide open, sure I was about to be assaulted by this winged-creature on top of everything else. As if losing to this one guy wasn't already enough.

Instead of coming for my face the bird shifted slightly as he approached the ground, and right as it looked like he was going to crash into the sidewalk in front of me that same bird turned into an incredibly good-looking man.

He stood six feet tall, with shiny black hair and lean muscles that while physically less impressive than those of the guy whose hand was still on my shoulder, looked like he had earned them through a genuinely physical life rather than lifting heavy objects repeatedly at the gym.

My heart was already in my throat as the second man turned toward us. He wore blue jeans that wouldn't have been out of place in a western, and a polo shirt with short sleeves that gripped the muscles of his neck and shoulders. His expression was impossible to miss, angry. But it wasn't me he was watching, instead he locked his gaze on the man behind me.

"What the hell do you think you're doing?" the newcomer asked. He didn't wait for a response, instead he barreled toward the both of us at a run. I was certain I was about to be squished between these two mountains of men. Instead, my attacker shoved me out of the way. I tumbled to the ground, catching myself on my palms as gravel scraped against the delicate skin of my hands. By the time I managed to right myself and look back over at the scene behind me, both men were already swinging punches.

It was safe to say that the second guy was not a friend of the first, but I wasn't about to wait around to know for sure.

I stood up and ran as fast as my bare feet could take me. The street around us had mostly cleared out, other people having the same idea that I did. Whoever these guys were, nobody wanted to get in their way. Me, more so than most.

I turned on to a side street the first chance I got, hoping both men were still too preoccupied with each other to be following me, but not willing to take the risk of letting myself slow down.

Turn, turn, turn. I didn't bother trying to keep track of where I was coming from. There was no way I wanted to go back to that park anytime soon, if ever.

Really, I just wanted to go home. Even if home was where Darren and Kelsey were starting their lives together, it had to be better than the pain and exhaustion my feet were experiencing, let alone the confusion of everything else that was going on around me.

I had to get away.

Eventually I turned into what looked like a busy commercial area and forced myself to slow my pace to better blend in. I was still wearing my fuzzy blue pajamas, so there was only so much blending I could do, and as a fun update, my pants had streaks of blood where I'd wiped my hand. But if I acted like I belonged, no one really looked too closely. At least that was what I kept telling myself.

It was as my pulse began to settle down that the rest of my body's complaints really started to register. Everything from my hands, to my knees, to my left foot hurt like nobody's business, and my stomach was beginning to growl in protest from the lack of food. Still, the most overwhelming sensation was the dryness in my throat. Considering I was dangerously lacking in water, an intense cardio workout was the last thing I needed.

No, I reminded myself, *the last thing I needed was kidnapping in the street by some psycho. Or, attacked by a birdman.*

But lack of water was coming in at a strong third.

Still, I had no money, I had no anything. Even the clothes on my back were getting increasingly worthless as I sweat and bled in them. I couldn't go much further without risking even more unwanted attention.

Not far in the distance I caught sight of a one-story pub squeezed between some retail stores. It was red brick, old, and had a thatched roof, and the sound of music was already floating in the air toward me. I couldn't quite make out the tune, but really, I didn't care what the music was so long as I could just sit and be closer to food and water.

As I approached, a few people sitting out on the patio looked up at me briefly, but no one took any real notice or objected to my being there. The only thing that caused me to pause was a blue chalky line, that glowed neon even in the daylight, that was drawn all the way around the building right from the sidewalk and back down toward the gap between the building and its neighbor. It was a clear reminder of how much there was going on that I still didn't understand. I hadn't even really let myself think about the man I'd seen turn into a bird or what that said about my new reality. Magic… the idea was both exciting and terrifying every time I thought about it.

More than anything my body needed sustenance, and I didn't think my brain was going to fully start working again until I got some.

I had to hope that not unlike restaurants at home, a glass of water might be free. If nothing else, getting some fluid in me might be enough to convince my body that I could run again, just far enough to escape from an angry waiter who felt stiffed on my bill.

No. I couldn't risk somebody catching me and drawing the attention of the police. I had to lay low.

Holding my breath, I stepped across the blue line in the dirt. Absolutely nothing happened. I convinced myself that it was just decorative, though I couldn't imagine why anyone would take the time or effort to put it there.

Once I stepped inside, the bar greeted me with a more intense version of the music I'd heard earlier and a strong smell of meat and bread. A hint of stale beer lingered as well, and together the aromas formed what had to be the best thing I'd smelled all day. My mouth started watering at once, as I tried to push down the shaky feeling that threatened to overwhelm me.

For second, I stood near the front door, pretending to study the menu pasted to the wall, not sure I was fooling anyone. There was no way I looked like I belonged there. I needed to get rid of my pajamas, and find something to wear that was both more practical and less noticeable.

It looked like the pub served everything from

sandwiches, to stew, to chicken wings and veggie burgers. There was something for everyone, so long as everyone enjoyed pub fare.

More than once, I reminded myself that it didn't matter. I could get away with a glass of water, but I certainly couldn't afford food. The menu wasn't a luxury I'd get to enjoy.

Not wanting to waste a table, I turned toward the interior of the building, spotting the bar across the way with a few empty stools standing beside the long marble counter.

A series of long tables and booths occupied the bulk of the building, with some smaller tables tucked near the window. People enjoying lunch filled a third of them, but it was the waiter that caught my attention. A dark-skinned man dressed in ripped jeans and a band-T flitted from table to table, refilling drinks with a snap of his fingers. And I meant that literally--both the snapping his fingers and somehow refilling empty cups, and flitting. Or more specifically, flying! He couldn't have been more than three feet tall and had wings about the length of my forearm extending from his back, translucent but shimmering, metallic looking in their strength as they carried him through the air.

After refilling a pitcher of beer, he looked up at me, his brown eyes locking onto my own. His smile faltered right away, and I realized my mouth was hanging open. He looked at me like I was just another bug to crush, but didn't stop to say anything and continued his path from table to table, leaving me to my own devices.

A few men sat at one end of the bar, talking animatedly about a soccer game they'd watched the night before. One other woman sat on the other end, hunched over a plate of nachos, and shoving one after the other into her mouth. Her skin was the color of cream, unnaturally pale, while her hair was a shock of white in a pixie cut that didn't look like it had been styled recently. I sat down, one barstool away, and did my best not to stare hungrily at her plate.

"What can I get you?" A female bartender moved toward me. She was a large woman, but well-dressed and with her graying-black hair pulled back into an elegant bun. Her voice had more than a hint of a Russian accent.

"Just a water for now," I said. "Still deciding."

While I waited for my water, my legs vibrating with anticipation, I couldn't help but look back over at the nachos. And of course, that was the very same moment that their owner looked up at me. Unlike her skin and hair, her eyes were a vibrant blue. But it was the smear of red on her lips that was the most alarming splash of color against her pale features. I looked away, apologetic. This was not the time or place to be staring at people and making an ass of myself. I needed to get my water, and get out.

When the bartender brought back my glass of water, I grabbed at it, losing my cool for a moment. A second later she pulled up a menu from under the bar. "Only the water is free," she said, staring at me knowingly. "If you don't want any food, drink the water and go." The tone of her voice made it perfectly clear she knew I couldn't pay for food, or anything else, but somehow, she didn't manage to sound unkind.

I can imagine I looked homeless. And at least she hadn't kicked me out entirely. A minute later, she even returned with more water after I finished the first in one long draught. It felt like she'd saved my life with that one gesture.

Not ready to go back outside, and half convinced I'd run into either of those men as soon as I did, I forced myself to take my time with the second glass of water, sipping it slowly before leaving my elbows on the counter to support my tired head. I was feeling a little more myself after the first drink but still lightheaded.

I looked up again, and this time it was the other girl at the bar watching me instead of the other way around.

Except, it wasn't my face she was studying. The sleeve of my pajamas had fallen down to bunch around my elbow, and the girl's eyes had focused in on my wrist.

"You're going to want to cover that up?" she said, quietly, urgently. A few feet away, the bartender looked up at us, but didn't comment.

I did as she asked, and tucked my hands onto my lap, moving the fabric back up as I went. Heat rushed to my face, though I couldn't explain why I felt like an idiot. I was hiding and running from so much at one time, I couldn't keep track of anything at all.

I hadn't thought much about the scar marking my wrist since I'd first seen it, and part of me had just assumed it was part of this new life. But, that wasn't the case. I tugged at my sleeve again, double checking I completely covered the sun shaped design before taking another sip of my water trying desperately to look natural.

It must not have been working because the white-haired girl had moved on to studying my face, watching my every expression and flinch. She opened her mouth to speak, and I thought she was going to say something to me, and sat up a little straighter.

Please, let whatever comes next be answers.

Instead, the girl waved over the bartender. "Valyria. She's going to have something to eat." The girl cocked her head toward me. "It's on me."

I sat there, dumbstruck for a second, before the girl nudged the menu back toward me. "Come on, dealer's choice. I'm either going for the fish and chips or a sandwich, but the stew looks pretty damn good as well."

My stomach only grumbled in response, and I picked up the menu.

CHAPTER THREE

Together, we moved to an empty table in the corner of the room, an alcove wall behind me blocking out some of the music and noise.

Once our food arrived, the two of us ate in silence and I would've sworn I was having a religious experience as each spoonful of hearty beef stew passed my lips. I thought I had known what it felt like to be hungry before this, but the shakiness that almost went to my bones, promised my body was far more famished than it had ever been before.

Even after finishing the large bowl, I still wasn't full. It wasn't enough, it would never be enough.

A moment later, the blonde girl sitting across from me finished her BLT and leaned back in her seat, tilting her head up toward the ceiling with a happy sigh. "That was amazing."

I nodded along. "Thank you so much. You have no idea how much I needed that."

At once, the girl's gaze flicked to my wrist even though I had it safely tucked away behind me, trying to look natural. "Actually, I think I do. And if I'm right, I know you wouldn't say no to more food. I'm almost full, if you want something else, don't hesitate to ask."

The girl produced a thick black wallet from her pocket, and held it up in front of her. On her right wrist sat one of those leather-banded bracelets, with cheesy metal studs, though somehow the accessory suited her look. "I'll be honest, I'm technically not the one paying either. So seriously, if you need something else, go for it."

My eyes widened a little as I took in the wallet, thick with paper bills. "Where did you get it?" I whispered. Stolen money had paid for the food I had just eaten, but right away I knew I was forcing myself to care. More than anything, I was still just grateful.

Reading my expression, the girl in front of me put the wallet away. "It's mine, don't worry about it."

I shook my head a little, finding myself again. "Sorry. It has just been a strange day. I think I need to sleep for about a week before I start thinking straight again. I meant what I said before, thank you so much for the food. No judgment here, you're basically my new hero."

The girl grinned, revealing a row of white, but slightly crooked teeth. "In that case, how would you feel about splitting a pizza?"

I laughed out loud, and the action seemed to shake a little of the weight from my soul. "If you're my hero, then pizza is probably my superhero. All hail pizza."

"I like the way you think." The girl stood up only a little, moving to take off the bracelet she was wearing as she rose toward me and then extending her hand across the table, looking pointedly down at her wrist. "I'm Harper. Nice to meet you."

"Kadie." I shook the girl's hand, noticing in that moment that the skin underneath where her bracelet had been sitting had the same symbol as my own wrist. "I'm pretty damn glad I ran into you. And I have a few questions."

"Unfortunately, I don't have any answers. I've been making things up as I go along ever since I got here."

"This morning?" I asked. Harper nodded her response, and I forced down the feeling of disappointment that came with realizing I was just as in the dark as I ever was. We both sat back down, and a second later Harper had waved over the flying man. He didn't speak, but smiled at her politely. He refused to even look at me.

"We'll have a pizza," Harper said. "Large. Meat lovers?" She looked over at me for a second as she placed the order, and I gave a quick nod. Even if I had been a vegetarian, I think I would've made an exception in that moment, putting my own survival ahead of anything and everything else. Was I just a crappy person? Mostly, I was hungry.

"Whatever you want sounds good to me."

The man nodded and zoomed away, but not before casting me one last withering glare.

I kept my voice low, not wanting to piss anyone off any further. "Okay, the little flying guy. Do you know what that is?"

Harper chuckled but shushed me. "Don't, that's probably rude. But also... I know! I mean, I saw a guy today who was seven feet tall with long pointed ears that stuck out from the side of his head. I don't think I understand what anything is in this place."

My suspicions were confirmed. "Please tell me you have some idea what this place is" I asked. "I just showed up here this morning, with a letter in my hand and no idea what was going on."

Harper shook her head before pulling out the wallet again then, rifling through it before pulling out a piece of paper. After unfolding it, she handed it over to me. It was an identical letter to the one I had received, but with the name Harper Mitchell written on the top instead of my own.

A little embarrassed, I reached my hand down the loose fabric of my top, and pulled my own letter out of the sports bra I'd worn to bed the night before. My pants didn't have pockets, so it had been my only option. "I won't make you deal with my boob sweat," I said, turning the letter to face her. "But I got the same thing. It all seemed so weird. Impossible. And I don't know what to make of this," I said, holding out my wrist.

All the humor seemed to melt from Harper's expression at once. "Seriously, put that away. It was when some guy saw the mark on my wrist that things started going south for me. I grabbed his wallet and ran before he could start any trouble, but I got the distinct impression that I shouldn't be flashing that around."

I put my wrist down, admonished. "But yours is new too, right?" I couldn't help myself asking. "I definitely didn't have this yesterday."

She shook her head. "Me neither."

"So, you've been letting that guy fund you all day?" I looked around the room to see if we were being watched, then back at Harper with an obvious hint of admiration. "I've been walking around in my pajamas for hours and people keep giving me weird looks, but no one's exactly stepped in and offered to help. The letter said there would be help. Instead, some guy tried to grab me too." Over the next few minutes I filled Harper in on everything that happened to me since I'd arrived, but the two of us mostly stopped talking once the pizza arrived, saying little beyond how great the food was. Soon, eating became the most important thing. Every bite of pizza I took tasted like pure magic, though I couldn't say if that was simply because it was pizza or if there was something special in the recipe.

It took a while to get to the last slice, but we were both fully committed to polishing that bad boy off despite Harper having already said she was full. After the last bite, I slipped out to the bathroom, and took a real pleasure in cleaning myself up. There was a lot to be said for washing my face, and just feeling human again.

Still, I felt better. Not good, still wary, but better.

I was visibly relieved to see Harper still sitting at the

table when I got back. Part of me had been afraid that with just how jumpy she seemed, she'd take the first opportunity to go out on her own again. But she didn't seem any more eager than I was to face whatever was waiting outside for us again by herself.

"Did you need anything else?" the bartender from before asked, showing up at our table just as I sat back down.

Harper looked over at me, but I just shrugged. At some point over the two courses and a half dozen glasses of water I'd managed to eat my fill and then some. "I'm good if you are."

"I guess we're ready to pay." Harper answered the original question with an earnest smile.

"I'll be back with your bill." The woman turned and moved faster than I would have guessed she was capable of. As soon as she left, Harper's expression fell again.

"Weird favor," she said, handing me the wallet she'd been hiding behind her, "but would you mind paying when the bill gets here?"

I almost opened my mouth ask her to answer the obvious question, but between how uncomfortable Harper looked and the fact that she had already done me a much bigger favor, I kept my mouth shut and did what she'd asked. The money didn't look like anything I'd ever seen before, with each denomination of bill tinted a different color and decorated with figureheads I couldn't name, but it was easy enough to match up the numbers on the pieces of paper to the total on the bill in front of us.

It was hard not to draw the moment out since the giant question mark hanging over what came next was enough to have me squirming with anxiety all over again, but, too soon, I had paid the bill and handed the wallet back over, leaving Harper and I both staring at each other expectantly, both waiting to see what the other would do next.

"So," I said finally, drawing out the word. "Where are

you headed next?"

"Honestly," Harper said with a shrug, "I have no idea."

"I'm in pretty much the same position," I admitted. "Before this, basically all my body wanted was to get to some food. Now that that's covered, who knows?"

"Yes!" Harper said a little too loudly. "I don't know if it was just the stress of today, or all the running around, or maybe it's just part of the process of showing up here, but I've never been that hungry in my life."

"Well, thanks to you, I'm feeling a whole lot better." I braced myself for what I wanted to say next. "And if you're open to it, I wouldn't mind sticking together, at least for a little longer. Before, I'd been trying to find someone who looked like they had some authority to see if they could help. But after everything, I'm not sure I should be confessing to my ignorance. It would probably just put a huge target on my back."

"If I've learned anything, it's that we're all born with targets on our backs either way. But until we know more, keeping quiet is probably a better idea. Maybe we're being paranoid, and the fact that we were both attacked on our first day here is a massive coincidence. Yet somehow I'm having trouble seeing it that way."

I looked down at myself. "Well, playing it cool or not, anyone who might be looking for me can probably spot me a mile away. Look here, new girl without a clue who doesn't even have real clothes."

"That much we can fix. We'll just have to go and find a store to buy you something decent to wear. The shopping opportunities in this city are like... I've never seen anything like it. And it seems like anything goes in this place. If you want, we can find you some medieval looking gear, since I've seen more than a few people who look like they're straight out of the 14th-century."

"Honestly, even jeans and a T-shirt would be heaven right about now. But..." I didn't say anything next, I had already asked for too much.

Harper shook her head emphatically. "No, this is totally on me. Or at least on that asshole from before. Having someone else here to figure all this out with me is way more valuable than a few extra bills and a wallet that isn't mine. So, if you're willing to stick with me for a while, then I'm totally happy to buy you some clothes that will help both of us blend in a little better. I mean, I don't exactly want to be the girl walking around with the lunatic in pajamas." Harper laughed easily and I found myself following suit. She made all this sound easier than I thought it could ever be.

I nodded in agreement as relief swept through me. Harper stood up right away, but as soon as I tried to do the same I found myself glued to my seat, sweat beading on my forehead.

"What's wrong?" Harper was looking down at me, her forehead bunched up, she seemed puzzled as to why I hadn't stood up too.

I took a deep breath. "I'm not sure. I just keep thinking about those guys today. I mean, that one dude changed from a bird into an ass-kicking superhuman. And that first guy? I have no idea what his plans were for me, but I don't exactly want to find out. They're both probably still out there somewhere, unless they managed to kill each other."

"Well, we can always hope. You can't stay here, right? I mean, I've seen the way that little guy has been looking at you and I don't exactly think you're welcome." Harper did her best to keep her tone light, but I knew she was only trying to make me feel better. Lucky for her, it worked anyway. I still didn't want to go back outside, but I did really want to find something new to wear, and unless I mugged some of the pub's customers and stole the clothes from their bodies, this was my best plan. Plus, the sooner I found something new I could wear, the sooner I'd feel better. At least in theory.

Harper offered me her hand and pulled me up from my seat, and the two of us left together. I only looked back once at the pub that had fed me when I'd been at my lowest. I didn't even know what its name, but would remember it for the rest of my life as the place with the best food I'd ever tasted.

Stepping back out into the daylight, heavy afternoon sun greeted us. There were more people around than there had been earlier, which made it easier to act like we knew what we were doing.

"I think I saw a department store a few blocks back," I said while trying to remember exactly where I'd seen it. I'd seen a lot of things as I'd run from block to block, trying to lose myself, to lose the two guys fighting by the park.

"No way, I know exactly where we are going to find some clothes for you. And probably a few other things we could use."

I looked in trepidation back in the direction I'd come from originally. I wasn't sure I was ready to go exploring again quite yet.

"Trust me," Harper said, locking her eyes on mine. "You're going to want to see this."

CHAPTER FOUR

I followed Harper through the city for a few blocks. It was hard not to be impressed with her confidence walking such unfamiliar streets. We ended up in an area that seemed residential, though still so unlike anything I'd ever seen before. One block looked suburban, with rows of townhouses lining the streets, another was made up of mid-level apartment buildings, and the next had small huts that seemed to come from a different century. Mothers walked with small children either strapped to their bodies, in strollers or toddling beside them, each person far more at ease than I felt.

I was all too aware of the fact that I could have been out of my pajamas for twenty minutes already, and yet Harper seemed intent on her destination.

We just passed the school that was hovering a story in the air, with a sign out front that read 'no prosaics', when Harper finally stopped and pointed. "See, there." My eyes followed Harper's finger across the street. It took me a second to realize what she was looking at as my eyes drifted across an ice cream truck and over to the corner store next to it. But then I doubled back. The vehicle I was looking at was certainly part ice cream truck. In the middle

29

a bored looking teenager sat at the window, with pictures of various ice cream treats I'd seen a million times before painted underneath him. But at both ends of the truck were a set of white stairs leading up into the vehicle. On one side, people piled up into the vehicle, sometimes in groups and sometimes alone, and from the other side people walked back down. Completely different people than the ones I'd seen go in. And the closer we got to the ice cream truck, or whatever it was, the easier it was to see that there was no one walking in between the two doors in the actual ice cream selling part of this thing. This impossible thing.

"What is that?" I said, hoping Harper would have a better sense of what was going on here than I did. She was the one who had brought us here.

"I heard a few people calling it the bazaar last time I was here. And look, most of the people coming out have shopping bags."

I glanced over at the exit side and saw she was right. The people coming out varied in outfits, ethnicity, and age, and most of them were carrying bags or parcels.

"That doesn't necessarily mean people are shopping in there." I wasn't sure of anything anymore.

"But they might be. And doesn't part of you want to see what's going on there, no matter what it is?"

Harper sounded excited but I struggled to find the same level of enthusiasm. "I don't know, I really need to change out of these clothes and don't want to waste any more time." What I didn't say, probably because I felt a little embarrassed, a little naïve, was that whatever was going on in front of us had me feeling entirely unsettled.

The phenomenon had to be magic. Same as a grown man flitting around the bar with wings, or another changing from a bird into a human. There was magic here, but I still wasn't ready to face it. I still wasn't sure it wouldn't be the end of me. "I'm not sure it's safe."

"You worry too much."

I gave Harper a surprised look. If anyone had a good reason to worry, it was us. After everything we'd both been through that day, a little caution certainly couldn't be anything but an asset. "I don't know…"

Finally, Harper stopped bouncing excitedly on the balls of her feet and looked at me. "You don't have to go in if you don't want to, but I want to see what's in there. I don't know what it's like where you're from, but magic isn't something I'm used to. It's the kind of thing you read about in stories, things that shouldn't exist outside of fairytales and daydreams. If there's magic in there, I want to see it. I want to see all of it. You can wait here if you want, and I'll come back for you. I promise. Or I can even meet you back at that tailor shop we passed a few blocks ago. But I'll never forgive myself if I don't have a chance to go check this out. Today has been the strangest day of my life, bar none. But if somehow this isn't real, or if I'm simply lying in a coma somewhere with a bump on my head and imagining all of this, then I want to see as much of it as I can before I wake up." Harper watched me, waiting for my response.

I held up my forearm to her, and for second she looked at me, unsure. I turned over my arm until a small purple bruise was visible. "I've been pinching myself all day, trying to wake myself up, to see if this is real."

"I thought maybe I died, and this was the weirdest heaven ever."

Yup. There wasn't anything at all I could say to follow that up, but if nothing else, Harper's confession was enough to push me to follow her through that ice cream truck and into whatever came next.

During our last few hours together, I'd never even considered that the world or book she came from had been different from my own. Yes, I'd seen so many people who would have fit right in my hometown, or in a lecture at my college, or in one of my yoga classes. But there had also been so many people who were distinctly…other.

Races other than human, clothes from other times… I must have passed countless people who would have had me doing a double-take if I'd met them even a day earlier. But my brain refused to process them.

I still hadn't truly understood that there could be places so fundamentally different from what I'd known. Even though the evidence was increasingly stacking up to prove that I'd never really known anything at all.

I knew that wherever Harper had come from hadn't had magic either, but that didn't mean much. She could've come from somewhere in the past, or the future. Her book might have been a murder mystery, and she lived in a city full of serial killers and stalwart detectives. Or a country with riddled with war. Even without magic, the possibilities were endless.

And for every genre that didn't feature in Harper's life before, I was standing surrounded by people who'd come from those kinds of stories. There was more diversity on the street corner I was standing on now than I'd ever experienced in my life.

It was incredible. And I was still desperately trying to get back to the familiar, to change into some clothes like the ones I'd worn a million times before, and as a bonus, to pretend like none of this ever happened. Harper was right, this was a beyond unconventional afterlife that no one had ever considered. But no matter what was happening, it was time for me to start appreciating the possibilities it offered. I'd escaped whatever had almost happened to me in the park, got a free meal, and already made a friend. At least I hoped so. I'd more than earned the chance to explore and see something truly cool. I couldn't even imagine where the people disappearing into the side of the ice cream truck were going, but suddenly I wanted to find out for myself.

"I'm in," I said, grinning. "You go first."

Harper laughed and happily obliged. I was relieved to see there wasn't anyone standing at either door, stopping people from entering. Everyone around us was simply acting like it was a completely normal passageway from one place to another, so I tried to do the same. There was no real line, so we simply merged with one group as they went in, matching their pace. One second, I was going up the stairs into a hallway cloaked in darkness, and the next I was exiting into a massive room showered with light.

Right away, I could tell from the air pressure that we were somewhere far higher up than we had been a minute before. Wherever we were, it was open and airy, but still enclosed. Interlocking stones lined the floors, and around us were more people than I could count, milling between stalls and carts and the few normal shops that looked like they'd come from every corner of the world, all filled with goods for purchase. Someone bumped into me, and I realized I'd stopped to look a little too long. I moved with Harper off to the side.

"Okay, so this is new." Harper didn't look at me, her eyes still focused on everything going on around us. Nearby, a small woman exchanged a handful of coins with a man behind the counter of a slushy stall. Beside them was a tent that seemed to be full of handmade jewelry.

Harper took a step forward to start exploring, but something else had caught my eye. The two of us made our way over to the very edge of the room, to a glass window that took up every inch of the wall. We were standing at the top of a skyscraper, over a massive city that stretched out in every direction. To the south, a stretch of wooden docks met a massive body of water. I reasoned that was the source of the salty air I had smelled earlier. That was, if we were even still in the same city.

"Wow," Harper said without a drop of cynicism in her voice. "This is really something else."

"A minute ago, we were on the ground, somewhere out there. And now we're here." The thought came out of my mouth before I'd realized that I was stating the obvious, but it was safe to say my mind was trying to wrap itself around whatever had just happened.

There was no question it was magic.

"What do you think that is?" Harper asked, nodding her head to the west. She was looking at the same white building I'd noticed right before I had run into that jerk in the park. Even from all the way up high, it still looked huge. "No idea, I saw it before and kind of wanted to go. I thought maybe it would be my best shot at finding some help, or some answers."

"It looks pretty official, right?"

I nodded, still admiring the building from afar. I was looking at a different side of it than I had been before, and could see just how massive it was, stretching for multiple city blocks.

"It's funny," Harper said quietly. "But the city isn't at all what I expected when I first showed up and read that letter. I mean, they said I'd be somewhere not that unlike where I'd come from. And I can promise you, this is nothing like where I came from. But maybe there isn't anything like that here."

I laughed a little to myself, not because the situation was funny but because I hadn't even considered it. "You're right. This isn't at all like home sweet home for me either. I mean, would it have killed them to ease me into the magic thing a little? I grew up near a big city, but anything that remotely resembled the real world, or at least the real world I was used to would've been nice. Just one more thing to add to our complaint forms later." I laughed, trying not to sound like I was whining about any of this.

"So, what now?" Harper asked, turning back toward the busy area we'd entered. "I'm guessing we can probably find you something to wear in here, if nothing else."

"Honestly, I'm suddenly in a whole lot less of a rush to do anything at all. Let's just wander for a bit, and check things out. No sense wasting any of your money until we see what our options are, right?"

"Sounds like as good a plan as any."

So, we wandered, stopping every minute to get a better look at something or someone though Harper was good at reining me in when I was staring a little too obviously.

"Sorry," I mumbled after she caught me a second time in only a few minutes. "There are just so many people here that I never imagined could even be real."

"I know what you mean. This is so impossibly different from where I come from."

Okay, time to do better. "So where did you come from?" I asked.

I wasn't looking directly at Harper as we walked, but I could almost feel the shift in her mood and instantly regretted my question as she paused. "Sorry, ignore me. You don't have to answer that." I couldn't imagine why it might be awkward to describe the place someone had come from, but it was making Harper uncomfortable, and I knew there were no guarantees as far as our friendship was concerned. Not yet.

"No," Harper said, waving me off as I turned to face her. "It's fine. It's just, I let everything today push all of that back so far, I think part of my brain was trying to repress it. I'm from New York."

"Oh, I've been there." Probing my memory, I tried to come up with something more specific. But absolutely nothing came to mind. New York—I know what it looks like, I know where it is. I know that I've been there. But I don't remember when or why.

Harper shook her head and smiled. "Somehow, I don't think the New York you know is quite like the one I do. World War III broke out a few years after I was born. New York is a bombed-out wreck of a city, not really a place to go visit."

That time, I felt like an idiot for opening my mouth yet again. Even when I was aware of my own assumptions, I couldn't seem to stop them. "I want to ask questions, but I don't even know where to start. It's weird, I keep assuming everyone else's experiences before were like my own, even though my brain is screaming at me saying that they weren't."

"Ask away. Until this morning I'd never even considered that there could be places all that different from my New York. I'm in pretty much the same boat you are."

"Is there a lot of fighting where you're from? Country against country, that kind of thing?"

"Not really, the war ended a long time ago, before I was really old enough to participate. Now, everyone just fights to survive. Against each other, against invaders, against wild animals and warlords. It was pretty bleak." Despite welcoming questions, Harper's tone was clipped and abrupt.

I didn't probe much further, and Harper didn't seem all that keen to volunteer more information, so soon enough the conversation died away and we continued our endless wandering between the stalls.

Maybe I had gotten a little greedy from the magical transportation to the bazaar, but I was hoping to see the kinds of things you only heard about in fantasy movies sold here among the snacks and handcrafted items.

But there were no magical lamps, magic rings, enchanted swords, or anything else of that nature. At least nothing quite so obvious that it jumped out at us, as neither Harper nor I really stopped to talk to anyone who didn't talk to us first. After an hour, we found a blue tarp tent filled with an eclectic mix of clothing both on racks and stacked on tables. There didn't seem to be any method to the madness in terms of what went where, but both Harper and I enjoyed losing ourselves in the treasure hunt. There was a changing room in the back made up of little more than a curtain on a rod that I could pull open and closed, but that was more than enough for me to wiggle into a pair of jeans and a plain gray tank top. I should have gone for something a little warmer, but didn't want to press my luck since I was still missing a key piece of my outfit that may well cost more than the rest of my clothes combined. Thankfully, the tiny black woman with short cropped hair and a brightly colored outfit, also had a few choices of shoes at her register. I tried not to look too surprised when she asked me what size I was and then quickly altered the pair I'd been looking at with a few mumbled words to become the size I needed.

"That will be one eighty-five, or a wish per fifty."

"A wish…"

"Here," Harper said, cutting me off and handing the woman cash. As the shopkeeper moved to make change Harper shot me yet another look suggesting that I was saying too much. Her motto in life seemed to be don't ask questions.

"That last woman was an idiot," the shopkeeper whispered to us conspiratorially as she handed Harper a handful of coins. "Honestly, I don't even know what she's doing here. Damn prosaics don't appreciate that just because they *can* go where they like doesn't mean they should. They're just not equipped to deal with the realities of our city. So instead I have to end up haggling for my wares like some sort of common shopkeeper because the librarians don't have enough justification to simply kick the likes of them out of Sanctum."

Harper and I shared a glance. I was confident that she didn't have any better idea than I did what this lady was talking about, but she didn't seem happy. And I didn't want to do anything to piss her off.

The woman must've caught our expressions because she stopped rambling at once and gave us each a withering look. I could tell she was wondering if we were like the customer that came before us, if we were some of *them*. Whoever they were.

I smiled and rolled my eyes, trying to look like I was commiserating with her. I didn't know if it worked, but it at least got her to finish bagging the socks I'd purchased without any trouble.

"Did you want to throw out those old pajamas?" Harper asked once we left the tent. "There's a garbage can over there."

I looked down at the bundle in my hands, knowing I should just get rid of it. But instead, I shook my head. "No, it's kind of all I have left of home, you know? Maybe I can get them cleaned or something and use them later. Besides, it's not like I have anything else so throwing things out probably wouldn't be my best plan ever."

Harper didn't argue and instead doubled back to the same tent we'd just been in, coming back a minute later with a backpack slung over her shoulders. "Here, shove them in so you don't have to carry them around. We'll try to grab a few other things while we're here, so the bag won't hurt either way."

After buying two new toothbrushes and a tube of toothpaste, plus a hairbrush at a cart that sold things usually found at the convenience store, alongside an elaborate collection of teacups, we stopped and counted her money. Harper's money. I still couldn't believe how generous she was being, sharing her windfall with me.

Unfortunately, we were starting to run low on cash. I tried not to think about figuring out where we were going to sleep that night, and instead put on my biggest smile. There was still just over a hundred left, which would feed us both another day or so, hopefully lasting long enough to find some real help. Assuming Harper ever let me speak to anyone ever again.

"What do you say?" Harper asked. "Time to get out of here and back into the world?"

"Sounds good to me." I looked around the room, trying to find the door we came from. Instead, I found half a dozen doors all spread evenly throughout the room, pressed back against the clear glass of the walls.

"Any chance you made note of which of these we came through?"

Harper glanced up and noticed the same thing I did.

"Nope. But worst-case scenario we end up in a different part of the city, far away from the guys we ran into today. I'd almost say let's aim for going somewhere new. What's the worst that can happen?"

I didn't feel like I could answer that question.

"Okay, what's the worst that can happen in one part of the city that couldn't happen in another?"

"Fair point."

We decided on a door with a sign over top of it labelled West End. I forced myself to keep breathing as we stepped through the dark passageway with another group of people and back down onto the street. At least this time the odds were in our favor and we ended up somewhere completely new from where we first entered the bazaar.

I heard the rush of nearby waves before I noticed anything else, and it wasn't long before we found the docks I'd seen from up high. Ships lined endless piers moving off into the distance. I looked up to see a signpost, one direction pointed toward the theatre district, another to the Archive, and the third to the Reclamation Center.

It was strange, I hadn't even thought about the idea of a Reclamation Center since reading the letter. At any time, I could've sought it out and escaped this whirlwind of a day to go back to mild life. And yet, the idea wasn't at all appealing.

Every time I thought about my life before, all I felt was sad. Sad because of Darren and Kelsey, and sad because I didn't know where my parents were. They could be in the same city I was, even only a block away, and I had no way of tracking them down. But I couldn't ignore the fact that simply going into a Reclamation Center to return to my story would mean throwing away any sort of future with them here. And saying goodbye to any real future for myself. I'd live on forever in a familiar world going through the same motions repeatedly, but I knew how that story ended and I didn't like it. Sure, there were other parts of my life that I loved. My job, my friends. Books, movies, board games. And I couldn't argue that life there was easier than it was here, at least so far.

But I wasn't ready to give up on the idea of more. The Reclamation Center would always be there if the time came when that was my only option. But all things considered, my day had taken a pretty positive turn and things were going far better than they had been back at that park.

If Harper didn't decide she would be better off without me, I could convince myself I might be okay.

"What are you looking at?" Harper asked, drawing my attention back. I nodded my head toward the Reclamation Center sign.

"You." Harper made a face. "You're not thinking about going in there, are you?"

"Not a chance. Just kind of got lost in thought."

"I hear that happens when you're hungry." I laughed appreciatively, not at all surprised that Harper was hungry again already. My own stomach was starting to gurgle again. "Any chance you want to help me track down a grocery store and maybe we can find some cheaper food that will help our money last a little longer?"

"I'm getting the impression you're always hungry." It was only as I said those words that I really took in her tiny frame. She had said the world she'd come from had been a hard one. It was all too possible that she hadn't been getting enough to eat before arriving here. But Harper didn't seem to take any offense at my comment. Instead, she grinned. "That sounds about right."

"And you're not worried about running out of money?"

"Nah, there are more wallets where this one came from. Well, not specifically. But I'll figure something out, I always do."

I didn't mention that I was not that kind of person. But for now, I had Harper on my side and we were on our way to a well-earned dinner. And let's face it, the idea of a good meal always made things look a little better.

CHAPTER FIVE

The store we stumbled onto had perfectly fit my mental image of a typical grocery store, but had its name written in an indistinguishable script above the door in a language I didn't recognize let alone understand. The food inside wasn't much better. Half the fruit I spotted when I walked through the door came in shapes and colors I didn't recognize. The meats looked even more mysterious. Thankfully, a little hunting through the aisles left both Harper and I with a couple of meals worth of goodies.

Although, to be fair, I was sure Harper would eat absolutely anything put in front of her.

We ended up at a park, unpacking Harper's backpack full of food while we settled in under a large oak tree. The sun had almost disappeared behind the skyline, and I tried to get comfortable as blades of grass pricked against every inch of my exposed skin.

I reminded myself repeatedly that this wasn't the same park I'd been in earlier that day, but I still found myself looking around every minute just to be sure we were truly alone. Thankfully, the park only had streetlights around its outer edges, leaving its interior dark and gloomy. There was still a little light coming across the skyline, but my eyes were quickly adjusting to the growing darkness.

On our way in, we passed another blue line in the dirt, identical to the one that had was around the pub where we had our first meal together. Neither Harper nor I said anything about it but I suspected we were both wondering the same thing. Something this random couldn't be a coincidence.

But Harper's priority was food. We'd gotten a loaf of bread and some fixings for sandwiches that wouldn't hold up all that well in a warm backpack overnight. Harper had also thought to grab some fruit for the morning so we wouldn't have to go looking for more right away. Hopefully, that would give us some time to come up with a better game plan than living meal to meal and hoping no one noticed us.

We still had a little money left, but nowhere near enough to get a room in the one hotel we'd passed. I'd have loved to find some sort of directory in case there were any cheaper accommodations that might have been an option for us in the future, but at least for that night we were committed to sleeping in the park. At least, Harper was, and I was too tired to argue. I was usually too much of a wimp to spend the night sleeping in a park, but it had been a day of firsts and I was feeling a little more confident than I had that morning.

As Harper took out our limited supply of food and spread it out on a few paper towels in front of her, I set about taking off my shoes. Putting them on had been one of the best feelings of the day despite how worn down and battered my feet were, but taking them off wasn't nearly as much fun. The blisters I'd noticed earlier had already bled through my socks, and more were already forming all over the soles of both of my feet. A few stray bruises also decorated my skin here and there. It wasn't a pretty picture and felt even worse.

I'd never given much thought to my shoes before, but I promised myself I'd be grateful for them every day from that moment forward.

"Ooof," Harper said waving her hand in front of her nose as swallowed down a bite of her sandwich. "Put those bad boys away."

"I'm sorry," I whined. But I didn't put my shoes back on. Instead, I grabbed one of the two remaining pairs of socks from the package I'd purchased at the bazaar and moved to put those on instead, hoping the bleeding had stopped and I wasn't about to ruin a second pair.

"Don't be dumb, I was just kidding. Your feet need to breathe. And eat. Or you need to eat to feed your feet. I don't know, I'm really tired. Weird day."

"Weird day," I agreed. Thankful, I stuffed my new socks back in our backpack before handing it over to Harper. I left the bloody ones beside the trunk of the tree we were leaning against, not willing to put them anywhere that might touch our food.

The temperature had started to drop a little but the air was still comfortable. I had to hope it would stay that way overnight since all I had to cover me was the thin fabric of a sweater Harper had insisted on getting at a discount bin near the front of our mystery grocery store, at least unless I was willing to put my now seriously grimy pajamas anywhere near me again. We should've considered a blanket, but we never seemed to stop to figure out our next steps, instead Harper seemed intent on going from A to B and planning as she went. And I was just grateful to be around someone who had any plan at all.

"You know, you don't have to eat all of that now," I said, breaking the silence after we both finished our sandwiches and split an entire cucumber, as Harper started stacking together another. "We've got more food tomorrow. And we'll find more after that.

"Are you sure?" Harper said with a pointed look that ensured I knew the question was rhetorical. "Anything could happen tonight, anything could happen tomorrow. It never hurts to make sure you have enough fuel to get you through whatever's coming."

I couldn't argue, though I didn't see our situation as quite so bleak as Harper did, at least not anymore. So, I changed the subject. "My last memory from before all of this was pretty much at the same time yesterday, when I was about to go to bed. Everything was awful, or at least what I'd thought was awful back then. Back then, damn, it feels like so long ago."

"A lifetime ago," Harper said, not looking at me. Her voice was soft and I was almost certain that she hadn't realized she'd spoken out loud.

"I mean, is there any way you could have ever even imagined that this was where you'd be today?"

Harper shook her head. "Actually, I wasn't sure I'd be anywhere today." A long silence hung between us but I knew better than to speak up. "Before I got here, I was in the basement of this long-abandoned skyscraper. It was close to the one my boss, Elaine, used as her headquarters, and I was supposed to get her a package. I was running late; my sister had just fled the city and I didn't know where she'd gone. It knocked me off my game somehow. Alayna—the under Lord of Manhattan—was less than pleased with my performance. The last thing I remember is one of her flunkies running me through with a broadsword."

My mouth dropped open a little but I snapped it back up again, trying to keep my expression neutral. Inside, I was horrified, and a little afraid that my reaction to Harper's story was obvious. But what do you even say to something like that?

"When I got here, I was pretty sure it was heaven. Either that or the blow hadn't killed me and I was hallucinating somewhere in a coma. But that thing damn well felt like it had killed me. And I didn't know what I'd done to deserve this afterlife, but I was convinced. I guess it's easier to believe that than the fact that my entire life had just been a story someone was telling. A story where they didn't see fit to keep me alive."

"God, Harper. That's tough. I'm sorry." As far as condolences went it was pathetic, but it was the best I could manage.

"Not your fault. I just hope my sister fared better, that she managed to get away. Though, I guess in the end it doesn't really matter. She's here somewhere too. Although I guess that means Elaine is as well, same with Jonas, the bastard who killed me."

"Well, this seems like a pretty big place. Maybe you can find your sister and the two of you can start over here, avoiding any assholes from your life before. Like the letter said, this is your chance at a new life, to create something for yourself. You don't have to work for anyone you don't want to, or deal with any crap." I said the last part remembering vividly how few people had run to help me when the man in black grabbed me. Maybe people here just sucked, but I wasn't about to say that Harper. "Your life here can be better than it was before. I promise." That much at least I was confident in. Even if there were no guarantees in the After, I'd already seen so many incredible things in one day that a better life had to be at least possible. Anything seemed to be possible in this place. "But first, we are probably going to have to get some sleep."

"I don't even know what time it is," Harper admitted. "The sun hasn't been down that long, so it's probably not that late but I am so beyond ready to sleep."

"We're pretty well tucked away here. No one will see us, and, with luck, tomorrow will go a little more smoothly since we won't start it off waking up in a strange place, with no idea how we got there. There must be help somewhere, there must be more than this. So tomorrow we'll find it. Even if we just get ourselves to the nearest police station, make sure the uniform isn't long black coats and red sunglasses, and then see if anyone there can help us."

"Or, we can go to that big white building. Like you said, it looks official."

"See, we've got options. So many options."

"But first, sleep."

"Sleep," I agreed. Harper set about putting everything back in her bag and then propped it up at the trunk of our tree as a pillow. I only had my new shoes to keep me comfortable, and I would've been better off with just my arm to cushion my head from the ground, but didn't want to risk someone finding us in the middle of the night and sneaking off with my unprotected new shoes. If anything, Harper was the one who owned them but they had quickly become my most important possession.

I tried to imagine what my parents might have been wearing when they'd arrived in the After, or if they had anything on them that would serve as a reminder of home when I found them.

But it wasn't my parents, or Darren, or my friends, or anyone else I'd known in my life before that I thought about as I drifted off to sleep that night. Instead, the last image I could remember circulating through my head as my eyes got heavy and my thoughts slowed down, was a large brown bird, feathers soft and elegant. It watched me from overhead before swooping down to save the day.

Soon after, I fell into a deep and dreamless sleep.

At least a few hours must've passed before I woke up again, jostled slightly as Harper moved beside me to stand up. The sky overhead was still dark and filled with stars, with no signs of morning.

"Sorry," Harper grumbled. "Just need to pee in the bushes like the classy lady that I am."

My mind barely registered what she said. Everything was fine, and I could go back to sleep.

I must've been out again seconds later, but the next thing my mind registered was the sound of someone screaming in the distance.

Harper!

I was completely awake all at once, sitting up before I even realized that I'd moved. My eyes adjusted quickly to the dark around me but I still couldn't see much of anything. It was why we'd chosen that spot, we didn't want anyone to see us but our oh so brilliant plan had quickly backfired.

I considered calling out for her, but in the end kept my mouth shut. I knew it was what Harper would've told me to do and my own mind didn't have a clue about what to do.

I rushed to put my shoes on knowing that every second I wasted was one that could cost Harper everything, but I had no choice. Stuffing my feet back into their confinement was painful, but I knew the alternative would be worse.

The park wasn't large, just poorly lit. I didn't let any thoughts of staying hidden hold me back as I sprinted toward the direction I thought the scream had come from. Nothing, nothing. No one. I could see the streetlights in the distance, but not much else. At least until a flash of movement caught my eye. And there they were, Harper struggling against the grip of a lean, beanpole of a man who towered over her. I couldn't make out any of his features, but Harper's hair was unmistakable, as was the long sweeping cut of the man's black jacket. He was pulling her away from me, and she was fighting with everything she had…but losing.

I put all my remaining strength into pumping my legs and getting to them, but too quickly they reached the edge of the park. One moment, they stood on grass, struggling against one another. The next, they passed over the blue line in the ground, and disappeared. Completely and totally gone in what looked to be a puff of ash.

I kept running, pushed myself to get there as quickly as possible. It took me ten seconds, but I knew already that I was far too late.

Right away, even in an empty street lit by stars above us and a few streetlamps, it was obvious that both Harper and her attacker were long gone. It was only once I looked down that I realized Harper had left something behind, losing it in the struggle. Her bracelet, the same leather band I'd noticed when we'd met in the pub was sitting on the ground, just on the inside of the blue line separating park from sidewalk.

Picking it up, may have saved me from giving up entirely because as soon as I leaned down closer to the ground I noticed a faint trace of residue, particulate and gray. More than likely, it was the same ash I'd seen in the air only seconds before, there was a trail of it bleeding from the edge of the park and down the street in a straight line, enough of it that I could make it out under at least a few of the lights ahead.

Harper was gone, but either she or the man who had grabbed her had somehow left a trail behind. Something I could follow.

It wasn't much, but it was something. And I latched onto that something with every part of myself. I couldn't accept that Harper might just be gone.

Dammit, dammit, dammit. I thought, pacing in place for a moment. There was no choice but to follow. I couldn't say how fast they were moving, where they were going, or how any of what had just happened was possible, but I needed to go.

At first I tried to run, tried to give it everything I had to catch up and make up for lost time. But the faster I moved the harder it was to see the ash on the ground. Finally, I forced myself to slow and follow as close to the ash as I could, knowing one misstep or wrong turn would mean I'd be far too late to do anything at all.

CHAPTER SIX

The trail got a little easier to follow as I learned what to look for, continuing through the labyrinthine streets of the city. I tried to stay focused as I moved, not letting myself wonder if I was already too late. Few other people were out this late at night, but those that were seemed intent on staying out of my way, on staying out of anyone's notice, ducking into the shadows of nearby buildings as I moved toward them. No one spoke to me or offered to help. Although I guess it's not all that fair to put the burden of helping on people who only saw me as a crazy person following a dust trail through the city in the middle of the night.

Really, I was just glad to be wearing shoes.

I tried to keep track of my surroundings as I went and soon began to recognize a few of the buildings I passed. I didn't have enough energy to truly focus on specifics but I was sure I was getting closer to the docks where Harper and I were only hours before. As I moved, the streetlights were my only allies. On some streets, electric lights stood three stories high and made what I was looking for easy to spot. On others, only gas lamps illuminated my way, making it harder to focus on much of anything without straining my eyes to the point of blurry vision.

Soon, the now unmistakable smell of the ocean, if that's what it even was, assaulted my nose.

Eventually, I reached the docks themselves and the endless blackness of water on the edge of the city during the night. There weren't many other people around, and those I spotted managed to keep themselves scarce. A blue line glowed in the distance, drawing my attention. On the building above it a sign read "Reclamation Center".

I glanced down to confirm I was still standing on top of a thinning line of ash. It extended off into the distance, headed straight for the Reclamation Center, which was the last place I wanted to go.

I was already wheezing from the effort of keeping up my pace. Even with slowing down to follow the trail, my body had had enough. Enough running, enough hiding, and not nearly enough water. Despite being beyond exhausted, both physically and mentally, I forced myself to keep moving.

And then I saw them. Right beside the blue line emanating light from the ground, Harper and her attacker reappeared in a fresh puff of ash that looked like a hazy blur from where I was standing. After having known Harper for only a day, I already felt like I could spot her anywhere.

She was still fighting every step of the way, but her attacker quickly forced her beyond the blue line.

Once again, for what I hoped would be the last time for a while, I ran harder, promising myself that if I just moved faster it would all be over soon.

Unwillingly, my body continued to slow. I was moving at a pace that was barely a jog. At least Harper and the man beside her weren't going much faster, but I wasn't catching up either.

Even if I managed to make it to Harper, I'd have almost no fight left in me.

But I had to keep trying. Harper had given me so much

in that one day, and I couldn't let myself stop moving, stop trying.

My pulse quickened as in the distance Harper broke free from the man holding her. She got a few feet away and already I was hoping for a happy ending. A happy ending that never came. He had her again a few seconds later. By then I was close enough to hear her frustrated yell but not nearly close enough to do anything about it. I had to hope that someone else was even closer, close enough to hear her scream and to come to her rescue when I was so entirely useless.

This time, Harper's assailant wasn't taking any chances. He hoisted her tiny body up and over his shoulder, moving her in a fireman's carry as he took the steps up to the Reclamation Center two at a time.

Mentally, I tried to prepare my body for what I knew I had to do next—move faster than I ever had before. Whatever was about to happen to Harper behind the doors of that elegant stone building couldn't be good. Whatever was coming, she didn't want it. And that was all I needed to know.

I passed a row of darkened stone buildings as I moved for one final sprint. But instead of propelling myself forward, something grabbed me from behind and forced me back. I recognized the feeling of strong hands at once.

They have me too. It was all I could think, repeatedly, as I struggled against an impossibly strong grip. It was right when I realized that screaming was my only option, that a second hand reached up and grasped around my mouth, silencing me.

I fought with every ounce of strength I had, trying to remember every defense lesson I'd had but it wasn't enough. As I struggled to wriggle loose and to clench my teeth around a stray finger of whoever was holding me, Harper disappeared behind the front doors of the Reclamation Center.

Gone.

She was gone, and whatever was coming next for her would be my fate shortly after.

The grip on my arms and mouth only tightened, holding me against a firm chest so that I could barely move at all.

As my heart continued to race in my chest, whoever stood behind me turned my body so I was facing them, doing their best to keep total control over me as I shifted.

Instead of coming face-to-face with one of the black jackets, as I was starting to call them in my head, I found someone I recognized. It was the man from earlier who had shifted from a bird into a human before attacking a black jacket hopefully, on my behalf.

Or was he attacking the other guy so he could get to me first?

Either way, he was right there, inches from my face and glaring down at me. "I'm not going to hurt you," he said, voice firm and steady. "If I take my hand off your mouth will you stay quiet? The last thing we need is to attract any more attention."

I thought about it, and nodded. Worst case, I could always go back on my promise. At least by agreeing to this I'd get his hand off my mouth.

As soon as I moved to bob my head his grip on every part of me loosened until I was standing up of my own free will, staring at him in disbelief.

But there was no time for formal introductions, Harper needed my attention far more than he ever could. I turned back to continue my race toward the Reclamation Center, but right away the man's hand tugged against my wrist, not hard but enough to keep me from going too far. "You can't go in there."

"What are you waiting for? She needs my help. And let's face it, we could both probably use *your* help." I didn't want to assume he'd jump to our rescue but wasn't about to turn down an extra pair of hands either.

The guy shook his head, as though apologizing for

something. "I'm sorry. It's too late."

"You don't know that, she could be in there bleeding to death, or worse…" I didn't let myself finish my mental list of things that could be happening to Harper in that moment.

"She'll have been forced back into her origin story already. There's nothing we can do."

I blinked. "What?"

"They went into the Reclamation Center. All that's in there are receptionists and portals that take people back to the books that they came from. And once that happens, there's no undoing it. Going in there now will only cause a fight, and one I'm not ready for. I need to figure out who it is I'm fighting, and why. And having you forced back into your story too isn't going to help anything."

I started to fumble out an argument, a desperate plea to get him to change his mind as I recapped out chase through the city. Before long, no words came out only stuttering and then silence.

"We have to get you out of here." It sounded like he already thought the discussion was over.

"Please," I said at last. "She's my friend and they took her. That guy grabbed her and then just disappeared… there was this blue line on the ground and as soon as they passed it, they were just gone. I couldn't catch up."

"He is a member of the Order of Pheneus, so he almost certainly has abilities that let him travel faster than normal. Blue aeon-lines deflect magic within them, but once he had your friend beyond the lines, he would have been impossible to catch for most people." His voice softened a little. "There was nothing you could have done. I really am sorry. But it's too late. She's gone…"

I looked back over at the Reclamation Center. I wanted to go, to know for sure or to help if I could. I didn't want Harper to have to be alone. But at the same time, I was afraid to do anything at all. Afraid for my own life. For whatever was going to come next. And still, my body seemed to be pulled toward the Reclamation Center like a magnet.

I felt pulled in both directions, toward the last place I knew my friend had been, and toward this guy who had stopped me from saving her. Instead, I stayed in place. Both options were equally appealing and terrifying. I needed both, and neither.

And I didn't want to say goodbye.

At least the guy standing with me knew well enough not to press matters. He stayed silent as I was caught in my own thoughts. Harper was gone, forced back to the life she'd come from. She would live through that miserable existence repeatedly. And die repeatedly.

She was gone, and I was alone.

I forced a deep breath as my body still struggled to reclaim control over itself, but it came out in shuddering waves. I could already feel the hot prickle of tears forming behind my eyes as I tried to get a grasp on my emotions. I couldn't do this right now, there was too much else going on.

But my mind and my body seemed to have different plans. They were done, exhausted and broken.

I heard myself crying, sobbing even, before I realized what was happening. Humiliated, I buried my face in my hands and tried to shove the massive influx of emotion back down inside me, but it wouldn't go.

Harper was gone. It hadn't been that long ago that we'd settled in for the night and I told her that her life here could be better than what she left behind. Instead, she got up to go to the bathroom and in one moment, had everything ripped away from her before she had a chance to even enjoy her new life.

And as much as what Harper had been through was infinitely worse than any of my own troubles, they were overwhelming me at the same time. Maybe because I knew that what happened to Harper could just as easily happen to me. Or was I just done? I hadn't prepared for any of this. The letter I'd read when I'd first arrived had promised things like help and a world that was both familiar and welcoming, and instead I just had this bullshit.

I sobbed harder as both emotions and tears flowed out of me for a few solid minutes, crying into my own hands while simultaneously trying to pull it all back in.

It was the gentlest touch that I noticed first, a hand on my shoulder, calm and reassuring. I flinched a little at first, but soon leaned into the touch. It didn't help to stem the flow of tears but was somehow welcome all the same.

A moment later strong arms encircled me, not holding me in place like before. Warm, and soothing. It didn't make anything better but it did make me feel just a little less alone.

CHAPTER SEVEN

I couldn't say how long it took me to catch my breath and calm down. Strong arms still wrapped around me, but as soon as I did I felt super uncomfortable about what was going on around me. The stranger holding me must've felt the moment when my body tensed because a second later he let me go, taking a long step back as though to deliberately give me my space. He looked away uncomfortably, and I did the same. I didn't really understand what had just happened between the two of us, but the time for hugging things out had passed.

"Sorry about that." I gave a helpless shrug. "I didn't mean to lose it."

"I'm not one to judge, and I can certainly imagine that you've had an intense evening." The guy looked back over at me and forced a small smile. "Well, now that we've done that I guess we should get through introductions so I can convince you to let me get you out of here. Protectorate Avos, Hand of the Archive."

"Kadie Meyer. And I don't know what that means." I shot my eyebrows up a tick in challenge. The last thing I was in the mood for was any more ominous dancing around whatever was going on.

"You can call me Grayson. The rest can wait until later."

I stuck my hand out and Grayson mirrored my action. Our two hands touched slowly before his completely enveloped mine and we shook in greeting.

"Nice to meet you Kadie Meyer." Grayson's expression shifted a little as he watched me. "I'm sorry for everything that has happened to you so far. I wish I could explain but we don't know enough." A tinge of frustration edged his tone. "For now, we just need to get you somewhere more secure to give you your best shot at making it through the next few days."

I shook my head, alarmed. "Wait, what?"

"You don't need to worry. Everything will be fine. Just follow me and we'll get you somewhere safe."

I did as I was I was asked and followed Grayson through the streets of the city, but my mind was stuck on one of the last things he said. Everything was going to be fine. First... define fine. Second, I could've sworn that same phrase was in the letter I'd read when I first arrived in the After. And so far, the statement had turned out to be a complete and total lie.

I wasn't sure where I was expecting Grayson to take me, to a bunker or to the police perhaps. I didn't know what it meant when he referred to himself as Protectorate—but it sounded official. Instead, we ended up at a train station. There were still a few lights on inside, and I could hear a locomotive moving away in the distance, so it was open for business despite being the middle of the night. But that didn't explain what I was doing there.

I wanted to ask, to demand an explanation, but Grayson was already holding the front door open for me. I stepped inside and he followed behind me.

While the building I entered was far smaller, it held much of the same elegance as Grand Central Station with marble floors and elegant designs etched on the walls.

It was a little after three o'clock in the morning. No wonder I felt exhausted.

Okay, to be fair there were all sorts of reasons I felt exhausted but that had to be one of them.

"What are we doing here?" I forced myself to ask the question as Grayson made his way toward the information desk.

"Hemingway Station is the central transportation hub in the city. You're getting a train, and you're going far away from here."

His statement gave me pause as I bristled against someone telling me what to do and where to go. "You're going to have to give me more to go on than that. I mean, nothing about this day has gone like the letter I got, promised it would. What the hell is happening?"

I felt silly as I stomped one of my feet against the ground but it was too late to take the action back. If anything, my mini temper tantrum seemed to show Grayson that I wasn't just going to be some lost little lamb who went wherever he told me to go, at least not without more to go on.

"I've seen you twice today, and both times you were moments away from being taken against your will and shoved back into your origin story. Is that not reason enough to go somewhere else? Anywhere else?"

"That's not an explanation. I think there's been a mistake. None of this should be happening to me."

"Honestly Kadie, that's the question of the day. You, and others like you... you aren't supposed to be here in the city. And yet here you are. You have us scrambling for answers where there shouldn't even be questions.

My eyes narrowed as I dissected his statement. I couldn't say why but the tone of his voice had me more than a little insulted. What did he mean I wasn't supposed to be there? "I arrived here this morning," I explained, not sure how much he knew about me. I was already aware that it had to be more than a coincidence that this guy kept finding me right at the perfect moment. "I had this letter"—I took a second to rifle through my pocket, glad that at least I was no longer carrying my welcome letter around in my bra—"and it said all this stuff about me being a character in a book. And that I could start a new life here and that people would help me and everything would make sense and be fine."

Grayson watched me. In the bright lights of the train station I could make out far more of his features than I'd been able to in the dark, or in the blur of the fight earlier. He had deeply tanned skin with an olive tint to it, and his eyes were a slightly darker brown. His hair was nearly black, with curls that framed his face. "And let me guess, your day hasn't quite gone the way you expected."

I shook my head.

"Fair enough. To start, this is the city of Sanctum. It's one of the four capital cities of the After, situated in the Western Realms. Until today, at least for generations, new characters didn't arrive in the capital cities. Instead, they turned up in some of the more genre specific places throughout the world. No one is forced to stay where they first arrive, but many do as they end up feeling the most comfortable. Those places are set up to take in new arrivals. In Sanctum, everyone has been in the After for years, if not their whole lives. They choose to come here. So technically speaking, you really shouldn't be here. Yet, for some reason, over the course of ten minutes today, we started getting new arrivals all over the city. No more since then, but it was enough. No one knows what this means."

"Is that why people are trying to shove us back through Reclamation Centers, to pretend like this never happened?"

Grayson opened his mouth, but then closed it again in short order like he was rethinking what he wanted to say next. "We don't know. Your friend wasn't the first person to be disappeared since her arrival."

"And what about this?" I was about to pull my sweater

up from my wrist and shove it in his face, but Harper's words of warning earlier still rang in my head even if she wasn't there to speak them. Instead, I tried to subtly place my wrist in between the two of us so he could see it. The symbol etched into my skin was still there, as clear as ever. Despite the scar tissue, it still managed to look deliberate, almost artistic.

"That's the third of those symbols I've seen today. We're doing everything we can to figure it all out, but we don't know what it means. The people I work with are convinced that it must have some greater purpose or meaning, because the Archive doesn't make mistakes. But I'm telling you, the best chance of keeping you safe, of keeping you out of whatever is coming, is for you to go far away from here where no one, including me, knows where you are or where you're headed. Maybe you'll end up in a city more like wherever you came from, and you can settle in there like any other new arrival and start a life for yourself."

I looked around, suddenly nervous that somebody might be watching us but the few other people in the train station waiting for late trains all seemed to be minding their own business. Either that or fast asleep on nearby benches. It was a bit of a relief to have at least something explained to me, to learn the name of the city I had been running through all day. Sanctum—it wasn't the first time I'd heard it mentioned, but now the name held so much more meaning. It certainly hadn't felt all that much like a sanctum or sanctuary for me so far, but giving the place a name made it just a little more real.

Grayson must've taken my lack of answer as agreement. "Stay here," he said, before taking off toward the ticket counter. Feeling too exposed standing in the middle of the room, I wandered over to a large map that took up a few feet of wall space.

It was the kind of map you'd see in the opening pages of fantasy stories, dark lines etched onto faded parchment.

But the places this map showed me were well beyond anything I'd ever seen in a book. Unlike what I'd seen before, the ocean made up far less of the available space. There were undeniably four major landmasses, but I wasn't sure I would call them continents because each one was connected to the others in some form or another. There were still large swathes of water in between some of the spaces, but from a cursory glance at least there was no visible end to the land.

I found Sanctum on the map easily enough, even though it didn't have a large gold 'you are here' sticker. As promised, it sat near the western corner, on the edge of one of the larger bodies of water. Between Sanctum and the next city, which appeared to be New London, was a massive forest with no discernible landmarks besides trees and more trees. I tried to take everything in all at once but the number of things to see was overwhelming. So many forests and mountains and cities and open spaces and castles. And there had to be so much the map didn't show. I was mostly focusing on the main destinations that I could get to from Sanctum, but this map promised that and so much more.

There was no question that it was a big world out there, and it still wasn't one I could even begin to understand.

I heard Grayson come up behind me before he said anything. As I turned, he handed me a ticket and a small leather pouch. "There's money in there. For now, I've gotten you on the next train out of here but get off at whatever stop you want and get another train to anywhere you like. I'm sure you can recognize which cities will be most suited to you. But either way, there's enough here for you to do a little moving around. And then to make a start for yourself with whatever help you're able to find. I promise, if you go somewhere else, anywhere else, there will be people to help you. The After isn't in the habit of bringing in new people and simply leaving them to their own devices, unless that was exactly what they came from before. And even then, the help is there if it's needed or wanted. What happened to you today, it's inexcusable and inexplicable."

I looked up at the map again and tried to figure out where would make the most sense for me to go, but I could feel resistance building in my gut. There were so many different options, how could I possibly know which was the right one? After the day I'd had, the last thing I wanted was to get on a train by myself and shoot off in a direction of someone else's choosing. Yes, the decisions from there would be my own but I'd still be alone and clueless. There were so many things that could go wrong.

"And what if I don't want to go?" I asked, holding my jaw firm to try to hide a slight quiver of my lip.

"That's a mistake. We don't know enough about what's going on here or how you're involved. It's too risky."

"What do you care? You don't even know me." I knew it wasn't fair, that he'd already gone out of his way to help me, or to save me from myself. But that didn't change the fact that it wasn't his job to send me off like some wayward child to the countryside.

Part of me suspected that what he suggested was really was my best choice. Everything he was saying made sense. And I'd seen with my own eyes that this city wasn't exactly my good luck charm. So far, I'd had more bad luck than good, though I certainly counted meeting Harper strongly in the positive column. But at least I was starting to know my way around. Granted, not really a big win in the positives column, but it was something. Leaving would mean starting all over again.

"Is there another option?" I asked. "Is there any way I could stay here and still avoid getting myself killed or whatever. I don't want to be looking over my shoulder for the rest of my life, wondering how all of this played out, never knowing if I'm really safe."

I expected a snapped no right away, but instead Grayson considered my question. "There's no 'or whatever' about it. Let's be very clear here, if this is something you're considering. I know you're new and this will be more than a little strange for you, but finding yourself forced back into a Reclamation Center is a damn big deal. Being sent back is in some ways worse than death." Grayson paused, appearing to brace himself. "That being said, death isn't always a bad thing and some people do choose it. But dying in the After and being reclaimed to your origin story are two different things. If your friend had simply been killed, she'd wake up again without any memories back in whichever city made the most sense for her character. She would've started fresh, like her story had just finished and there was a world of possibilities in front of her. But reclamation is permanent. She's gone and will never be a part of this world again. So, if you take that train ride, and you end up in trouble, or even dead, it's probably still a better fit for you than if what happened to that girl happens to you."

"Harper. That girl's name was Harper." My tone was angry but I was doing my best to take in what he was telling me. On one hand, death wouldn't be the worst thing ever—which was a weird thing to even think to myself—but on the other, losing all my memories and starting over was a kind of death all on its own. And yes, maybe I'd wake up where I was supposed to be with no memories of everything that happened today, but I couldn't make myself see that as a good plan. I wanted to make the decision for myself, and to get the chance my letter had promised, to build my own life. I didn't know for sure that I wanted to build it in Sanctum, and deep down I knew that if my only other way was being left alone in a train station, then I'd do as I was told and go. But it wasn't what I wanted. Hell, I left Harper's backpack at that park along with whatever there was left in her wallet, and our breakfast and my pajamas from before. So now even the one thing I'd had when I'd first arrived was gone, probably forever.

Shit. There really were no obvious answers and I resented having to decide at all. I certainly wasn't in the right frame of mind for it.

Which meant I wasn't in anywhere near the right frame of mind to take a solo train trip in a world I didn't understand. There were going to be countless rules and laws of physics that were completely foreign to me.

No, I wanted to stay and I said as much aloud to Grayson. "If I stay, what does that mean for me?" I didn't ask if he'd leave me there because I didn't want to make it obvious that that was something I was considering.

"Then whatever happened here in the city today, you'll now officially be a part of it, for better or worse. You should come with me, to where I work. From there, it's mostly out of my hands, but I can at least promise protection. And we'll do our best to get you answers."

"Well, shit. That sounds way better. Why didn't you offer this in the first place?"

"Because I don't know what having you with us is going to accomplish, and there are no guarantees of your safety. This has already been tumultuous enough, and one less moving piece might have made things a little easier. Or you may offer the clue that we're looking for before we even know we need it. Honestly, at this point no one really knows what's going on and if you're prepared to put yourself in the middle of it, then I can't stop you. But if you want out, all the way out, then getting out of Sanctum is your only real course."

Apparently, the passageways that Harper and I found to the bazaar weren't the only shortcuts in the city. I did my best to keep up with Grayson's long stride as he practically charged from street to street, through doors that stood in places where they shouldn't be and out into different corridors that were instantly recognizable as being far away from where we started. It didn't take long at all to reach our destination, and when I found myself staring wide-eyed up at the giant white building I'd seen all day, I knew I made the right decision.

"This is where you work?" I asked.

Grayson was standing on the steps, watching me as I took in the sight in front of me. Before, I'd only seen the building from the back and one side, but the front was even more impressive. Large glass doors, easily three stories tall, stood in the center, and flags of a hundred different nations flapped above the entryway. The white stones seemed to glimmer in the moonlight, reminding me I was in a place shaped from fairytales.

"Come on, I've already been gone longer than I should've. If something has happened, then I need to get up to speed fast. But first, we'll get you somewhere to sleep and go from there."

I was surprised to find the front doors unlocked as we slipped into a massive lobby. Thick, red carpeting met my shoes, and in front of me were at least four different fireplaces each lit but with no chimneys overhead. I wasn't sure how they were avoiding getting smoke in the air, but I chalked it up to being along the same lines as Grayson turning into a bird or magical doorways to everywhere.

I only took a few steps inside the building before it became all too clear what this place was. From the lobby, I could make out glass railings on various floors circling up around a massive staircase. And through each of the railings I could see endless rows and rows of books. Bookcases stretched out in every direction, no wall separating the lobby from where the shelving began. There was plenty of seating, and an unmanned help desk close to the entryway. But most of the space was taken up by an impossible number of books. My university library had been impressive, one of the best in the country. But it had nothing on this, and I'd barely even gotten inside yet.

To my surprise, I looked over and found Grayson smiling at me, and a flash of color melted over his cheeks when our eyes met. "Come on. You'll have more than enough time to look around later. The others are already waiting for us."

I quirked an eyebrow, curious how anyone could be waiting for us when Grayson had only spoken to me since we'd run into one another. But he was already gone, it seemed he was less concerned with making sure I kept up now that we were in the safety of the building. It took me a second to spot him as he disappeared down an aisle of bookcases. Once I caught up, he turned again down a long hallway, lit by torches on the walls.

I yawned against my will, my body having had enough but my mind still on high alert. It was hard not to think that if I went to sleep again, yet another bad thing would happen to me.

I was getting sick of things just happening to me.

Finally, we stopped in a large open room by a desk manned by a female receptionist who looked even younger than I was. Behind her sat five heavy wooden doors, equally spaced out in a semicircle.

"Wait here," Grayson said. He nodded toward an armchair.

I sat down without argument and tried to smile at the receptionist but she was frantically typing away at the keyboard on her desk.

Instead, I watched as Grayson slipped into the center doorway. "We've got another one," was all I heard him say before the door clicked shut behind him.

CHAPTER EIGHT

Sitting in the sleek, leather-backed chair, I felt like I should've quite literally been twiddling my thumbs, trying to entertain myself to pass the time. Instead I did my best to sit still and look like a perfectly respectable adult human.

The receptionist seemed to be making a point of looking anywhere other than directly at me, giving me far too much time to study her from a distance. She had warm-toned brown skin and unnaturally white hair, cropped to almost exactly chin length. A few stray freckles dotted her complexion. Besides the color of her hair she didn't look anything like Harper, but my mind couldn't help but draw a comparison.

Harper should've been there with me. She was gone and I was still waiting for answers. None of it was fair. None of it was right. The white-haired receptionist looked up at me as I was still studying her, and I reminded myself for the dozenth time that I shouldn't be staring at people as often as I was. Yet another thing Harper had had to remind me of; I was starting to doubt whether I'd even survive in the After without her. But unlike all the other people whose attention I'd unwittingly drawn that day, the receptionist smiled, broad and genuine. "Hey," she said from the other side of her desk. "I'm Eliza."

"Kadie. But at this point I'm mostly just lost."

Her grin only spread further across her face. "It may have been suggested to me that I leave you alone, but I have to ask... Are you one of those people they've been talking about all day? One of the marked?"

At once my eyes flicked down to my wrist, too late I reminded myself to play it cool. This wasn't the kind of thing I should be advertising. But Eliza caught my reaction. "You are! Everyone has been on high alert all day, talking about new arrivals, and you're the third person they've shuffled in here, trying to stay under the radar. But I wasn't sure how much of what I was hearing was true, at least until now."

"There are more of us? Like me?"

"Two guys. At least, there were two guys brought in today that I didn't recognize. But no one tells me much of anything, so that's not anything new. I'm doing the best I can with what I've got."

"Girl, do I feel you on that one. That's basically been my entire day."

Eliza opened her mouth as though to ask something else, but it snapped shut again a second later. I wasn't ready to go back to sitting alone with my thoughts so I asked her, "What is it you do here?" Too late I realized I should've started with asking where here was.

"Apprentice librarian. I've only been dedicated to the Archive for three years, and I kind of lucked into this gig for the week." She gestured to her desk. "Usually, no one really trusts me with anything interesting. I'll get there."

I nodded like that made perfect sense. "Wait, you've worked here for three years already? You don't look like you could be much older than eighteen. Shouldn't you be in school or something?" Okay, I knew exactly how stupid it sounded as soon as the words tumbled from my mouth. I didn't know anything about this girl or where she'd come from.

"All right, so I'm starting to get the impression that what they've said about the marked having just arrived in the After today might be more truth than rumor. I'm guessing you have a lot of questions."

"Yes, and I would love you forever if you could answer even one of them. Like seriously… how old are you?" I winced a little, realizing right away that my question was both rude and potentially the waste of a chance to get real information.

Eliza grimaced, clearly that was just as rude a question here as it was where I was from but if I was dealing with some sort of child labor situation, I wanted to know about it. "Older than I look. Time passes differently here, but you'll adapt to it. Or you'll get used to just ignoring it, because honestly, I couldn't even explain to you how it works. I'm sure some of the archivists have a better handle on it, but aging is definitely not an exact science around these parts."

I must've blanched a little because Eliza chuckled. "Really, it's a good thing. You'll live a longer life than you ever would have before. And you get to do so much more cool stuff."

Of course, what she didn't say is that I only get to live longer if I managed to survive the next few weeks, or however long it took to get all of this figured out. "What else can you tell me?"

Eliza glanced over her shoulder at the door behind her. "I'm really not sure. I mean, you're in a tough spot and I'm kind of bad when it comes to inserting myself into situations I shouldn't be involved in. But at this point, I really don't want to lose my job."

I slumped back into my seat. Another dead end. "Tell you what," Eliza continued. "Once things are a little more sorted, and I get something of a go-ahead from the bosses, then you and I will take this on together. If they tell you anything, or if I learn anything, we'll swap secrets. At least that way we'll both be a little less in the dark."

"I'll take what I can get." I smiled at her, grateful that someone else was being friendly, a feeling that was still more bitter than sweet after losing Harper.

Losing everyone. I hadn't even considered until then that since I'd arrived in Sanctum by mistake, my friends and family, really everyone I've ever known, had gone somewhere else. Okay, yes that meant that Darren and Kelsey were snuggling in some quiet café far away from me, which was both nice and gross at the same time. But I had no way to know where everyone else had gone or if there was any way to find them. Could be I'd made the wrong call by not getting on the train and at least giving myself a chance at finding them.

Something electronic buzzed in front of Eliza and she looked down at her desk. "They want to see you." I didn't know what to make of the look in her eyes as she watched me stand up before waving me past her desk to the doors beyond.

The center door opened before I was even three feet in front of it.

Well that wasn't ominous at all.

I moved into a large, dimly lit office. Across from me was a long desk with four people behind it, all wearing serious, tired expressions. I took one of the two empty seats on the other side without an invitation, not looking at the panel who seemed to have assembled to meet with me. Not one of them saying anything until I sat down. At least Grayson was there, a face I recognized if not one I was all that comfortable with.

Two men and two women sat across from me, each wearing simple white robes, smudged with lines of gray. Grayson was on the end beside a woman who was seventy years old if she was a day, with dark skin and wiry grey hair pulled up into a topknot. Beside her was another woman, younger, say forty-years-old. She had pale skin and sleek black hair that hung in layers around her shoulders. Her brown eyes studied me more suspiciously than the others.

On the opposite end of the table from Grayson sat a boy who couldn't have been older than seventeen. He had the perfect skin of an unusually blessed teenager, and wavy blonde hair that was almost picturesque, like he should have been modeling for shampoo or at least be the default photo in a picture frame. But something about him suggested that he was far older than he looked as he leaned into the table to study me—or maybe what Eliza had said about time passing differently had just gotten in my head. "So, I believe introductions are in order," the youngest at the table said, looking at me and smiling.

No one else spoke so I assumed they meant that I was the one meant to introduce myself. I went through the motions of saying who I was for the third or fourth time that day. It was getting a little exhausting.

Thankfully, Grayson jumped in. "This," he said, indicating the woman at his right, "is Joanna Nyce. Beside her is Marissa Dorset. And on the left, is Jonathan Credence."

I didn't do much more than stare, my brain moving in slow motion. "Nice to meet you." My greeting came out as more of a question but it was the best I could do.

It was the older woman who spoke next, and she sounded kind which I wasn't expecting. "We are the heads of this branch of the Archive of Ink and Soul. Where you are now. The Archive is the true heart of the After. Between the walls of its four branches you can find every single book from which the people who populate this world first came."

I just managed to stop myself from swearing in disbelief. So, this building housed, what, every book ever written?

"I'm sure you have a million questions," Jonathan said. "But first, we have a few for you. We found ourselves in quite a dilemma today, and would like to know why. At this point, anything we could learn might be helpful. So, if you don't mind sharing with us a few things about yourself, it would be very much appreciated."

I looked over at Grayson and he nodded slightly. It's not like I had any choice. And I'd missed my shot to get on that train and avoid all this. "What do you want to know?"

"Anything you can tell us, really." Jonathan's hand moved from the table into his lap as he watched me. "Information about yourself, where you came from and then your experiences today. I promise you, no detail is insignificant, especially any special talents you might have. We want to know all of it."

I wasn't sure how I felt about sharing all of it, but if there was any chance he might help I was willing to take that risk. I started talking, rambling more like it. I didn't go into that much detail about my life because I just couldn't find a natural place to start. But I did tell them the last thing I remembered, and a little bit about me. My job, going to school, my parents. I didn't see it coming but unsurprisingly they did ask a few questions about where I'd lived, treating it more like a setting than a real city that I'd lived in my whole life.

"No magic," I said again, after the fourth roundabout question about my abilities, and the realm of possibility from where I'd come.

They all nodded not quite as one, and let the subject drop, but more than one expression read at least a little wary, like they didn't quite believe me. Hell, I would've signed up to be from a place with magic in a heartbeat.

I continued with everything from my arrival in that alleyway, to almost getting run over by a guy in a kilt and seeing bubbles in the air, to meeting Harper right through to losing her. For that part, no one interrupted with anything to add or ask. They just let me talk. And I impressed myself that I managed not to cry. My body was starting to remember just how tired it was as the adrenaline of yet another new situation wore off. The longer I sat the harder it got not to just lie down and take a nap on the floor.

I finally finished my story, getting caught up in it until I reached the end. I took in a long breath, relieved, when Jonathan circled back to the same question he asked before. "So, you're absolutely certain you don't have any preternatural abilities? Nothing out of the ordinary, no spells, no wishes, no elemental control or the ability to talk to animals?"

I shook my head emphatically. "No, two days ago, magic wasn't real. Not for me. It was the kind of thing you read about in books, sure. Or that you wished you had. But no one I know can do anything all that spectacular, and I've never seen any signs of it in my life."

"What about since you arrived in the After? Have you done anything out of the ordinary?" The young man's eyes lit up as he waited for my answer and I was sorry to disappoint him.

"Well, it's probably safe to say that I've done quite a bit out of the ordinary today. Absolutely everything about my day has been nothing like what I would call ordinary. But the closest I've come to doing anything magic is seeing this guy shift from a bird into a man." I cocked my thumb over at Grayson who barely managed to push back a smirk.

I was starting to feel like something of a disappointment.

"I find it hard to believe that if the Archive somehow intended to show us something by bringing new arrivals here, that it would have bothered with prosaics," the younger woman, Joanna, said.

"Alas, that is not really your area of expertise," the older woman responded, but the slightest tick of a frown at the corner of her mouth suggested she agreed with Joanna.

Joanna nodded her head. "And so, the question is what do we do with her now, and the others?"

Marissa answered, frowning a little. I tried to convince myself it wasn't worry I was seeing on her features. "They're here now, so we might as well keep an eye on them until we can get some answers. If we send them back out there in the morning, they'll be tracked down just as quickly as they were today. And I have to wonder how many more are out there that weren't found by those Literati mercenaries, that just managed to slip through the cracks. We're not even sure how many people we're looking for and until we know more, I'm hesitant to do anything we can't take back."

Grayson answered. "The good news there is that if we don't know about them maybe the Literati don't either. We still have time to put all of the pieces together."

I wanted to raise my hand and ask exactly what it was they were trying to figure out but I kept my mouth shut. I was starting to think I was so tired that all of this around me was a dream all over again. I stopped myself from pinching to be sure, I didn't need another bruise or another disappointment.

CHAPTER NINE

What was left of my night passed in a blur. Grayson ended up staying with the others in the small office, where they talked in hushed voices and cast me a few furtive glances before Eliza ushered me back through the door before she escorted me upstairs to what she called the dormitories.

She said that the block of bedrooms included in the building weren't used as permanent housing for the people who worked in the building—librarians—but were mostly for when someone got lost in a project or needed to be in early.

And now, there were three of us living in one row of bedrooms. Eliza pointed out that the two beside me were already occupied before bringing me into my own room.

It looked like every hotel room I'd ever seen. A queen-size bed in the middle of the room with an end table on either side and two identical lamps. There was a dresser against the opposite wall, but no television on the top of it. In the far corner of the room sat a beige armchair with another side table, and an empty desk. It felt a little cramped, but at least I had a bathroom all to myself.

I was even more grateful for the bathroom when my door locked with a click as it shut behind Eliza. A second later, another click grabbed my attention.

I turned the doorknob a few times, hoping the sound was only a figment of my imagination. But by that point I had no fight left in me. I was locked in, but it wasn't like I had anywhere else to go.

I went back and forth a few times on whether to shower right away or in the morning, but no one really told me what to expect the next day and I didn't want to risk being woken up with no warning, still looking like I'd crawled out of a dumpster.

Having hot water rush over my body in torrents was a glorious experience. Thoughts and memories kept trying to creep up on me, reminding me of everything I'd been through but I pushed them back repeatedly. Absolutely everything was out of my control and I just needed time to rest and regroup.

It wasn't long before I was fast asleep.

Waking up, I was immediately assaulted by a rush of memories and confusion. It felt like I'd slept for a long time, which was potentially great news, but if I'd been asleep for well over eight hours how come no one had come for me yet? I slipped back into my clothes and then took a few minutes in the washroom to freshen up all over again, still not feeling entirely clean.

Ready as I was ever going to be, I knocked on the door to my own room, hoping someone would answer from the other side.

Nobody came.

I was still stuck there, essentially a prisoner.

No, literally a prisoner.

Letting out a low groan of frustration, I walked away from the door, completely out of ideas. No one I'd met the night before had hinted that their plan had simply been to lock me up and throw away the key, but it was hard to feel even a hint of optimism.

"Urrgghhhh!" Before I knew what I was doing, my feet were carrying me back to the door. I banged my fist against the frame several times, shouting incoherently as frustration poured out of me. It didn't do much to make me feel better, but at least I was doing something.

And then someone knocked back. Except, the noise wasn't coming from the door. I tempered down my outrage, listening. Nothing.

With a few quick raps of my knuckles, I knocked on the front door again. This time, the response came right away. Someone was knocking on a wall of my room.

The sound came again and I did my best to follow it to the exact spot where someone was trying to get in touch with me from the other side. I knocked a few times, trying to tap out a catchy beat. Yes, sometimes my priorities could be off.

"Hello," a muffled voice came through the wall.

"Hi," I answered, likely sounding a little overexcited. I wasn't sure how loudly I needed to speak to be heard through drywall.

"Do you work here? Any chance you could let me out?"

"No luck. I'm stuck too. Were you brought in yesterday?"

The voice came through more clearly this time and there was no question that its owner was a guy, one with a bit of a southern accent. "Yeah, long story but I'm pretty sure I've been trapped in this room for almost a day now. They brought me food a couple times but won't answer my questions. Or you know, let me go."

"I know that feeling. I'm Kadie," I volunteered.

"Devon. And it's nice to meet you because the guy at the other end of my room, Marc, has been a bit of a dick so far. Not exactly helpful, or chatty."

I groaned loud enough for Devon to hopefully hear me from the other side of the wall. "Don't you hate when your fellow hostages aren't the friendly chatty types?"

"And you know what, it happens to me all the time. Plus, as a bonus, I'm pretty sure I'm being mocked by all of this taupe wallpaper."

I chuckled, grateful for the distraction. The fact that I was glad to have someone else stuck with me wouldn't win me any humanitarian awards any time soon, but I'd take the company all the same.

I shifted so my back was leaning against the wall, head tilted up slightly to stare at a white ceiling and a generic looking light fixture, making myself remember where I was. This wasn't the time to get complacent just because I had someone to talk to. I was still a prisoner in some strange building. A fate I was convinced I'd volunteered myself for.

"Devon. Question. I wish I could say this was going to be the weirdest thing that has crossed my mind recently, but you're on board with this whole, we're all book characters thing, right?"

"I guess."

"Any chance you came from some sort of super thriller where you have epic skills that might help us escape?" It was a long shot but I figured it was at least worth asking. I'd seen some strange things the day before and knew it was entirely possible that I could run into someone with the exact skills that I needed and never know it. If he did have some sort of ability like that one and I didn't ask, I'd feel like a moron for a very long time.

"No luck. I'm just a university student from Texas. How about you?"

"Yoga instructor from Pennsylvania. I've learned pretty quickly that my list of useful skills is too damn short."

"Well, that's not that helpful. And I don't know about you, but my room doesn't even have a window I can try to jimmy open."

"Same here. No windows, just two doors. One to the bathroom, and one I couldn't open if my life depended on it." And for all I knew, it did.

"What about the other side of your room?" Devon asked. "Try knocking over there and see if anyone else answers. I mean, we're probably still not going to get a jewel thief, but who knows."

I briefly remembered my conversation with Eliza the night before and how she'd mentioned that there had only been two other people like me who came in, but I'd been tired enough that I wasn't going to trust my own memory. I went across the room and knocked. Immediately, I felt the difference in the wall, far heavier than the one I shared with Devon. There wasn't another room on the other side.

"No one there. I think my room might be at the end of the hallway, so there wouldn't be a room there anyway."

"You don't remember if you're at the end of the hallway?"

"Hey, it was really late when I came in. And before you go judging me, shouldn't you remember whether you were the second to last room in the hall?"

"Fair point. I just…"

"I get it. It's safe to say that yesterday was the strangest day of my life. Or even of my new life, because I can't imagine anything else happening here that would be as bizarre as what I went through yesterday." At least, I hoped not. I couldn't afford to lose anyone else. Hell, I didn't have anyone else to lose. Off the top of my head, I knew a grand total of seven other people's names in the After.

"Okay, so we're on our own. But that doesn't mean we just sit around here and wait." Devon's voice came through calm and reassuring. "Is there anything in your room that might be small enough to use to maneuver the lock on our doors open?"

"Is that something you know how to do?"

"No, but I've seen it done in the movies a lot. And the way I'm looking at it is that a lot of the movies I watched were based on books, and even the ones that weren't, were influenced by them. In the movies, people can pick locks all the time no matter how much actual experience they have. So, if this place is based on stories, then maybe we can pull off a miracle."

"And then what?"

"That is a very good question. But let's go one thing at a time on this one, shall we?"

"Fair enough. So just look around for small things and then go for it?"

"It's the best plan I've got."

I spent the next few minutes searching every corner of my room looking for anything that was either small and metal or I could break apart to become the same. But honestly, it was more a way to distract myself than anything else. Not only did neither Devon nor I have a chance in hell of picking the lock and escaping, but neither one of us had anywhere to go. Even if we somehow managed to find our way back out of the library, that would put me right back to where I was yesterday. No answers, no friends, no food, and no money beyond what Grayson had handed me, which I wasn't exactly sure I could keep.

I didn't really want to go anywhere, but I also didn't want to stay locked up. So, I searched. I searched until I was certain that apart from shattering the mirror in the bathroom to try to get a tiny glass shard, I was completely out of options

I was more than ready to admit defeat. And kind of hopeful that Devon would continue to keep me company until something new happened, just so I wouldn't have to be alone with my thoughts anymore.

No Darren. No parents. No Harper. Nothing.

I tapped on the wall in the same spot where Devon and I had been speaking. There was no answer after a few seconds and I knocked again. I'd been thorough in my search of the sparsely decorated room and couldn't imagine that Devon's hunt would take much longer. I waited for a minute and then knocked again more enthusiastically, sure there was no way he wasn't hearing me. But he still didn't answer.

I pressed my ear close to the wall and listened for the sound of his voice but only got a gentle hum. Could be there was something going on nearby but I couldn't guarantee it was coming from Devon's room or even this floor. This building was probably ancient, and kind of strange so I wasn't about to bet anything on what I was seeing or hearing.

I knocked one last time before flopping backwards onto my bed. He was gone. And I almost had to wonder whether if I'd imagined him in the first place, desperate not to be alone anymore. Could I have conjured up another prisoner in the room next to me so I'd have someone to talk to.

And now I didn't even have that.

My heart felt heavy in my chest and already I was tired all over again like I hadn't just slept for several hours. And really, who could say how long I'd slept? With no windows, I was only going on my own feelings, and with everything I'd been through, those were as upside down as everything else.

I reached up over my head, intending to grab a pillow and press it over my face so I could scream out my frustrations in false privacy. But as soon as my fingers grasped around a cotton pillowcase I heard a faint tapping from somewhere nearby.

I sat up, and right away it was clear that the sound wasn't coming from where I'd been talking to Devon. It wasn't coming from the wall at all. Someone was knocking at my door, and a second later I heard a lock snapping open.

They were coming for me, whoever they were. And I had no idea if that was a good thing or not.

I scrambled up and ran a hand over my hair in the process. At least I'd showered the night before, not that I would consider myself or how I looked even remotely presentable. But it would have to do.

The door swung open slowly, as though the person opening it was waiting to see if I would react badly. But I stood and waited, not wanting to do anything at all. Not wanting to make the wrong impression.

It was Eliza's face I found on the other side of the door, smiling at me. "Good morning," she called into the room, voice teasing. "I hear you were planning a great escape."

I blushed a little but before I could answer I caught sight of two figures standing behind Eliza, both taller than she was and unmistakably masculine. Had they sent armed guards to wrestle me into submission?

While both men behind Eliza were tall, neither one of them wore the white robes she did. Besides their height, they looked almost nothing alike. The taller of the two had short black hair, and dark eyes that glowered at me. To my eye, he was undeniably Asian, but I reminded myself not to make any assumptions. For all I knew he came from a fantasy world or a human colony on Mars.

The other guy looked much more approachable, smiling at me already. He had shaggy brown hair and green eyes that seemed to reflect laughter. Everything about him screamed surfer. I'd never seen either one of them before, but there was something oddly familiar about the latter of the two.

"Devon?" I asked, smiling because I was just that confident I'd guessed right.

"Kadie," he answered back, tipping his head slightly as though playing with an imaginary cowboy hat. "It seems as though our plan has worked brilliantly. They've set us free and without our having to do any work at all." A moment later, he was laughing maniacally, the sound the pinnacle of an evil super villain laugh.

Seconds later, both Eliza and I were almost doubled over laughing along with him, though the noises we made sounded at least a little more natural.

The other guy had taken a step back from Devon, and as I looked up I could have sworn I saw him roll his eyes.

Note to self, pretty safe bet on which of these guys I didn't want to bother being friends with.

Once we'd caught our breath again, Eliza ushered me out of my room and into the hall.

"Alright, you all have everything you need?" she asked. "I'm not sure if you'll be back here again until the end of the day."

I looked over at Devon who just shrugged. "That would probably be a no," I answered. "But I've got everything I own on me right now, so that's about as good as it's getting."

Eliza winced. "Right, sorry. Well, off we go, all the same, right?"

Devon gave a thumbs up while I shook my head, still both amused and perplexed. It was going to be an interesting day.

CHAPTER TEN

"On our left, here we have the main lobby. The front entry to the Archive is on Cuthbert Street, but there's a secondary door on the other end of the building as well." Eliza led the three of us past the stairwell overlooking the front of the building where I'd first entered the building with Grayson the night before. Our rooms were on the third floor, and a quick look upward promised that we weren't even halfway up the building. The promise of books, books and then still more books was even more overwhelming in the daylight, and based on how big the Archive looked from outside, it would be all too easy to get lost in the vast labyrinth of shelves this place held.

"Fantastic," Marc said from somewhere behind me, voice completely deadpan. "And I'm all for getting a tour of the building rather than being locked up like hostages. But when are we getting out of here?"

Eliza stopped walking and whirled back toward us in an instant, her eyes locking onto Marc's. The two of them stared one another down for a few seconds before she finally spoke. "Look, buddy. I told you this when you first got out of your room and nothing has changed since. You're not a prisoner here…"

"Then let me go."

"That's not my call to make. People who know far more about what's going on than I do seem to think it's particularly important that you stay put. And since, from what I've heard, you about got yourself killed by being out on your own yesterday, there is no reason you can't be at least a little more cooperative. Enjoy the tour, we'll grab some lunch. Make this easier on all of us."

Marc opened his mouth to argue, but shut it before responding. I wasn't even sure what outcome I was rooting for. Grayson had warned me that coming back here with him would have consequences, but there was no longer any question that I didn't have as much freedom as I had a day ago. Still, staying in the Archive, at least for a while meant I wouldn't be waiting to be attacked all the time.

Eliza nodded, satisfied. "The councilors are taking the morning to come up with a plan, or at least a plan to help them make a plan. You'll know more about what's next by this afternoon."

I was willing to play a game of wait and see, and from Marc's sullen silence I could guess he was opting to do the same, at least for the time being.

The silence that followed us as we passed by the central stairwell and between two long rows of bookshelves was nothing if not awkward. For a full minute, no one said a word and I let my eyes wander to the spines of the books surrounding me. I only caught a few titles here and there, and not one of them I recognized.

I had never been an especially great reader but had tried to pick up a few titles beyond those I'd been assigned in school. Still, here I felt woefully outmatched. And still, it was fascinating, seeing all these books in one place and realizing that they meant so much more than I'd ever realized. Of course, I hadn't had any chance of taking in just how necessary books were to my existence back in my old life, and now it felt impossible to truly appreciate everything they'd given me.

"Are the books here organized by genre?" Devon asked, his fingers trailing over several books as he walked, finally breaking the silence. "Is it a Dewey Decimal kind of thing?"

Eliza chuckled but didn't slow. "Good old Dewey didn't exactly have a system like ours in mind when he started organizing libraries back in the day. He was a lot less concerned with fiction than we are, so we had to come up with our own system over the years. We end up adapting it more often than you'd think as the book world evolves out there in the other world."

"The real world, you mean," Marc said, a hint of scorn in his voice.

"What is real?" Eliza said, sounding both whimsical and philosophical all at once. Her tone remained light, but there was an edge to it, promising that her patience with Marc was already running thin. "I mean, we're here. This is happening. That's real enough for me. But overall, there's not actually a consensus. Some people in the After call it the real world, some call it the other world, lots of us don't think about it at all."

All of this was going on as we continued to move through the building, trusting Eliza to take us wherever we were supposed to be, but my attention was only half focused on the conversation going on around me. The rest of my mind kept tugging at threads of ideas forming from what Eliza had told us. Even admitting to myself that I believed I was a book character, or that I had started out that way, didn't mean I'd even begun to come to terms with what all of that meant for me. For my life, both before and now.

As I stared at the countless books we passed, I kept getting stuck on the idea that I had come from one of these. Somewhere in this building was the book I'd been formed in. My whole story, cover to cover. And not just mine, everyone I'd ever known.

I took a few quick steps to catch up with Eliza. "What exactly is your system for placing books in the Archive?" I asked, wanting more of an answer than what Devon had been able to get.

"Yup. Mostly genre based. Different sections for different kinds of books, but you know there are authors out there who are making it their life's mission to make things more challenging. You wouldn't believe some of the random stuff I've read…"

Any other day whatever tangent she was about to fall into would have fascinated me, but for once I felt the need to interrupt her, to stop the flow of information before it began. "So, can people come in here and look up the books they came from?"

Eliza's expression scrunched up as she considered the question. Eventually, she just shrugged, like it wasn't something she had ever given much thought to, an idea that seemed completely absurd to me. "In theory. And there are librarians who train to help people find their origin stories, but there isn't that much call for them. Most people in the After never venture out past the region they start off in and probably don't even realize Sanctum is here."

"But it's possible?" To my surprise, it was Marc who had joined the conversation, taking a quick hop forward so he was out in front of Eliza and me, walking backward to watch Eliza as he moved down the aisle. "Could I look up the book I came from and… I'm not sure. But could it happen?"

Devon had squeezed in beside me as well, noticeably hanging on to every word of our conversation. He had to be just as curious about this possibility as I was. With just one book we could learn everything that had been written about our lives, learn things about ourselves we'd never considered.

Eliza turned a little, taking in each of us in turn. Whatever she saw must have been enough to really grab her attention. "It's not as simple as that. I mean, we have a database with titles, authors and genres, but can any of you tell me the name of the book you came from?"

Huh.

Well, that was something I hadn't considered. And no matter how hard I searched my memories, nothing jumped out at me. Neither Devon nor Marc had an answer either.

"Don't feel too bad. No one ever does. Figuring out an origin story is rarely simple."

"If you could, figure it out I mean," Marc said, sounding sincerer than he had since first being let out of his room, "could someone here maybe tell us which city we were supposed to have started in? The city where the people we knew would have been brought to?"

At last, Eliza stopped, facing all of us. "In theory… but, it's a little more complicated than that." She paused to check a rectangular device in her pocket. "We probably have time for a quick detour." She didn't bother waiting for an answer. "Yeah, we've got time to do this. I mean, no one here seems to know what to do with you yet anyway. What do you guys say, are you dying for food or do you want to see something potentially kind of cool?"

"Food can wait," I said immediately. Both Devon and Marc nodded their approval.

"In that case," Eliza pumped her fist into the air, "turn around and go back the way we came!"

The trip to wherever we were going didn't seem to take long, though I wasn't focusing enough that I could have made the trip back in reverse. All I could really think about was that somewhere nearby was *my* book. I only really started to see past the endless books when the four of us left behind the well decorated décor of the main library and headed down a cement staircase into a basement. The flight of stairs came out into an equally spare hallway that curved slightly as it stretched out in the distance. We passed several open doorways to empty offices filled with books and I couldn't help but take a peak in every one as we passed.

"This way," Eliza said, calling out to us, and I realized that I'd fallen several paces behind everyone else in my attempt to explore.

We all stopped in front of a set of double swinging metal doors, each with a small round window, displaying yet more books on the other side.

Without any fanfare, Eliza pushed the door on the left open and held it while the three of us entered the room. Once we were inside it was clear that it was more of a warehouse than a single room. Concrete walls spread out in the distance and neither the floor nor the ceiling offered much in the way of aesthetically pleasing décor. Which made sense since no one had bothered to do anything besides fill the with books. If I'd thought the shelves on the floors above us were overwhelming, this was something else entirely. There were no shelves, no tables, no chairs. Nothing but books. They sat stacked in massive piles one on top of the other, pile after pile in only a vague semblance of rows. I'd called it a warehouse, but most warehouses I'd seen had been significantly better organized. And that was saying something.

"What is this place?" I asked Eliza. Part of me had been hoping that she was going to take us somewhere that we could just look up our origin stories and find all the answers we'd been hoping for. Instead, she had brought us to pure chaos in book form.

"See up there?" Eliza said, pointing to a nearby stack of books that wasn't quite as high as the one beside it, only coming up to about my waist or so. It was hard to imagine how someone had managed to put that many books in one place without the entire collection toppling downward. "Watch it carefully."

I wanted to ask more questions but did as I was told, keeping my gaze fixed on the pile of books Eliza had pointed out. Because Marc wasn't making a fuss beside me, I had to assume that he and Devon were doing the same.

It only took a second to see what Eliza had been waiting for, as a thick hardcover book popped into existence on the top of the stack. Except, pop was an exaggeration. One moment it hadn't been there, and the next there it was. Like someone had just placed it on top of the pile.

No, like magic. Laughter bubbled up out of me, surprised and delighted.

But if I'd been excited by the book appearing out of nowhere, Devon's reaction was ten times stronger.

"Holy shit," he said, barely able to contain the laughter in his voice. "That was incredible. How did you do that?"

"I didn't do anything." Eliza didn't sound as impressed as I felt. "That's the Archive at work. As new books are completed, they arrive here to be sorted by librarians. You'd think a place like this would be able to drop a book in its rightful place on the shelves as easily as placing it down here, but no such luck. Instead, we get new books all the time. Sometimes thousands a day, and they all start here then they have to be sorted and brought upstairs so they can be found easier later. It's a bit of a process."

"There. It happened again." I turned toward the direction Marc was looking and didn't see anything out of the ordinary. But then again, I wouldn't have. But I certainly believed him, and that wherever he'd been looking there was now one more book there than there had been a minute ago.

"So, the books don't all go in that stack then?" I asked, my eyes drifting back to the original pile we'd been looking at. Because Eliza had pointed it out, I'd assumed that all the new books were appearing on that same place. Which would mean all the books that had come in yesterday would be all in the same place, and hopefully easy to find.

"Alas, no. That would be too easy. We can usually tell which piles are active based on the size, but it's not always quite that easy. On some days, the books seem to appear in piles that correspond to the sections of the Archive that they will be sorted into. Other days, it's completely random. And then on the days when the Archive is particularly annoyed at us for whatever reason, we start getting new books scattered around the building. Never a title left in the right place, of course. But a never-ending Easter egg hunt that no one can ever see coming or really figure out the right answer to. And because of how quickly books are being published now, there's always a backlog. Always. I don't think I've ever seen this room more than half empty, and it's not the only warehouse in the building. So, there are always books to be sorted, and never enough people to see to it. I figure, once I finish off my rotation playing receptionist for the Council, then I'll end up stuck back sorting again for a few weeks. They have us, apprentices, do a bit of everything so that we have a decent sense of what our options are before we pledge to one order or another."

I was still barely hearing anything Eliza was saying, though I tried to remember as much as I could to really think on it later. My book might have been in that room. My friends, my family, Darren.

"Okay, but you guys all saw that book just appear out of nowhere, right?" Devon's voice still held a giddy note. "That was freaking incredible. It was magic! This is too damn cool."

At last, I made myself look away from the piles of books and focused on my new friend's face. Before, I would've guessed he was in about his mid-to-late twenties. But with the way he was grinning at the piles and piles of books, I now pegged him as just out of his teens.

"Right. I keep forgetting you guys are all probably prosaics. None of you came from worlds with magic, right?"

"I didn't," I said, and looked over at the guys who were both shaking their heads.

"I saw some pretty crazy stuff yesterday, so you can call me a believer," Marc said, "but before that I was just a cop in Chicago. But some guy yesterday called me that too. Prosaic. He didn't exactly make it seem to a good thing."

"It just means someone who came from a world without magic. Or sometimes someone non-magical in a magical story."

"I don't care what you call me, I just want to see more stuff like that," Devon said.

"Well, we should probably get going. I promised Keeper I'd get you guys fed and then up to the classrooms to meet with Joanna. Lucky you."

Eliza didn't wait for us and instead pushed her way back out of the warehouse and into the hallway. I cast one last look back at all the books, just at the right moment to see yet another pop into existence. I could almost feel it in my bones that my book was in that room somewhere, but could do nothing about it.

CHAPTER ELEVEN

"Any chance you have a map or pamphlet of some kind we could use to find our way around this place?" I asked as the four of us traversed yet another set of stairs. Even though we just left the lower level, we'd had to go all the way back up through the lobby to get to our new destination which was in a completely separate basement.

"Not really. We have a map near the front lobby so people can find the genres they're interested in, and there are librarians around if they still need help finding something specific. No one's ever needed any more than that," Eliza said, while Devon and I shared a look like she was clearly a crazy person. There didn't seem to be any rhyme or reason to how this place was set up and I didn't relish the idea of poking around without a personal tour guide. Although, left on my own, I'd find some interesting things just by picking a direction and walking for a while.

No part of me thought that the Archive was boring, but it definitely required a map.

We ended up in a large staff room decorated with sofas, a few small televisions sitting on desks, plus of course more books. A passion for reading was clearly a prerequisite for becoming a librarian. Deep blue throw rugs under a matching set of coffee tables formed a focal point around the three seating areas in the middle of the room.

From the other end of the staff room we entered a large area that could only be described as a cafeteria. It was smaller than the one I remembered from my high school but was arranged in the same way, with endless long tables and chairs filling most of the room. There was a long row of stoves, microwaves, and counter space, presumably for the use of anyone who needed it. And in the corner sat a few different appliances that at first I thought were refrigerators, but at a closer look were far wider than what I was expecting.

There was only one other person in the room and he didn't so much as look up when we came in, intent on his plate of pasta as he shoveled spoonful after spoonful into his mouth. He wore the same white robes as everyone else but I could see his were spattered with red sauce.

Eliza deposited us at the end of a row of tables close to the kitchen area and took off at a jog toward one of the appliances I couldn't put a name to.

Devon, Marc, and I sat in bewildered silence as we waited for her to return, each staring off at something different, lost in thought.

When Eliza came back a minute later, she was carrying something I absolutely recognized. A cardboard pizza box whose lid we quickly flipped open. My mouth started to water right away. I was even more impressed when she set it down on the table and I could see steam coming off the combination of sauce and cheese. Eliza deposited four water bottles onto our table from a paper bag she'd been carrying along with the pizza.

"You get delivery to this place?" Devon asked. Eliza only nodded, already intent on picking up a slice of the pizza for herself. "How cool is it that this place has magic, and still has pizza delivery?" Devon grinned but a second later his mouth was busy tearing into a slice of pepperoni pizza.

I could only mmm my agreement as my mouth was already full. The pizza wasn't quite as good as the one I'd eaten at the pub the day before, but the fact that it was hot enough to have just come out of the oven moments ago, was more than enough to make up for the slightly bland taste.

Just as I was leaning in to grab a second piece, a commotion came from the other side of the room. A large group had come in through the same door we'd used, talking amongst themselves. There had to be at least a dozen people, a mix of men and women all dressed in workout clothes rather than the attire I was finally getting used to seeing.

The moment the crowd saw us, their voices hushed. They were still talking, but far quieter than they had been a moment before and at least half of the group seemed fixated on ours. They were talking about us, I was sure of it.

"Ignore them," Eliza said in a whisper, as soon as she swallowed what had been in her mouth. "Nosy bastards, all of them."

I didn't respond, worried I'd be overheard, or that I'd just say the wrong thing. I had never minded a little extra attention, but ever since arriving in the After, the attention I was getting never seemed to be the right kind. It was possible that this new crowd was just interested because we were outsiders, but I'd already seen enough to know there was more to it. These guys knew who we were, and why we were here. At least as well as anyone else did.

As the four of us ate in silence, the feeling of strangers watching my every move was almost palpable. It only felt slightly less unnerving than the sensation of being hunted, which I'd experienced the day before. Neither was much fun.

Despite our discomfort, we still managed to finish off the large pizza in record time. I tried to ignore the little voice in the back of my head that was already wondering where my next meal would come from as I swallowed my last bite.

I missed regular meals, and knowing where my food was coming from. And not having to feel gratitude towards those who took enough pity on me to make sure I had something to eat. Not that I wasn't grateful, but I did miss just being able to go into my own kitchen and make my own dinner without it being a highlight of my day.

"What do you guys say, ready to get out of here?" Eliza didn't wait for an answer as she hopped up from her seat, confident the three of us would follow quickly, which we did without hesitation.

As we passed the big group, very few of them bothered to feign an interest in their own lunches long enough to stop studying us. My gaze darted down to my wrist as I covered my new scar with my other hand, trying to look inconspicuous. Was this the thing that made me so interesting?

I still had Harper's bracelet from the night before, but I had put it on my other wrist, not giving the action much thought at the time. Now, far more deliberately, I unsnapped the claps and then reattached it over the scarred sunrise on my wrist. I forced myself not to look away when I caught the eye of a brown-skinned woman who watched me with an intense level of concentration, but I still felt guilty somehow.

"Hey guys, how's it going?" Eliza said with a wave as she reached the door. She didn't wait for a response, but her face had been plastered with a toothy grin that didn't quite seem genuine.

"What was that about?" Marc asked. "What happened to 'nosy bastards'?"

"Those guys are the Protectorate, essentially law enforcement for the Archive. Since I haven't decided yet which order I'll be pledging once I graduate, no point in pissing anyone off."

"You might end up working with those guys?" I asked.

"Probably not. I'm leaning toward becoming a Scholar, but we're not supposed to get too attached to any one order over another until we have experience with all of them. Next year I can actually try working within the orders and see what I like best."

Eliza took a different route to get us back up to the main level, and I was starting to suspect that she was keeping us deliberately confused about how to get around inside the Archive.

We took off for the back of the building, and soon I caught sight of a large clearing of shelves in the distance that seemed to have seating and even a coffee cart, but I lost track of it before long.

"So, there are Scholars and the Protectorate. What else?" I asked, both out of a need to fill the silence and a deep desire to know *more*.

"There are four orders, each headed by one of the councilors. Protectorate, led by the Hand of the Archive. The Head leads the Scholars—they focus on using the incoming books to learn as much as they can about the other world and their technology, and how we can implement what they've learned in our own world. Then there are the Archivists, led by Eye. They're focused on tracking the characters who enter the After and how the world changes because of these new additions and new books."

Eliza paused only long enough to unlock a heavy oak door at what looked to be the back of the building. But instead of reaching sunlight, we slipped through the door into yet another block of rooms. These were decorated more like a house than a public building, with plush furniture and portraits on the walls. "Then the Heart of the Archive leads the Keepers. They're a little harder to explain, almost like religious leaders, interpreting the will of the Archive."

I nodded along like all this made perfect sense as I did my best to commit everything to memory while I took in our new surroundings. The four councilors I'd met the night before were clearly the leaders of the Archive. Who did what exactly was hard to say. Even if Grayson hadn't already outed himself as the Hand, he would have been the obvious choice for the person in charge of protecting the Archive. But everyone else... And what any of that meant for me, I couldn't say.

"So, now what?" Marc asked. He still managed to sound ruder than I would've liked but I couldn't help but be grateful that he was asking the very same question I was thinking.

Having had something to eat, I felt a lot steadier on my feet. And I was so ready to be done with all the stalling and non-answers. Not enough that I would've signed up to go back into the story I'd come from, but enough that I was beginning to contemplate taking my chances on my own out there in the city.

That didn't seem to be an option anymore. We weren't being given any options at all.

Eliza was being great, but if her job was to keep us busy so we'd stop asking questions, it wasn't going to work for much longer.

"We're meeting Archivist Nyce. She should be able to tell you what's next."

From the entry hallway, we climbed up a narrow flight of stairs that took us up to yet another collection of rooms. The first room we passed was empty, at least of people. Two rows of simple wooden desks faced a chalkboard on the far wall.

"Is this a school?" I said.

"Sort of. At least, it used to be an academy for new librarians. But in the last few years we've been running out of space to store actual books, so we've started moving some of the lectures across town to a separate building, turning classrooms into offices and conference rooms, so the offices closer to the library could be opened to the public and store new fiction that comes in. We know we're going to end up using this area for more bookcases, or a new genre, or something eventually. And sooner rather than later. So, they're trying to stay ahead of things."

It wasn't long before we heard a murmur of voices coming from up ahead. A minute later we stopped in front of the door to one of the classrooms right as a group of six streamed out of it. They ranged in age from young adult to middle-aged, but all were holding stacks of textbooks as though they were students.

Joanna Nyce, the stern looking woman I'd met yesterday, sat behind a desk at the front of the newly empty room, flipping through a stack of papers. "Good, Eliza. You're here," she said without looking up. "I know this wasn't exactly what you were expecting for your rotation with the councilors, but we appreciate your stepping up as a tour guide this morning."

Eliza nodded respectfully and approached the desk. "Happy to help. If you need me to stay on past this weekend..." Eliza stopped talking when Joanna finally looked up at her, eyebrows raised.

"Ambition is good, but don't push your luck. Now more than ever we need to stick close to our traditions. They are what will see us through the other side of this. Now, let's see what we're dealing with." I felt like a deer in the headlights when the woman's dark eyes focused in on the corner where Devon, Marc, and I had positioned ourselves. Authority had always made me nervous, and the idea that this woman had some serious sway over what happened to me next wasn't making it any easier.

"Which brings us to the question of what to do with you all now. There's been quite a bit of debate, and suggestions range from leaving you to your own devices to see what the Archive has in store for you, to keeping you in the rooms we provided until we know more, for your own safety, of course."

Devon raised his hand beside me, looking a little sheepish.

"Yes?"

"Keep us safe from what exactly?" He paused for a second, pressing his lips together. "Nothing was really explained to me yesterday. And I'm sure you're like, mucho busy, but if you could clear any of this up…"

Not speaking, Joanna flexed her fingers out in front of her, her gaze dropping to watch the joints move. "That is fair," she said finally. "I shall do my best to put this in terms you will understand."

"Great," Devon answered with a grin. I nudged him to be quiet.

"As librarians, we serve the will of the Archive, and as such, the will of the After. Your unexpected, and unprecedented arrival yesterday represents a shift in the Archive's plan, one that we don't yet understand. Your presence potentially represents a chance, though there has yet to be a consensus on how we are expected to react to this shift. Above all, we serve the will of the Archive. Our new aim is to determine how you factor in to that will."

"And you're keeping us safe from the black-coats from yesterday," I said, thinking out loud.

Joanna nodded. "Those black-coats, as you say are members of The Order of Pheneus. Mercenaries. We suspect they were hired by those who believe that it is not the Archive and the stories it holds that should shape the After, but the people who are in it. By removing you, they would have thwarted the will of the Archive. Until we know more, we must ensure that doesn't happen. By any means necessary."

At that, I stood up a little straighter. There was no part of me that wanted to spend any more time behind a locked door, and especially not by myself. "In the end, we've come to something of a compromise." Joanna continued. "If the Archive has brought you here, we must assume it's for a reason. But since there are still sightings of mercenaries out in the city, we can only assume that their intention is to thwart that will and return you to where you came from. So, you'll need to stay here for the time being. It will give us time to learn more about you, and to uncover why you of all people were brought to Sanctum."

"No, no," Marc said, raising one of his hands up as though to ask a question but not waiting to be called on. "You can't treat us like prisoners. We haven't done anything wrong. I want to get out of this place, and now. I can figure things out for myself, thank you very much. I do appreciate the help you provided yesterday, but enough is enough. I need to go."

"You really don't. At this point, your safety is paramount, and everything else can wait. As I was saying, you'll be staying here in the Archive. But we will give you free access to the building, an honor rarely bestowed on non-librarians, let alone prosaics such as yourselves. But because your abilities are limited, we expect that there is little damage you can do."

I grimaced a little at that one. We hadn't done anything to warrant being treated like pests, as far as I knew. It didn't sound like we were going to be kept as prisoners any longer, but we weren't exactly honored houseguests either.

"You'll be able to visit any section of the Archive that is open to those who work here. We ask that you be respectful and stay out of the way as best you can. But even if someone should come looking for you here, they will not be able to get to you because of the protection of the Archive. You'll be safe for now, and hopefully within a few weeks' time we will know enough that we can put you somewhere more permanent. Somewhere closer to where you belong," she said, the last part with a bit of a condescending sneer but I did my best to ignore it. Even though no, I didn't have any magic to speak of, I was already beginning to resent the term prosaic, and the penetrating stares cast my way.

"What are we supposed to do with ourselves then?" Devon asked. "Just read all day, every day? I know this is the wrong crowd for this, but I'm really not much of a book person."

"How you entertain yourselves during your private time is up to you, but we intend to take full advantage of your presence here in the coming days."

"You're going to study us," Marc said, his expression wary.

"We are librarians. Study is what we do. We will learn as much as we can as quickly as we can, and go from there. And while we can't stop you from interacting with those who come in from the city to enjoy the Archive, we would highly recommend that you keep to yourselves. Your ignorance of Sanctum is readily apparent, and we'd like to avoid any further attention."

Joanna stood up from her desk, picking up the stack of paper as she moved. She handed one to each of us. "We have put together extensive questionnaires to learn as much about your backgrounds as possible. Have these filled out by tomorrow. Beyond that, your time is your own."

I took my survey and folded it in half, not bothering to look at it yet. It was heavier than I expected, several pages long. I was a little impressed that they'd managed to come up with something quite that quickly.

With a wave, she dismissed us, leaving me feeling both worthless and heavily scrutinized at once. It was clear that no one at the Archive would be rolling out the welcome wagon for us, but at least I had somewhere to stay, that from the sounds of it wouldn't involve being locked in my room again. Which was something.

I still couldn't guess whether I'd come to regret not getting on that train when Grayson had given me the chance, but the people in the Archive seemed to want answers about what was happening to me as much as I did, so as far as I was concerned, that meant we were all on the same side. At least for now.

CHAPTER TWELVE

"Well, this is where I leave you," Eliza said after she had returned us to the main section of the library, only taking us so far as the door that separated the staff-only academy, and the part of the building that is open to the public. "I only get one week assigned to the councilor's office, so I have to get back to it. But thanks to you guys, I'm pretty sure I got the best week possible."

She waved goodbye, promising to meet up with us again later, leaving Devon, Marc, and I standing together, awkwardly huddled in a group.

"I think I'm just going to go back to my room for a while," Marc said, shoving his hands in his pockets and not looking Devon or me in the eyes. He stayed, standing like that for a few seconds. I guess he was waiting for one of us to say more.

Part of me wanted to just let him go without speaking up, already looking forward to a chance to hang out with Devon without a wall between us, and without Marc making snide comments at every turn. And really, I wouldn't have guessed Marc wanted to spend any more time with Devon or me than he had to, since the guy had been a bit of a jerk so far. But he was one of us. And from the look of him, he wasn't enjoying what was happening to us than I was.

And if it was me, there was absolutely no way I'd volunteer to go back to my room and be alone for a second longer than I had to. And it wasn't like I had a giant gaggle of friends to choose from. I needed every ally I could get.

"Did you want to meet us for dinner?" I asked, right as he gave up and started to turn away. "We can meet in the cafeteria or something." I did my best to look like his answer didn't matter to me one way or the other. But after losing Harper I was more intent than ever on building up some relationships in this place. If I could lose anyone at any moment, I couldn't afford to be picky.

A big part of me expected Marc to say no but instead he answered, "Are you sure?"

"Why not? We all have to eat, right?" I guess I should have asked Eliza before she left how exactly we were to go about getting food for ourselves while stuck in this building. But since we've had delivered pizza appear out of nowhere, I was at least a little more confident that I'd get to eat again before the end of the day. It was something.

I looked at Devon, hoping for backup and got nothing. "Maybe we can all run over what happened to us yesterday. Exchange information and see what we know. Because at this point, it seems like information is the only weapon we are going to get. Everyone here can do all these incredible things that none of us ever imagined. And we don't even know which way is up." My little speech had started out as an attempt to engage Marc enough that he wouldn't retreat from Devon and I entirely, but the more I spoke, the more I had to say. "And if we're looking for information, we are in the best possible place to get it, right? If we had arrived where we were supposed to, our lives would have been way more boring. We would probably already be back to lives exactly like our ones before. At least here, we have access to *more*."

"I was perfectly happy in my life before," Marc said. "But your first point is valid enough. I don't want to be stuck in this place forever, and I'm not loving the lab rat vibe that people seem to give off when they're around us. Plus, I'm not totally convinced anyone here actually knows what they're doing. Or what's going on. So, if getting some answers of our own is the fastest way out of here, I'm all for it."

His response wasn't exactly the rah-rah, go team enthusiasm I was trying to muster, but it was a start. I turned to Devon. "Are you headed back to your room, too?"

Devon shook his head, making his shaggy hair flow from side to side as he moved. "No. I don't really know what I want to do next. But all there is to do in my room is nap. I must've had four naps yesterday between being locked in and going to bed later that night. No thanks."

"Well, I'm going to go look around. See if I can figure out where everything is in relation to the lobby. I don't even think I could find my way back to the cafeteria at this point. I mean, worst-case scenario, I'm sure I can ask for directions but with the way everyone's looking at me, I'd rather just work it out for myself."

"I'm in," Marc said, though he hadn't technically been invited. So much for him going back to his room, but I wasn't going to turn down a little support.

"Sure, me too."

"Alright, so where do we go?" I asked, looking around me. We had exited back to the ground floor, and every direction seemed to offer little more than books, books, and more books. I knew if we walked straight for long enough we'd be near the front of the building, which I hoped would at least help reorient us toward the non-public areas like our bedrooms and food, but for now I was willing to try going somewhere else entirely. To see something new.

"We could go right out the front door," Marc said, and

I didn't think he was entirely kidding.

"No way," Devon said. "I bet they have some sort of crazy magical system in place to make sure we don't go anywhere."

Completely on Devon's side, I nodded. "Plus, if you leave now and get yourself killed, that's going to be on us for letting you go. So today we're staying put. Eliza said that this place is sorted by genre, so let's see if we can get the lay of the land and figure out what goes where. It might make it easier to orient ourselves later if we have a decent idea of what the bigger landmarks are."

Nobody argued, so I took the silence as a signal that that was our plan at least until we came up with something better.

Soon, we took a random left turn into the stacks and started picking up books on the shelves closest to us, looking for a common theme.

"Hey, this one is set in Texas," Devon said, his accent more apparent than ever.

"Westerns maybe?"

"Nope," Marc said. "This one's about a widow in Ireland rebuilding her life."

"I wonder if any of us even know what the actual sections of a normal library are?" I said. "I mean, is there a chance we're just in a general fiction section?"

Nobody answered, and I suspected that the others were as clueless as I was. A better plan probably would've just been to ask Eliza for a run down, but at least we were passing the time.

We moved slowly, picking up books one by one and pausing to read the backs or admire the covers. We eventually made it from one row to the next, to the next. It was at least an hour before I realized that Devon hadn't put down his Texas book.

"You're never going to be able to find the right place to put that back properly," I said, pointing to the title in his hands.

Devon looked down, an expression of mild surprise crossing his features. "Good point. I just kind of like having it with me. Maybe I'll read it tonight once I'm back in my room. It might give me a taste of being back home."

"You're from Texas?" Marc asked.

"Born and raised. I mean, I guess. As much as I was born and raised anywhere."

"Do either of you guys have any ideas about what kind of book you came from?" I asked on a whim, flipping through the pages of the book in my hands. "I'm pretty sure I was in a romance, or at least there was a romance involved. But I guess that could mean anything. Even taking out the possibility of magic, that still leaves so many options, right? It's not like falling in love is all that genre specific."

I looked around me, trying to guess at just how many books were in this building, filling every nook and cranny. They were countless, and every single book that was here had brought its characters with it, populating the world outside the Archive.

It was a lot to take in.

"Are you still stuck on the idea of finding your own book?" Devon asked, with an unreadable expression.

"I wouldn't say stuck. And come on, don't tell me you wouldn't love to read the story you came from just as much as I would. I mean, the things you could learn about yourself... Or about the people in your life. It's worth considering."

"So, what's the last thing you remember, then?" Devon asked.

It didn't take long for me to give both guys a quick rundown of the patheticness that was my life before, all the while pretending to be completely fascinated by each of the books I picked up so I didn't have to watch any looks of pity come across their faces. So far, I wasn't really seeing any commonalities between the stories I was looking at, other than none of them seemed to be set outside a reality like I was used to.

"My life was pretty lame," Devon said. "The last couple of days I remember was just more of the same. Going to classes, hanging out with friends. I met these girls at a party a few nights ago, and they were telling me about this epic road trip they were on, visiting potential schools across the country and trying to decide where to go next year. But I only hung out with them for an hour, maybe less. I saw one of them a few days later, but she said like three words to me, and that was it. Then I was here."

"My last week was way more interesting than that," Marc said, setting himself to tell his story. "It was my first week on the job, and my partner and I ended up sucked into this epic manhunt for a serial killer. I'll say, I think I held things up more than I helped, and my partner was definitely the one saving the day. But I can say with some level of certainty that the book I came from was not a romance of any kind." I looked up at Marc just as his expression shifted from guarded to worried. "The last thing I remember was leaving the station to go home to my wife after we caught our guy."

"You're married?" I asked in surprise, looking down at his ring finger. He wasn't wearing a wedding band.

Marc caught my look and raised his hand up, examining the empty finger for himself. "I lost it on the last night I can remember. It's a long story. But yeah, happily married. Very happily. We were coming up on our first anniversary. And all I've been able to think about since I got here is that Meg probably showed up in the city where she was supposed to, and is looking for me. She'll have no way of knowing I'm here, maybe halfway across the planet. And by the time we get out of this place, is there going to be any way at all for me to find her?"

I looked over at Devon and the two of us shared a guilty look. Yeah, okay, Marc had been a jerk all day. But it was possible that there was more going on underneath the surface than I'd given him credit for.

And I was a little jealous that he had someone who would be waiting for him. At least my parents would have each other, but Darren would be all about finding Kelsey. I wager he hadn't even thought of me since he'd arrived in the After.

If anything, I should've felt guilty about how little I'd thought about my friends and family since I'd woken up in the After. Were my parents looking for me? My friends from work, from school? Or were they all still just trying to figure out their own lives? I might never know for sure.

How many people reconnected with everyone they'd known before when they arrived in the After? Did people move on and start fresh?

If I could find my book, I could start to piece some of my life back together.

Together, the three of us left the row of shelves we'd been occupying and stepped into a what seemed to be an endless aisle. I noticed Devon was still hanging onto his Texas book, but didn't say anything else. Worst case scenario, some poor librarian was going to get stuck re-shelving it, adding a little extra work to their already daunting task. And since the Archive was open to the public, I imagined that was something they often had to do anyway.

We walked and talked for a while, and I was surprised to find that Marc was the one with the most to say. His storytelling clipped and abrupt, Marc gave us a play-by-play of him and his partner catching a serial killer on the mean streets of Chicago, bringing his story and his city to life with ease. Anytime I tried to jump in with an anecdote from my own life, I seemed to come up short. I told myself that it had more to do with my life being all too boring compared to Marc's, but it was hard not to feel like I really should have more to offer.

I loved my life before, at least everything before things with Darren came to a screeching halt. Reliving my memories seemed more important than ever, and yet I came up with next to nothing. I could vividly remember the first time I met Darren, in line for coffee after teaching a morning class. He'd been stressed about work, wound tight and anxious. But after we talked for a few minutes he visibly relaxed, and laughed along with some stupid story I told about one of the older women in my classes who refused to give up on mastering a particularly troublesome pose. But sharing that with Marc and Devon, especially when Marc was reliving what had to be the darkest time of his life, seemed trivial and silly. Something about the idea of coming from a romance book was already making me feel like I was less than the people around me. The focus of my story, of my life, had been about falling in love and relationships. And in the end, I hadn't even been able to do that much. I decided to let the guys think I was just a little more on the private side than they were.

Most of what Devon had to say was all about meeting those teenage girls at that one party that one time. No one said it out loud, but I think even Devon realized what that said about him. The story he'd been in wasn't his. He had been a side character, and the story had continued without him, leaving him to go back to his regular life like nothing had happened. One memorable night, and that was it.

I knew I was more than that, knew I'd met Darren on multiple occasions and we'd been together long enough for me to fall in love with him. Even if he was falling in love with someone else at the same time. And I could remember long dinners with my family, and how close I felt to them. But what if that was all there was to me?

The three of us hushed our conversation a little as we passed a group of women who were chatting excitedly, passing books to one another. They barely noticed us as we walked by but it was enough to pull me back to my new reality.

"Okay, I'm definitely lost," Devon said as we turned and found yet another endless row of books. "Do we backtrack or just keep going and hope we find something we recognize, or something that looks important?"

"I vote we soldier on," I said. "Not like we have anywhere we need to be."

Just then, two men came around the corner, and to my surprise I recognized them both. By then, I could've recognized Grayson just about anywhere. He was walking with Jonathan, the other male councilor I'd met the night before. Neither one of them was talking, and Grayson had his nose buried in a book he was holding in front of his face.

"Well hello," Jonathan said. Grayson looked up, startled by the other man's voice. "Didn't expect to see you three wandering about."

"Joanna set us free," Marc said hastily like he was worried he'd be banished back to his room if these two didn't think we had permission to be where we were. "We're just checking things out," I said, adding a little elaboration just in case we were in trouble. "We're trying to figure out our way around this place but aren't having much luck."

"What is it you're looking for?" Grayson asked. His brown eyes had locked onto mine and he tilted his head slowly, like I was a puzzle he was trying to decipher.

I blushed a little. It's not like I had anywhere specific I could ask him to direct us to, or any real reason for wandering the Archive at all. "Nothing really, just trying to see get acquainted enough with the place that we can get to anywhere we need to be without getting lost for a few hours at a time. Where we are now?"

Grayson looked around him and I got the impression he hadn't been paying that much attention where he'd been walking. "Fiction. The whole first level is general fiction. The next floor up as well. Stories about life and how we look at it."

"Good to know." Standing there in front of two of the most influential people in the Archive, I felt like a bit of an idiot. I didn't have anything intelligent to say or anything to add to the conversation. So instead, I decided to take a chance. "I wonder if this is where my book would be. The one I came from. Or maybe there's a romance section?" I finished off the sentence, rambling but hoping someone would jump in and save me from myself, filling in some of the blanks as they went.

"There is a romance section, but there's plenty of romance down here too." Grayson was still watching me, curious and wary. "But your book won't be out."

"Oh, I know," I said, trying to sound casual, like this hadn't become the most important thing in the world to me. "But eventually... It would be kind of cool to find it. Is there anyone here who could help me with something like that?" I knew I had already asked, but it never hurt to get another perspective. One I'd like the sound of a little better.

It was Jonathan who spoke next. "I wouldn't worry too much about it. The longer you wait, the easier it will be to track down. And with everything else going on, we had to pull people off shelving, so it could be a while."

"I'm happy to help out, since it looks like I'm going to have more than enough time to myself."

The younger man shook his head. "Only librarians, sorry. There's a lot of training involved, a whole system. Thankfully, if you're looking for something to do, there's always a good book around," he said, and chuckled, but I got the impression I was being dismissed.

My disappointment must have shown on my face, because Grayson was looking at me with far more sympathy than he had even the night before when he'd saved my life. "You never know," he said. "It will turn up eventually, and it's not like what's written is going to change. Be patient."

The five of us stared at one another for a while, until it got too awkward to handle. "Well, I guess we'll see you guys later."

"Sounds good," Grayson said, voice soft. "Let us know

if you need anything. I know it's a big adjustment." At the last second, his gaze flitted to Devon and Marc as well, including them in the offer.

I gave a quick nod and mumbled a response. Even I didn't know what I was saying.

As soon as they were out of earshot, Devon turned on me. "What's up with you and that Grayson dude?" he said, eyebrows wiggling.

I shook my head. "Nothing. I met him yesterday, he kind of saved my ass."

"Nope, I know these kinds of things. There is something going on there."

"You're crazy." But I couldn't help but smile a little at the idea, even though I wasn't exactly sure what he was suggesting.

And of course, Devon caught the smile. "See," he said, drawing the word out. "There's something there. And the dude is seriously hot, so you could do a lot worse." I went to laugh it off, but something Devon said grabbed my attention instead. I stopped moving, and gave him a suspicious side eye. "Wait, what? You think he's hot?"

Devon pursed his lips together in mock guilt. But then he looked over at Marc, waiting for his reaction before saying anything else.

Marc shrugged. "What?"

"Well in that case, yes. I do think that man is viciously attractive. I think a lot of men are all kinds of attractive. Did I not mention that in Devon one-oh-one?" He winked, and then quite literally jumped up and clicked his heels together before continuing off in the direction we'd been going, dropping the subject entirely but leaving me grinning.

CHAPTER THIRTEEN

When I woke up the next morning, the mantra of our time being our own seemed to have been forgotten by the councilors.

After breakfast, I handed in the questionnaire, I'd been given, and by lunch time I had already sat through an extended interrogation with Marissa about each of my answers—though the older woman never said so much as a single harsh word to me the whole time.

After eating lunch by myself—Devon, Marc, and I having stood in the corner of the cafeteria the night before, looking like we were deep in conversation until we observed enough people to figure out the clearly magical boxes where they were getting their food—I returned to the main library. But there was no sign of anyone I knew, leaving me to wander for hours, feeling both lost and like an intruder at the same time.

The next day was more of the same, with the three of us being split up for most of that day, but each still with far too much time to ourselves with nothing to do.

While the librarians were more intent on getting information from us than teaching us anything, we were still picking things up along the way, sharing information about what we learned and who we met at every chance we got. The problem was, I couldn't tell what information would really matter in the end, or what might be somehow related to our arrival in the After. And the librarians I spoke to didn't seem to have any more ideas about how I fit into the puzzle of their world than I did.

The Archive had seven stories, and more genres than I could count. There were devices all over the place I didn't understand the purpose of, and I still couldn't find my way between the offices, the bedrooms, the cafeteria and everywhere else without getting lost at least once. Lost was becoming part of my routine.

But at least I finally got my wish for regular meals. I could eat in any of the many gaps in my schedule, and it didn't cost me anything, an advantage I hadn't even had back home.

The appliances I'd noticed Eliza using before had turned out to be essentially refrigerators, and they were called the same even though they didn't quite look to the versions I was used to. And the Archive's fridges could keep things at any temperature at all. Each one was tied to a similar-looking machine in a restaurant somewhere in the city. They probably worked a lot like the passageways that I'd discovered with Harper. One side was hot, one side was cool, and the restaurants restocked constantly throughout the day, adding in new bottles of water, jugs of milk, freshly made tea and anything else in demand. Different restaurants had different specialties, but the compartment used for pizza seemed to get the most action.

It was on my fourth day in the Archive that I finally woke up to find that no immediate plans had been made on my behalf, giving me some real time to myself. Both Devon and Marc had already gone to appointments with a councilor in the morning when I rolled out of bed, and I didn't have anywhere to be until after lunch.

But I knew exactly what my body needed. First, I had

to get out of my bedroom. It was the only place I could be guaranteed any privacy, but I couldn't stay there a minute longer than I had to. Nothing about it felt like home.

Instead, I found an open sitting area on the fifth floor, with four couches sitting across from one another and a coffee table sitting in between them. It took a little work to get the coffee table out of the way, but at that point my body welcomed the extra effort. I spent the next hour going through my usual morning yoga routine, as my body groaned in protest and thanks. It wasn't long before I lost focus on the Archive around me and finally felt centered within myself again. There was still so much that was wrong, so much that I didn't know. But at least this much was entirely me.

Finishing things off, I moved forward to touch my toes, enjoying the stretch in my back. I let out a long happy sigh and held the position.

"Oh crap, excuse me." A voice came from behind me and I shot upward in an instant. I spun around to see a guy I didn't recognize standing behind me, a pile of books in his arms. Two of them tumbled from the top of his stack to the ground as he shuffled backward.

"I'm so sorry, I didn't know someone was up here. This floor is usually dead this time of day."

The guy had brown skin that looked like it didn't see much sun, and black spiky hair, the same color as the rectangular glasses that sat on his nose. His eyes were a pale, unnatural looking blue, which I tried not to look directly at for any longer than I had to, despite the friendly expression they held.

"My bad," I said. "You don't have to go. I just needed to find some space." I trailed off, not able to admit that I needed this space to work out because I wasn't allowed to leave the building. "Impromptu workout. Sorry about that."

Finally, the guy seemed to relax. "I just wasn't expecting..." His eyes trail down my body. I didn't have any workout clothes with me, so I was only wearing track pants and a t-shirt, Eliza had given me, but I suspected the view he'd gotten when he'd first walked into the section had been less than wholesome.

"Forget it, I'm done now anyway. Was just feeling kind of cooped up and needed to stretch it out. Probably not the best place."

"Don't worry about it. Usually you can go for hours in here without bumping into anyone. Just bad luck, or maybe good luck on my end," he said the last part with a cheesy wink, making me laugh out loud. "And to be fair, that's not even the weirdest thing I've seen hanging out here."

"Oh?" I asked, moving forward to help him collect the books that had fallen. It looked like if he tried to move even an inch to get them, he'd lose the rest in the process.

I put the books down on the table, feeling like an idiot all over again since it was pretty obvious I'd moved it out of the way in order to create my own personal workout space.

"Yeah, you know how it is. Authors."

"Uhh… sure?" I realized a second too late that maybe I should have been covering so I didn't sound completely clueless, but the guy didn't seem to think anything of my response.

"Here's the theory," he said conspiratorially. "No matter where you go in the After, there are things that are always going to be better than the versions we were created from. I mean, look at you," he said with a curt nod. "You're gorgeous," he said, like it was simply a fact and not a huge compliment, and I did my best not to react, though the conversation was getting stranger by the second and I could already feel a flush of heat in my cheeks. A second later I was all too glad I hadn't thanked him or something. "But gorgeous isn't that unusual here. We're looking at a world built from the imaginations of others. You don't get a lot of ugly main characters—

maybe the occasional girl who is plain but who everyone is inexplicably attracted to anyway. And love interests that aren't ridiculously attractive? No way. Sure, a lot of the secondary characters or whoever aren't inhumanly good-looking, but the averages are way off."

"Huh," I said, considering his idea. "Same with ages, right? Pretty people in their prime are basically a dime a dozen."

"You've got it. Most people never even stop to think about how these things might affect the world we live in. But I can guarantee that even deep in suburbia, our world does not look like theirs. Whoever they are."

"Good to know," I said, grinning. "Do you work here?" He wasn't wearing robes, but the things this guy was talking about made him sound just like the Archivists Eliza had mentioned.

"Nope. No stupid looking robes for me. I just like books... another one of those things. I bet there are way more readers in the After because authors by definition probably have a thing for books, so they write that into their characters. It's like their go to character trait when trying to make someone more interesting."

"Okay, wait a second. How did we even get here?" I laughed a little, realizing how quickly and comfortably our conversation had gone off the rails. "You were trying to make me feel better about getting caught working out in between the stacks."

"Right!" the guy said, moving to sit down at one of the couches. I moved to the one beside him and leaned against the armrest, not wanting to crowd him but entirely curious about whatever tangent he was going to go on next. "Haven't you noticed that people here... well, it all comes down to quirkiness. When authors are creating characters, there's only so much back story that they can include. So, what I've noticed is that a lot of them try to give their characters these memorable character traits. Everyone is a photographer or has a wicked temper or does origami in their spare time. Or you get the real weirdos who do yoga in the middle of public buildings."

I opened my mouth to defend myself but realized that probably wasn't my best strategy. There was no excuse I could give him that wouldn't out me as a random essentially living in a library. I shrugged. "Guilty as charged."

"No judgment here. I've noticed that for some of us, it doesn't matter how long we stay in the After, or how much we do to change who we are as people, there are always some things we can't shake. And usually, it's those weird traits that don't always feel like they make sense with who we are that are forever a part of us."

"Honestly, that makes as much sense as about anything else around here."

"Good. It always makes my day when I can convince somebody else to see my point of view. I'm Jamie by the way. Jamie Franklin, should you ever feel the need to credit that incredible theory to its rightful source." Jamie gave me a wide smile. As his lips parted to reveal his teeth, something looked slightly out of place. Not quite normal.

Not quite human.

But Jamie's teeth were covered again before I could get a closer look.

I froze for a second too long, thrown by his grin and my uncertainty about if I should give my real name or not but too soon the silence became awkward and I knew that remaining quiet any longer would only draw more of the wrong kind of attention to myself. "Kadie Meyer."

"And what brings you to the library today, Kadie? I mean, besides your workout?"

"I really just like it here. Best place in the city." I was guessing, but it was the best answer I could come up with but it was one that Jamie seemed to appreciate. "It's a beautiful building, there's never a shortage of entertainment, and you run into the most interesting people."

"I have noticed that." He looked at me again, forcing me to shift my gaze away as soon as his eyes met mine.

"How about you?" I looked down at the stack of books on the table. "Here for a little light reading?"

"Essentially. That's the trait I can't seem to shake, but I wouldn't want to anyway. And while there's a regular library by my house, let's face it, those places have nothing on the Archive. Anything I could want to read, it's here. I've been coming once a week for a while now, and picking stacks of books at random. I usually just keep reading the first chapters of a bunch of them until something catches my attention and I can't put it down. And it's funny, I've only lived in the city for a few years now, but I've learned a lot more about the After by reading these books than I have by actually going places."

"How do you mean?" I asked, trying to sound like I was just politely continuing the conversation while I was actually desperate for whatever he was about to say next.

"I dunno, you start to see patterns in the stories. Things that happen again and again in different books that you can easily relate to something out in the world."

"Such as…"

"Kadie." A deep voice called from nearby, snapping my attention away from Jamie. I turned to find Grayson standing at the other end of the sitting area, watching me. "Can I see you for a second?" he asked.

I turned toward Jamie and winced apologetically. "Looks like I'm being summoned away."

Jamie stuck out his hand and I shook it automatically. "It was very nice to meet you," he said. "Hopefully I'll see you around here some other time. And if you ever need a workout buddy, just let me know."

I said goodbye with a wave and made my way over to Grayson, my smile falling immediately. The two of us walked away from Jamie without saying a word to one another, it was only once we were out of earshot that Grayson said anything at all.

"What were you doing, talking to him?"

"Just that. I was talking to him."

"I thought Joanna told you that you shouldn't be interacting with the Archive's patrons. You might draw attention to yourself."

I didn't point out that I absolutely had drawn attention to myself, but that I didn't think it was a problem. "And you don't think summoning me over here like that didn't raise some red flags? Are most people that come here on a first name basis with, well, you?"

Somehow, Grayson didn't have a quick come back for that one but the set of his jaw tightened like he was grinding his teeth together.

"I thought it was worth the risk. Somehow you managed to strike up a conversation with not just any random person who came in to read, but with someone with known Literati ties."

"I have no idea what that even means."

"We're not talking about this here. With your luck, we'll be overheard in a matter of seconds. Needless to say, the Literati are people that *you especially* need to avoid. But they aren't really on friendly terms with anyone here at the library. They stand for the antithesis of everything we believe in."

"Jamie just seemed like a guy who likes books."

"By the same standards, I'm just a guy who likes books. Maybe you can accept that there's more going on here than you understand."

"And whose fault is that? We've been given the bare minimum of answers and basically told to just stay out of the way. To jump when you say jump, in case we can somehow help you. But no one's really looking to help us. Me, Devon, and Marc. We're just a science experiment to you people." And Harper, but I didn't say her name aloud. It was too late to help her. "We're the victims here. We're being treated like we're both useless and inconvenient all at once. Except for maybe when you need us. If you need us.

If our very existence isn't just some big mistake."

"I don't believe for a second that your existence is a mistake, Kadie. I know, believe me, I know that you were brought here for a reason. And not just you, everyone who arrived that day. There has to be a reason behind it, and figuring out what that reason is has become maybe the most important thing to anyone who works in the Archive. Our entire belief system stems around the fact that the Archive is the heart of the After. The After has a plan for all of us. The plan changes and grows as more books appear in our world, as the knowledge we have and the people who populate our world change, but there's always a plan."

Grayson was quiet, but only for a second. It would seem that once I got him started he was a lot more enthusiastic to chat than he had been any time before. "And the Literati believe the very opposite of that. They think that the characters should be the ones shaping our world, and that they know better than the After about what is best for everyone. Your friend wasn't the first person to be disappeared. It's been happening for years, maybe generations. People that the Literati deem unworthy, or too dangerous, are deprived of any chance to make a fresh start for themselves and are forced back into their origin stories, just in case their influence might taint the After. So, it stands to reason that those mercenaries who came after you had much the same thing in mind. If the After brought you here as a way to change things for the better, then they would be the ones who wanted to undo that change in an attempt to be the decision makers."

I was finally quiet, finally ready to stop arguing. Well, almost ready.

"Okay, and that explanation took all of two minutes. So maybe if someone had taken the time to tell us all of that before, I wouldn't have struck up a random conversation just because I was looking for someone to talk to. Don't you think this is the kind of thing that we should know? I get that everyone here is so busy, and so behind, but if our being here really is as important as you think, it wouldn't kill you guys to put in a little freaking effort. I'll do my best to be useful, but you gotta give me something to work with."

Grayson stopped walking, and turned to look at me. I noticed then that he had a long scar running just under his jaw. I wouldn't admit it out loud, but there was no way that anyone ever could describe this man as merely just a guy who likes books. He looked to me like a guy who could change the world.

And apparently, he was looking at me and seeing someone who could do that as well.

"You're right, I'm sorry. We didn't expect any of this. We were already struggling to keep up with how quickly things were changing, and then this threw us for a loop. Most of the time, leadership in the Archive is mostly ceremonial. Cities and countries govern themselves, but the Archive affects everything. Even then, most of the decisions we make don't have an immediate effect on the world around us. But everyone knows that this could be different. This could be the big one. We're doing the best we can."

"Please believe me when I say that that's what I'm trying to do as well. That guy today, he just stumbled on me so we started talking. He wasn't here looking for runaway prosaics who had shown up in the city when they weren't supposed to. He just wanted to read some books. And now, if I see him again, going out of my way to avoid talking to him will only draw more attention to me. So, I think"—I paused, trying to build a little suspense around my proposal—"the best thing you can do is to better arm me, and Marc and Devon, for whatever is coming next. Information is a powerful weapon, and we're surrounded by it here. Right? If the After wanted us to be here, it probably didn't want us running around blind and clueless."

"Well, that's one idea…"

"It's a damn good idea. Now what are you going to do about it?"

Grayson stood nearly motionless, his gaze drifting from my eyes to my lips and back again before he spoke. "We're already doing everything we can. But there is no room for mistakes here, Kadie. I would think you would know that better than most." Immediately, my mind jumped back to that moment near the docks, right after I'd lost Harper, when Grayson had held me as I'd cried, overwhelmed and exhausted.

I wanted to wish that he hadn't been there to see me like that, that this man who was now part of deciding what happened to me had seen me at my most vulnerable. But if he hadn't been there, it was all too possible that I never would have made it as far as the Archive of Ink and Soul.

But if nothing else, the memory did remind me that at least on some level, Grayson had been looking out for me since the very first moment I'd seen him.

"Fine. But this can only go on for so long. We're people, not puzzle pieces."

"Understood," Grayson said, his voice gruff. "It was never our intention to treat you as anything but guests, but this could be much bigger than any of us anticipated. It's better to be prepared for all possible outcomes.

And without another word, he was gone, leaving me standing alone and bewildered somewhere in the endless maze of library books.

CHAPTER FOURTEEN

I woke up the next morning, heart racing, to the now familiar sound of someone knocking on the door to my room. I couldn't say for sure what I'd been dreaming about but whatever it was had left me with an almost overpowering need to run.

I stayed frozen, still mostly hidden under the covers for a few seconds, trying to orient myself when my visitor knocked again.

Right. I was supposed to answer that.

"One second." I called out, springing out of bed at the same time. It was probably Devon, but we'd still only known each other for a couple of days and weren't exactly the see each other at our most ragged type of friends yet. I changed out of my pajamas in record time and into the first outfit I found on the floor, and took all of ten seconds in the bathroom to run my fingers over my hair, trying unsuccessfully to tame it.

With a huff, I finally made it to the door, swinging it open.

There was no sign of Devon. Instead, Jonathan Credence stood at my door—the Head of the Archive, and councilor for all the librarians who worked in the building.

He was carrying three parcels at chest level, each wrapped in brown paper.

He looked organized and together whereas I looked at least a little homeless, and not remotely respectable. Great.

"Sorry for the wait," I said, mumbling the words and unsure of what time it was and not wanting to admit I'd still been sleeping.

"No apology necessary. I shouldn't have popped by unannounced but I didn't want to miss you before you left to meet Doctor Maiz."

It was still a little unnerving, hearing someone who looked like a teenaged boy talk more like someone half a century older, but I nodded along, doing my best to keep my expression neutral. "What can I help you with?"

Jonathan waved his hand dismissively. "You've already done more than enough. I'm actually hoping I can be of some use to you. Since it looks like the three of you will be with us for at least a little longer, I thought the least we could do was to provide you with a few things to make you more comfortable."

Jonathan paused, his gaze dropping down to the packages he was holding.

"Oh. Did you want to come in?" I held the door open and he stepped inside before dropping the stack of parcels on the nearby dresser. As soon as the stack hit the wooden surface, the one on top floated back upward, drifting toward me.

My eyes went wide, and I reached out to grab the package before it could bump into my face.

To my surprise, Jonathan laughed out loud, the sound light and boyish. "So sorry," he said, catching my expression. "I'm so used to using magic, it's easy to forget that you lot might not be the most comfortable with it."

"It's fine," I said in a rush, not wanting to draw any more attention to all the ways I was *other* from the people who surrounded me. "Just takes some getting used to."

"Oh, I suspect that the longer you stay here, the more

accustomed you'll become to seeing these kinds of things. Go ahead and open that."

Without any need for further invitation, I ripped open the packaging, uncovering a simple cardboard box beneath the paper. The box itself couldn't have been any longer than my forearm, making it difficult to imagine what might be inside that would be all that helpful.

Inside sat a folded-up piece of white fabric, so thick it must have been forcibly shoved inside the box to fit. I sat the box down and pulled it out, unfurling a gorgeous sweater. "Thank you so much," I said breathlessly. It was a little strange to such an elegant gift from someone I'd barely spoken to before, but I was willing to go with it.

"That's just one piece, keep going."

I looked up, trying to be sure I'd heard him right. If there was anything else in that box it had to be tiny. But I put the sweater down and peered back inside the box. Another piece of cloth sat right near the top, visibly a pair of blue jeans.

It took nearly five minutes to unpack everything that had been magicked inside that one container—there was no way it hadn't been packed without magical assistance. I'd have trouble fitting everything Jonathan had brought me into my dresser, let alone get it back inside that one box. At the very bottom sat a hairbrush, a toothbrush, some soap, and a bottle of face wash. I'd been making do without... barely. And still, just seeing those items there sent tears welling up in the corner of my eyes.

"Let me or one of my aides know if there's anything else you're missing, or anything at all I can help with. I know this won't be nearly enough to actually have any of you feel at home here, but hopefully it can at least help make up for some of the inconvenience."

"Thank you," I said again as it was all I could think of.

"My pleasure. It was never my intention for you to be treated like this, and I see no reason to hold you here, but for now this is the best we can do."

Jonathan was watching me with a curious expression. On a whim, I decided to press my luck, "Is there any chance at all we'll be able to get out of here soon? It feels a little weird being inside all the time, and I'd love to see more of the city." I paused, trying to gauge his reaction, but Jonathan's expression remained passive, listening. "We would go as a group," I said, elaborating quickly. "And you could send someone with us, if you wanted. I know the guys are getting more and more anxious, the longer they're cooped up inside. It would be good for all of us."

"And that's fair enough. I appreciate where you're coming from. This transition is alarming enough without the extra stress that's been added on top of things for all of you. But for now, it's out of my hands. While the four of us can debate things until the early hours of every morning, we have to come to a consensus before anything is decided, at least when the safety of others is at hand. It's only been a few days, and I suspect we'll know more soon. For now, this is the safer option."

"And there's nothing we can do to help move things along? Or change people's minds?"

Jonathan shoved his hands in the pockets of his pants, gray and freshly pressed. "Well, maybe there's something. I can't make any promises, but pass me your shoes."

I looked down at the floor to where he was pointing, and sure enough my running shoes were sitting in the corner between my bed and the wall. It was a strange request, but if handing over my shoes could be a step toward getting a chance to stretch my legs somewhere other than the library, I was all for it.

I passed him the sneakers that Harper had purchased for me that day in the bazaar, hoping he wasn't going to do something to permanently damage them.

But they didn't seem to be in any immediate danger. Instead, he placed them down on the dresser, beside the two remaining packages. A moment later, he was waving his hands in intricate motions and mumbling under his breath. "There you go," he said, handing the shoes back to me. "I have no idea if that will work, I was kind of making it up on the spot. New spells aren't always winners."

"What did you do?" I held the shoes up, turning them over in my hands to see if anything about them was different.

"It was something of a tracking spell," Jonathan said, by way of explanation. "I've enchanted your shoes so that the councilors here in the library would have the ability to keep track of you, to an extent. While you're in the library, I'm not sure how much use this will be as the magics here are strong and unconventional. But if we get to the point where we can get you outside, this would help to make sure we're alerted right away if someone grabs you and tries to drag you off toward the Reclamation Center. It's not perfect, but it's an option. I'll do the same for Devon and Marc, then show the others and see what they think. Maybe this can help nudge things along. One more safety precaution is never going to be a bad thing."

It was hard not to think that this one more safety precaution would also help these people track my every movement, but for the time being I had to think that the benefits outweighed the loss of my personal freedoms. Freedoms I didn't have yet anyway.

"You did a spell on them, you said?" I asked.

"Essentially, yes."

"Are you a wizard or something?" I blurted it out, too curious for my own good.

"Or something. My parents were both magically inclined, and came from books where magical powers played a heavy role in politics. What I can do is a combination of both of their abilities, though my inability to physically pass into adulthood was all my father's doing, but I'm not sure there's a particular name for what I am."

"Wait, so your parents came from books, but not you?" My mind raced over the idea. So far, I'd just been assuming that everyone I met had come from a book, somewhat like I had even if the stories themselves had been vastly different.

Jonathan shook his head. "All librarians are second generation at least. The theory behind it is a little absurd, but it is supposed to ensure that we aren't secretly tainted by political affiliations given to us by our authors. So, in theory, those of us born in the After are more well-rounded characters than people like you, prosaics or otherwise. Librarians will have come from magical lineages, but not directly from books themselves."

"That's got to be at least a little insulting to everyone else," I said, before I could stop myself. But at least Jonathan had said that he thought the idea was absurd.

"Oh, absolutely. Some see the concept as outdated, but librarians do enjoy their traditions, if nothing else. And books of course, but while we may have had the opportunity to shape ourselves right from the beginning, that doesn't change the fact that over the course of years, or even decades, those of you who come from books aren't so different, not after you've started lives here for yourselves. So far, I've seen that the end result turns out about the same either way, but I'm in the minority on that opinion."

I shrugged, not sure I had nearly enough information to contribute my own two cents to this ongoing debate. And for the time being, I had other things to worry about. It wasn't like becoming a librarian had been on my to-do list. Still, it was a little strange to think that I would never get the opportunity. Or that others, who had been here for a hundred years or more would still be limited by their origin story.

"Well," Jonathan said, clapping his hands together almost silently, "on that note, I'll get out of your hair. Any idea what you're going to do with your time today?"

"I thought I might try picking up a few books at random and just reading through them, see if anything catches my attention. I'm working under the theory that the more I read, the better of an understanding I'll have of the After." I didn't bother mentioning that I was borrowing the idea from someone I met the day before, and Jonathan nodded his approval.

"Good, good. Make the most of your time here. And if you have any questions, be sure to flag down your nearest librarian. They certainly have plenty to do, but any one of them will be happy to hit pause on their work in order to talk books for a little while."

A minute later, Jonathan was gone, leaving me alone with my newly magic shoes and a pile of clothes covering my bed. The clock on my nightstand promised that it was still earlier than when I usually woke up, but my stomach was already rumbling, begging for breakfast.

Since Jonathan still had packages to deliver, I expected I'd be waiting a little while for Devon and Marc to be ready to get up and face a new day. I took a bit of time to change into one of my new outfits and put the rest away, happy to finally have some real options beyond a gray tank top and jeans that didn't fit that well. There weren't many pieces that I probably would have chosen for myself back at home, but it was nice to at least have options. And maybe if Jonathan could do a little persuading of his own, soon I'd be able to get out and maybe pick up some things to make my room a little more my own since Grayson hadn't asked for the money he'd given me back.

The next time someone knocked at the door for me, it was Devon, with Marc behind him. They were both wearing new clothes of their own, and quickly confessed that they'd each had their shoes enchanted as well. Marc didn't love the idea of having his every movement tracked since it would make it that much harder for him to leave the Archive at a moment's notice if he ever got the chance.

Me, I was at least willing to learn what I could with the time that I had.

After breakfast, I had a scheduled physical with someone named Doctor Maiz, who was set to meet me in an unused office near the front of the Archive.

I had to ask three different people for directions before I found where I was supposed to be, all the while, hanging on to the mug of coffee I'd grabbed from the cafeteria, which had been spelled to stay warm until it was empty. Now if only I could find a coffee mug that was never empty and I'd be all set.

I found the door I was looking for slightly ajar. Pushing it open and peering inside, I found a tall black woman sitting on a swivel chair, flipping through a binder. She looked up as I entered, her thick brown curls bopping slightly with the motion. She looked to be about twenty years my senior.

"Are you Doctor Maiz?" I asked. "I might be a little lost."

"Kadie?" she asked, her voice raspy and warm. I nodded, smiling a little. "You're in the right place."

It would have been hard to say if I was more relieved about finding the right place, or anxious about not knowing what was coming next. No matter how hard I tried to think about it, I didn't have any experience with doctors. It made sense that the book I had come from hadn't had any need for me to visit a doctor, but that left a giant question mark in my mind where a pretty normal life experience probably should have been.

"Please, have a seat?" The doctor said when I still hadn't moved, tilting her head toward a waist-high bench. Or was it a table? "The councilors have filled me in on your situation, so you're free to speak freely here. We just want to learn more about you."

Yeah, that wasn't exactly reassuring. Feeling stiff and awkward as I moved, I did as I was asked, looking around the room about any hints about what would be involved in a physical. For the briefest of instants, the doctor's brown eyes locked on my own, showing the strangest mixture of curiosity and sadness.

Not for the first time, I wished the Archive also held a collection of non-fiction that I could use as references for stuff like this. But no, of course those books were housed elsewhere, in yet another place I wasn't allowed to go. But maybe the doctor herself would unveil some new information for me. That alone would have to be enough of an incentive to get me through whatever the councilors had planned for me.

"Roll up your sleeve please," Doctor Maiz said once I was settled, bring over a tray of equipment I didn't recognize and placing it beside me. "Have you ever had blood taken before?"

Feeling a little nauseous, I shook my head.

"There's nothing to worry about."

"It won't hurt?"

"Not much." Well, that wasn't all that reassuring. The doctor picked up a sterile syringe and a few clear tubes from the tray before starting to piece together a complicated contraption that I could only assume was meant to physically remove my blood from my body, which didn't exactly sound like the best idea to me.

After tying a plastic ribbon around my arm, she seemed to be ready. But I definitely wasn't. "Okay, hun. I'm going to need you to relax a little." The needle she was holding was now hovering perilously close to my skin.

"Easier said than done," I said through gritted teeth. But the doctor didn't seem to be the type to chat and make me feel better. I squeezed my eyes shut as the needle pierced my skin.

"Okay, that's going to need a few minutes," said the doctor, her voice interrupting my building panic.

I forced myself to exhale and open my eyes, but made a point of looking anywhere other than at my arm.

"What's this for?"

"The councilors are looking for any physical anomalies," said Doctor Maiz. "And it won't hurt to have more of your physical details on file, blood type and the like. From what I can tell, at this stage the librarians are looking to gather as much data as they can."

"Are you one of them? A librarian I mean."

At that, my new doctor finally looked back over at me, the corners of her mouth pulling downward a little. "No. I'm not. But I've worked closely with them in the past, and they know I can be trusted with more... delicate matters."

"But you are a doctor."

"That's what they tell me. I was a medic in the story I came from, but I went to medical school after... in my thirties." The longer we spoke, and the more questions I asked, the more Doctor Maiz seemed to retreat back inside herself. But I wasn't quite willing to give up on a new source of potential information, so I tried a new tactic.

"Do I have a blood type then? Do you? If we weren't ever born, how does any of that work?" I hesitated a little, wondering if I was coming on too strong. "Sorry, but there's still so much I don't know."

"No, that's a great question!" Doctor Maiz was fully beaming at me by then, all her discomfort from moments before, long gone. "Everyone who arrives in the After from one particular book will have the same blood type, which as far as we know, means that it's something you inherited from your author."

"Huh," I said, accidentally catching a glimpse of the bright red fluid filling the tube coming out of my arm. But that actually was pretty cool. "Uh." I fumbled, too startled by what I'd seen to be able to form another question, or anything else to take my mind off what was happening to my body. "Quick! Distract me. Tell me something else. Anything."

For the next few minutes, the doctor was an unstoppable fountain of information, filling me in on all kinds of useful things which while they might never specifically come in handy, felt like the kind of information that everyone around me probably already had. All the while my blood was seeping out of me into a baggie, and I tried not to think about it.

Tried and failed, but I really did try.

But it turned out that a blood type wasn't the only thing I had gotten directly from my creator. All the general information that made it possible for me to be a walking, talking human, had also come from whoever she'd been—or maybe my author had been a he? Math, the ability to read, basic knowledge about how the world worked. Librarians had been studying incoming characters for years and had determined that while personality traits and memories were tied to the individual, all the filler stuff that no one ever thought about, but everyone needed, was shared between characters.

It was actually kind of neat, and it went a long way toward keeping me distracted until my blood draw was finally complete, and the doctor had popped a ball of gauze and a bandage onto my arm.

"Alright, are we done here?" I said, hopping off the bench and already hoping I'd never need to deal with doctors ever again.

Unfortunately, Doctor Maiz shook her head, grimacing a little. "Not even close. I still have to check your reflexes and your vision, examine your scar... and well, I've got a whole list. You're stuck with me for a while."

Shoulders slumping, I hopped right back up onto the bench. "Goody." But while my tone was sarcastic, I remained hopeful that maybe this would help. Maybe there was something buried in our physiology that would give the councilor's answers to the questions I didn't even know they were asking.

The next couple of days were uneventful, but still not boring. We found all kinds of places tucked away in the most unexpected corners of the building. A gym that was used mostly by the protectorate, but open to all librarians.

A coffee cart and quiet sitting area in a back corner on the third floor. A lost and found cupboard, filled with years' worth of items left behind by library patrons who had stopped by with everything from an enchanted toothbrush to a magic carpet that did little more than hover in the air. We each had our eye on something that we'd have liked to keep for ourselves, all loving the idea of having a little piece of magic of our own, but none of us had yet gotten up the nerve to ask if we were actually allowed to take anything.

Somehow, over the course of those two days, each of the Archive's councilors managed to find us at least once. They'd asked after everything from our health, to random facts about our histories, to the first moments we remembered upon arriving in the After, as if somehow reiterating things would change the answers we'd already given. They never seemed all that enthused with the answers we gave, but we tried our best to be helpful. Devon and I did so, I assumed, because we just wanted answers. Marc because he wanted to be let go sooner rather than later. I didn't think he had any sort of a plan for tracking down his wife once he was free of the Archive, but at least the councilors all seemed more willing than before to not only answer our questions but to volunteer information.

Apparently, if we made it to one of the more modern, contemporary cities, there were systems in place for people to communicate with each other over vast distances, and look up people they'd met before. But the Archive itself wasn't tied into any of that, and without finding our origin stories, it was still too wide of a net to cast to look for any one person.

I'd found a half empty notebook and a pen on the front desk and had swiftly adopted it when no one was looking. The front page of the book had a short list of people for me to look up once I had the opportunity. So far, there were only four names on the list. Darren, my best friend from work, and my parents. I had tried to come up with more names, but eventually decided that I wanted to start with those who were most important to me and build up from there. The rest would come with time.

But there was still no sign of my origin story, or Devon's, or Marc's. I found an excuse at least once a day to walk by the warehouse and peek inside, but if anything, it was only looking fuller than it had before. And without knowing anything beyond my life story and the love triangle I'd been caught in with Darren and Kelsey, my options were still limited.

Still, I was determined to find my book and to make the most of my time stuck in the Archive by doing so. I didn't know exactly what answers I was hoping to find within the pages of that one book I couldn't even name, but it seemed like my best option if I was ever going to have a chance of moving on with my life.

CHAPTER FIFTEEN

The one week anniversary of living at the Archive found Devon and I working with Grayson in one of the offices nestled in the west tower of the building. I wasn't sure how we'd managed to draw the short straw on being corralled into becoming the hired help, but secretly I was grateful to have something new to do.

"I thought you were supposed to be running around the city, enforcing the laws or something," I said in a huff as I dropped yet another box onto the rickety old table that sat in the center of the room. A cloud of dust unfurled into the air, tickling my nose as I started unpacking decades old file folders. Behind me, Devon was shifting boxes around, creating an organizational system I couldn't begin to understand.

"Don't worry," Grayson said, without looking up from the papers he was flipping through, "the city is well taken care of. It's been a long time since I've had the chance to get my hands dirty with some good old fashioned research."

"And what is it we're looking for exactly?"

It was then Grayson finally glanced up at me, his brown eyes focusing in on my mouth as I spoke. "City records," he said. "Specifically, how recently it was that new arrivals showed up in the capital cities."

"I thought you said that never happened."

"Not in our modern history, no. But the world hasn't always been as big as it is now. At first, there were only the capital cities – Sanctum, Asylum, Haven, Oasis. And everyone who was coming in from the regions those cities represented would arrive at one of these cities first since there was no variation, no opportunities to go where a character would best fit. Then the world continued to grow as needed, it still does. But the records being kept weren't as thorough back then, and while we've meant to back everything up digitally, it has yet to be a priority. We're behind on everything else, why not this?"

I shrugged, noncommittally. Not for the first time, I wished someone had taken the time to make a pamphlet, explaining the basics of the After to new arrivals. It was just one more thing for my to-do list.

Grayson mimicked my movement. "It probably won't get us anywhere, but it's one of a few ideas at this point, so we're going to keep going to see what we can come up with."

I looked down at the top piece of paper on the stack in my hands. "1890s," I said. It was the record of a girl named Delilah Jones. She'd arrived in Sanctum in eighteen ninety-two. She had been the housemaid of an English Lord, and the victim of a crime of passion. The paper said she had no known family, no friends. Her character had seemingly existed in something of a void. I wondered what had happened to her. I flipped through to the next person whose life story I held, trying not to linger too long on any one piece until I found something useful.

"Eliza told me that time passes differently here, that aging isn't always the same as what I'm used to. But do people just get old and die?" I thought of Jonathan, with his endlessly youthful face. "Or do people here just live forever?"

"Long story short... It's different for everyone. Think of aging as the natural progression of your story rather than a predictable force." He paused for a second to pick up a new stack of paper. "Eliza wasn't kidding when she said that things work differently here. My parents were both in their early twenties when they first arrived in the After. They both came from fantasy worlds, my mother getting here a few years earlier and then working as a courier in one of the larger elven kingdoms. By the time the two of them met, years later, they both looked the same as they had when they arrived. They were together for about a decade before my sister and I were born. But the way my dad tells it, as soon as I was born, things started changing for both of them as well. They aged as I aged. And then once I was full-grown, I stopped aging. I think they still aged for a few years after that, until my sister graduated university, but it's too hard to say for sure. But, I've been this way," he said, splaying his arms wide, "for most of my life. And my parents still look to be in their mid-forties.

"Still, I know of some places that are mostly home to prosaics, where time passes predictably for those who live there. People arrive at whatever age they were when their story finished, and they live their lives. They get older year by year, and then eventually they die of old age. Some come back and begin again, other souls never return to the After. We don't know whether they end up back in their origin story in the end, or if it's something else entirely."

"Wow," I said, mouth hanging open a little. "So how old are you?"

Grayson chuckled under his breath and shook his head. "I'm sure I read somewhere that that's considered a rude question in prosaic worlds."

"I think that only applies to women."

"Of course you do. And honestly, I couldn't answer your question even if I wanted to. Parts of the After track time differently, and in different regions time moves differently entirely. I am what I am."

"Where did you grow up?" I asked next, finding I was genuinely curious. I kept hearing about how many different places I could find in the After. Cities like the ones I'd known, suburbia, countryside. Post-apocalyptic wastelands like the one Harper had lived in before. Where she was again. But for all the talk of how the world I'd come from had lacked magic, I had yet to hear much about the places here that were built by it. I had to think that somewhere out there were magical cities, and dwarven mines. Cities based on Chinese myths, or ruled by Greek gods. Aliens.

"I was born in a town to the West of here, but we moved around a lot when I was young. My parents always wanted me to be a librarian because they couldn't, so they gave me the broadest experience possible of the world, so I'd understand the importance of it all."

Behind me, Devon let out a frustrated cough. I turned around to see him still in the corner, moving boxes around, glowering at them in frustration.

"Joining the Archive was my wish as much as theirs by the time I pledged. No matter where we lived, I was always nose deep in a book. At least until recently I would've bet good money that I'd read more of the books in this place than most of my colleagues. Maybe not Marissa, but it would be close."

"And yet somehow you ended up leading the protectorate?" I still had trouble imagining this tall, strong man as a bookworm. But I found I liked the image.

"It was what the Archive needed," Grayson said. "And I was the one best suited for the job. It took a long time to convince me to take it, but after the original protectorate was lost, Marissa and I had a long discussion. She'd been my mentor years before, and this was what was being asked of me. I wanted to do my part. I still get to spend more time surrounded by books than I'd ever thought possible. And the work I do benefits the Archive in the end, even if it wouldn't be my first choice. I'm good at my job, and I get results. Maybe this won't be my role forever, but for now I'm happy enough."

I wanted to argue that maybe happy enough wasn't happy at all, but who was I to judge this guy's life? He certainly seemed more fulfilled than I'd ever been.

The two of us worked in silence for a while after that, with me moving on to another box with records that went back farther than Delilah Jones. That meant handing off my finished box to Devon who didn't look all that thrilled to have yet another reject box to organize. In theory, he was taking whatever Grayson and I found unhelpful and was sorting the files so that when the time finally came to put these records somewhere other than in a dusty old attic, the work would be easier.

"Sorry," I said under my breath, handing him the box I'd been working through.

To my surprise, Devon smiled back, broad, and genuine. "No worries. It beats another day of trying to force myself to get into reading a book. And I like to be busy, to pass the time. Plus, if somehow this helps them, helps us, then I guess I can't complain."

"Well, you know I'm probably going to end the day complaining anyway. So, you're a better man than I."

Devon winked. "I could've told you that much."

I reached my elbow out to jostle Devon in the side before turning and grabbing yet another box of my own. I ended up placing it at my feet because we were running out of space on our table as endless stacks of paperwork spread out around us. Next time I went back I'd have to ask Devon for some organizational hints, because whatever he was doing was working better than my plan.

A few minutes later, my eyes scanned yet another character information sheet. This one featured a war hero who'd fought in some medieval battle. Thomas Decker.

The sheet should have had all the same information that all the others had, but this time, there was something that drew my eye.

"What about this?" I asked, holding up the piece of paper to Grayson. My finger drifted up to what I was trying to show him. Under the area where Decker's first arrival should be listed, someone had blacked out the information. I doubted I found anything truly valuable to our cause, but it was the most interesting thing I'd found all day.

Unfortunately, Grayson shook his head. "That just means that this guy went back to his origin story, almost right away. If you hold the paper up to the light, you should still be able to see where he first arrived. But we have lost some information due to bad planning back then. But wherever he came in, it's more than likely that same Reclamation Center was where he left as well. Whoever discharged him would've left that mark as a way to show us in the Archive that whoever this guy was, he hadn't had much of an impact on our world at all."

A little disappointed, I moved Decker's file to my ever-growing stack of useless information.

Just then, a loud crash came from behind me. Grayson and I both turned at once, to see Devon cursing under his breath. The box he'd been holding had fallen to the floor, spilling paperwork at his feet. In a matter of seconds, the dust in the air around him got twice as thick. I saw the moment when it reached the level of Devon's face and his whole body heaved as he took in a deep breath of musty air.

A second later, he jerked forward, letting out a massive sneeze. It would have been funny if it weren't for the fact that right after that, Devon disappeared completely. One second he'd been standing there, the next he was gone. In his place, hovering in midair at about the same level as his head had been a moment before, was a tiny bird, about the size of a chickadee.

"What the hell?" I said aloud. I closed my eyes tight for a moment and then opened them, but the image in front of me hadn't changed. More puzzled than worried, I looked over at Grayson, hoping he'd be able to offer some sort of an explanation but instead his face was contorted in shock, almost horror.

A flash of movement caught my eye and I whirled back to see that Devon had reappeared. He was standing there exactly as he had been a few seconds before but was looking entirely bewildered.

The three of us stood there for what seemed like forever. Finally, Devon shook his head a little and seemed to wake up before turning around to face us. But it wasn't me his eyes locked onto. At once, his expression shifted from scared to terrified. Instinctively, I turned to see what he was looking at.

Grayson was standing in the same place he had been before, but no longer was he confused, or distracted by research. Instead, he had stepped out from around the table and was standing right behind me, stance wide and steady. With a gun pointed straight at Devon's chest.

"Do. Not. Move." Grayson was talking to Devon but I found myself frozen in place at the same time. I couldn't understand anything that was going on around me. But whatever had just happened to Devon had clearly been magic, and a similar variety to what I'd seen Grayson do a week before.

"Who are you?" Grayson almost barked out the question.

Slowly, I turned back to face Devon, trying not to do anything too suddenly and set off an already tense situation.

Devon stuttered out a response that I couldn't understand. He was already visibly shaking and Grayson wasn't making this any easier. I couldn't say whether it was the gun pointed at him now or having been turned into a bird the moment before that had gotten to him more, but I didn't envy his position.

"Who are you?" Grayson said again, this time more

slowly. "Clearly, you're not who you said you were. And not a prosaic at all."

"I swear, I have no idea what happened to me. One second, I was sneezing. And the next everything was kind of a blur. I felt disconnected to my body, and like I was hovering almost. I kind of freaked out. In my panic, all I could think was that I wanted my body back. And then there I was, everything was back to normal."

Grayson scowled. "You're going to have to do better than that."

I took a long, slow breath trying to come up with something I could do that would make what was happening better. But there was nothing I could say. Instead, I settled on attempting to defuse the situation. "Let's just take a breath here. Could someone have done this to him?"

"In any other circumstances, maybe. But I know that magic he just performed all too well, and that's not something that would be out of his control. The odds of someone else transfiguring him into a bird while he's in the same room as me, after all this time? It's just too much of a coincidence. But something surprising happening and forcing his magic out... That I can believe. Which means he's been lying to us this entire time. All the assumptions we've been basing our investigation on have been based on lies."

Not moving his hand, Grayson's gaze briefly shifted to look at me. Gone was the easy-going expression from our shared conversation about his childhood. Instead, he was trying to assess whether I was just as much of a threat. But I still couldn't wrap my head around the fact that Devon had been lying this whole time. The pieces didn't fit. And looking at him now, he seemed as stunned as we were.

There had to be more going on, but Grayson did not look like he was in the mood for a reasonable discussion.

"I don't know what happened," Devon said again, as much to himself as to us. "I didn't do anything."

"Well, we're not taking any chances. Put your hands out in front of you, and don't make any sudden movements. It would also be in your best interest not to go muttering any incantations under your breath. I can't decide what happens next on my own, but we cannot simply let this go. But one wrong move and this is going to have a very unhappy ending for you."

CHAPTER SIXTEEN

At Grayson's order, I led the way back down to the councilors' offices, with Devon not far behind me, practically shadowed by Grayson. I tried to imagine all the ways this might have been a misunderstanding, how it could work itself out. But I kept coming up short, giving up entirely once Marc appeared beside us, shepherded by a librarian I didn't recognize, decked out in a white robe and a paranoid glare. He was guarding Marc, there was no doubt in my mind. Guarding Marc like Grayson was guarding Devon… and me.

I didn't know exactly what was coming, but the implication for what the end result could be was clear. If Devon had been lying about who he was and what he was capable of, there was nothing to say that Marc and I hadn't been doing the same. All anyone had to go on was what we'd said about ourselves, during the dozens of times we'd been questioned about our pasts. And maybe we wouldn't have been under suspicion before if the people in the Archive had thought we were magical from the outset, but the possibility that we'd been lying changed everything.

When we arrived in the foyer of the councilor's offices, it wasn't Eliza sitting at the front desk. Instead, it was a middle-aged man with dark skin and long pointed ears that protruded out from the sides of his head. He watched us from the moment we entered the hall leading to his workstation until Marc and I were seated in the lobby. Unlike the last time I was here, two armed guards who I suspected worked for Grayson were left with us while the Hand of the Archive himself marched Devon into the center room.

For a second we sat in silence, but eventually Marc leaned over and whispered, "What's going on? I was on my way to the gym when this guy"—he cocked his finger towards one of the two hovering nearby—"told me that the councilors required my presence. What he didn't say was that if I didn't go of my own free will, the decision would be made for me, but it was heavily implied."

Not bothering to keep my voice quiet as I assumed everyone around me would know what happened with Devon soon enough, I filled Marc in on everything from the dusty room to Devon's magical sneeze to Grayson's reaction. "And it's funny," I said. "Because Grayson can do the exact same thing. Or kind of. My first day in the After, I swear I saw him shift from a hawk into a human. I mean, if Devon had been hiding something this whole time, what are the chances that it's the same kind of magic that Grayson has?"

"No chance," Marc said. "I mean, I guess someone could just happen to rip off or have the same magical idea as Grayson's author, but the odds of that are just unreal."

I shook my head. "Grayson wouldn't have an author. Apparently, librarians have to be at least second generation citizens of the After. So, whatever Grayson can do, he got it from one of his parents. Meaning that the idea for those magical powers would've come from even further back. I guess it also means that Grayson wouldn't necessarily recognize anyone from the same book as his parents, so maybe Devon wasn't a new arrival after all. But... I don't know. None of this makes any sense."

"So, they're all pissed that Devon can do magic and didn't tell anyone?"

"I guess. But I honestly don't think Devon has been hiding anything. He looked as surprised as I was and seriously freaked out."

Marc sat back in his chair with a low hum, thinking to himself but not sharing with me whatever was going through his head.

"What do you think it means?" I asked, not willing to go back to sitting in silence. If Marc had a theory, I wanted to know about it.

"Well, do you have any special powers you haven't been telling us about?" Marc asked, turning back to lock eyes with me. We were both well aware that anything I said would be overheard by three other people, but I didn't have anything to share.

"I can't do anything. I can barely do long division. What about you?"

Marc hesitated for a second longer than I would've liked but soon shook his head and swore that everything he told me had been true.

"I guess it is wait and see?" I said, shrugging my shoulders.

"What choice do we have?"

If I thought the question-and-answer sessions I had been involved in before were an interrogation, the next few hours of my life were a rude awakening. No one took me into a darkly lit room with a long table and an unsheathed light bulb hanging overhead to create some sort of noir mood to intimidate me, but the result was the same. Devon had been moved away without being allowed to say anything to Marc or me, and then I was brought in.

Time seemed to stand still as I faced the four councilors all over again. The same old questions sprung most readily from Joanna's and Grayson's mouths. But while Joanna seemed intent on uncovering a plot, hoping to catch me in a lie, Grayson mostly just asked questions and intently listened on the answers.

But in the end, someone must've accepted that, at least for me, nothing had changed. And since there was nothing they could do one way or another to prove whether I was magical or not, and since I was already well under their control, it was determined that I, and later Marc, would be allowed to continue as we were, unencumbered. Nobody mentioned what would be happening to Devon.

They didn't even bother giving me a new guard to escort me back to my room, though they assured me that I'd be better off keeping to myself for the rest of the day while things settled down in the Archive. I wanted to wait for Marc, but the new receptionist and his steely gaze made it clear I wasn't welcome.

Yeah, it was probably going to take more than one evening for people around here to stop looking at me like I was a criminal. But I found my way back to my room easily enough, my week at the Archive and my new routine making it all too easy to go between my usual stops. But what I found when I entered our private row of rooms was certainly different than anything I'd seen before. Both my room and Marc's room stood exactly as they had been before I'd left this morning. But all the walls to Devon's room in the middle were gone. Instead, metal bars encircled all three sides of the room, adjacent to connecting walls rather than in place of them. Curtains had been hung where, I assumed, the bathroom walls had once been, at least offering him some semblance of privacy. Or at least it would, whenever Devon was brought back to his new holding cell. There was still no sign of him.

On the ground, surrounding all three of our rooms was a familiar bright blue line, the likes of which I'd almost forgotten about during my time in the Archive. Whenever we were locked in, magic would be completely impossible for us to use. Not that that changed anything for me.

I wanted to wait for Devon and Marc, to talk to somebody else who understood what I was feeling, but the need to follow the rules overpowered me pretty quickly. I slipped back into my room, glad I'd at least stockpiled a few books on my dresser the day before.

And when my door locked later that night, I wasn't even a bit surprised.

The next morning I was tempted to stay inside my room for as long as possible, hiding out from the world a little longer. But when I found that my door had been unlocked at some point while I was sleeping, I ultimately decided to venture out. High School had taught me that the longer I hid, the more attention I would draw to myself.

And I hadn't done anything wrong. I had nothing to hide.

And I was hungry.

As soon as I stepped out into the hallway, a flash of movement from beside me caught my attention. Devon had gotten up from wherever he'd been sitting and flung himself toward the bars of his room. He white-knuckled the metal rods, and stared at me with pleading eyes. "You're okay?"

I nodded. "I'm fine. Glad to see you though."

"You too. No one would answer any of my questions, but I got the impression that whatever happened to me yesterday put a target on all our backs."

"Any idea what happened?" I couldn't bring myself to ask if he'd been lying this whole time about having powers.

"I have no clue. It was the weirdest thing that's ever happened to me, and at this point, that's saying something. Eventually they explained what it had looked like from the other end, but I don't even think I knew I was a bird at the time. And I certainly didn't do anything to make it happen."

"And did they believe you?" The fact that he was

currently locked away in a cell probably wasn't the best sign, but seeing him there at all had to be at least a little encouraging.

"I don't think anyone knows what to believe anymore. But it looks like I'm stuck here for the next little while."

"That sucks, I'm sorry. Is Marc up yet?"

"Yeah, he's long gone. Didn't say where he was going. Didn't say much of anything at all. He mostly seemed to be in a mood, which is an impressive feat since he's still allowed to walk around instead of being treated like a spy."

"Well, that's Marc. Hopefully this will all pass quickly, and we can get back on track for getting us all the hell out of here.

Devon and I talked a little longer, and I felt terrible leaving him on his own but eventually my stomach growled loudly enough that he insisted I go get something to eat.

That had to be the fastest meal I'd ever had. I found a selection of bacon, eggs, and pancakes in one of the refrigerators. But the sensation of having everyone else in the cafeteria stop talking as soon as I entered the room was enough encouragement to have me shoveling down my plate of food as quickly as possible. My plan for the day was to basically stay out of the way as much as possible. And to not do anything that could even remotely, in any culture, be considered magical. I didn't know how, but it wasn't lost on me that whatever had happened to Devon could happen to me next. Or maybe it all was some strange fluke or misunderstanding.

Either way, I retreated to the stacks, heading for the fifth floor and the romance section which was becoming a favorite of mine. Yes, secretly part of me hoped I'd stumble on my own book, it somehow being missed during shelving. But with hundreds of thousands of titles surrounding me, I knew the odds weren't great. Still, the romance section had a little of everything, but always with the flare of love, or at least sexy times, flowing through the pages as well.

I headed for a stack at random, and almost immediately bumped into a metal cart that stood at about the height of my waist. It shifted forward slightly, knocking into the hip of its owner. Eliza.

She looked up at once, slightly alarmed. "Oh. It's you. I didn't expect to see you…"

"Let me guess, you didn't expect they'd let me out of my room this morning?"

"No, not that. I guess I just assumed they'd want to… okay, yeah. Keep an eye on you. I suck." Eliza shuffled her feet a little, looking downward. I hadn't seen her in a few days, but had to assume she'd heard everything that had happened the day before.

"I swear, I'm as harmless now as I was before." I held my hands up as though to show I wasn't hiding anything. "I figured I'd make today a reading day and get out of everyone's way until this gets sorted out."

"So, you're hiding out?" Eliza said with a knowing smile.

"Guilty. I can just take my books to my room, if you…" I didn't know how to end the sentence but right away Eliza jumped in to correct me.

"No way. Stay. I don't know exactly what happened yesterday, but I'm a big believer in innocent until proven guilty. And honestly, I'm not even sure what it is you guys are being accused of."

"Well, you seem to be the only one around here who thinks that way."

"Now, you are just feeling a little extra pressure right now. Mostly, people are probably about as confused as you are. Okay, maybe not quite as confused as you, but mostly, librarians are just a curious bunch. And not all that judging. Reading consistently teaches empathy, if nothing else. And we've all heard what happened to those of you who were caught on day one, forced back into their stories. Whatever's happening, it's not cut and dry."

While it wasn't a resounding vote of confidence, it was more than I hoped for. "Honestly, I'm probably too scatterbrained today to read much. Did you want any help?" I looked down at Eliza's overflowing cart of books.

Eliza hesitated, but a slow smile eventually played onto her lips. "Technically, I'm supposed to do this myself. But for all intents and purposes, anyone can put a book anywhere they want. So, if you wanted to have a look at these babies, and maybe see where they fit in on the shelves alphabetically, I can't stop you."

I grinned, so grateful for something to do.

Shelving ended up being about as tedious as I'd imagined, and I probably slowed things down a little by checking the back cover of every book for any hint of a name I recognized. But it passed the time quickly.

After emptying one cart and going back down to the warehouse to refill it, we ended up in the thriller section, shelving countless dark-covered titles, usually featuring knives or blood splatter. Not exactly my preferred reading material, but I made a mental note to double back if I got a chance later and at least check something out. The more I knew, the better prepared I would be.

Eventually, I took a large stack of books whose authors names ended in R and left Eliza alone with those from the front end of the alphabet.

We worked like that for a while, me coming back to refill my stack whenever I was empty-handed. But on my third trip, I found that Eliza wasn't alone.

Jamie looked up as soon as I came up behind him. It took him a second, but I saw the exact moment when recognition flashed in his eyes. "Oh, I know you."

I looked up to see Eliza watching us, and got a sharp flashback to Grayson scolding me for talking to this guy in the first place. He was Literati, or something. Something Grayson didn't approve of.

But if Eliza was under orders to report back anything I did that might be considered suspicious, I wasn't going to risk doing anything remotely interesting.

"Hey," I said in response, doing my best to keep my tone frosty.

Jamie's smile faltered at once. But he wasn't quite ready to give up. "Read any good books lately?"

I shrugged. Once again, my gaze flicked to Eliza, which probably made me look guiltier than anything else. But I felt like a deer in headlights, unable to decide my next move, and seeing pitfalls with every opportunity.

"Jamie here's a regular," Eliza said, her voice unreadable. "Usually tries to do us a solid and hand back his books in person once he's done with them, rather than re-shelving titles he's not sure about, and potentially making a mess of things. It's hard enough to find specific titles already as it is. Alphabetical only works when random patrons don't get lazy and put books back wherever it's most convenient once they decide they don't want to deal with them anymore."

I forced a tight smile. "Fair enough."

Jamie put down a small stack of books on Eliza's cart. "Well, I guess I'll see you guys later." He looked from Eliza to me and back again, looking more confused than anything. But I could remember all too vividly exactly how Grayson had responded the last time I'd seen this guy. Someone, somewhere, didn't trust him, and I had to think there was at least the possibility of a reason for that. And I didn't want any of that suspicion being transferred over to me.

Once he was out of earshot, Eliza rounded on me. "What was that about?"

Already, I was feeling like a jerk. Jamie hadn't done anything wrong any more than I had. At least not to me. And I knew all too well what it was like to be treated like some sort of freak of nature for something completely out of my control. Now, he probably just thought I was a bitch. And he'd been more willing to talk to me than almost anyone else around here.

It didn't seem like anything I could do would be the right answer, and I certainly didn't have a good one to give to Eliza.

"I don't know, I'm probably just being paranoid. But Grayson got weird last time I was talking to Jamie, and I didn't want to mess things up any more than they already are."

"Oh yeah, I get that. And Jamie's been under suspicion for a while now, though no one told me suspicion of what. But mostly, I think he's just a guy who likes books. But I definitely don't pretend to know everything that goes on around here. Which is probably why I'm still here stacking books when everyone else is coming up with plans and testing theories. And well, he's definitely a vampire, but I like to think the prejudice around that is at least a little less than it used to be."

"Wait. He's a vampire?" I should have known! I spun around to look back in the direction Jamie had disappeared, but he was long gone. Eliza smiled, like she knew how excited I'd be at the idea. "Are you kidding?"

"Nope. Definitely a vampire. I don't know if he started that way or he was turned since he got here, but for as long as he's been coming around here, he's a hundred percent undead."

"How can you tell?" I whispered. The idea was exciting even though I knew that in theory, vampires were people I should probably be afraid of.

At that, Eliza laughed out loud. "It's not a secret. And the signs can be a little different depending on the specific strain, but the fangs are a pretty big giveaway."

A memory of Jamie smiling at me from the couch flashed through my memory, but I had never even imagined that his teeth were used to... Weird. "No way." Also, gross.

"Yup. With a lot of people around here, who or what they are isn't immediately noticeable, but you learn to pick these things up after a while. You'll get there."

"Cool." It was all I could come up with to say. Already I was excited about the idea of reporting back to Devon that I knew a vampire. Or, at least I had known one before I'd decided to be kind of a jerk to him for no real reason I could come up with. And then proceeded to give him the cold-shoulder when he might have been perfectly happy to let me pepper him with questions about life as a blood-sucking fiend.

Yup, I'd definitely screwed that one up. Surprising no one.

I promised myself that Literati or not, if I saw Jamie again, Grayson's ideas about who I should and shouldn't be talking to, weren't going to get a vote.

CHAPTER SEVENTEEN

The announcement came that night, Marissa's voice booming throughout the cafeteria while I was doing my best to eat my BLT as quickly as I could so I could retreat back to my room. I'd been on the lookout for Marc all day, hoping to press him more about what we'd been talking about the day before, but there was still no sign of him.

"Attention, librarians." I looked up, trying to find the source of the Heart's voice. There was no sign of her, and no speakers above me. "As we are all aware, for some time now the Archive has been woefully behind on some of the tasks entrusted to those who work here. While some might argue that our falling behind is due to circumstances outside of our control, I feel differently. It is our sacred responsibility to keep this place running as smoothly as possible, so that it can continue to run our world. Today, we make a change. It's all hands-on deck between this very moment, and a time, hopefully not too far in the future, when we have finally shelved all our outstanding titles. All your other projects will be put on hold indefinitely, with only a few minor exceptions made for those in the protectorate, required to keep peace within the city. We will of course still be open to the public during this time, but we will be encouraging as many of our patrons as possible to come back at a more convenient time. Information that we desperately need is hidden within the pages of some of our yet to be catalogued titles. As soon as we find these titles, you can all get back to the daily routines that you know and love. But for now, I hope you all remember your time as apprentice librarians. Because it is that skill set that is going to get you through the next few days, or weeks. Whatever it takes to get this job done.

"Please report to the heads of your order for further instructions. Those of you not yet pledged to a particular order, you are likely among those who know best what to do next. Finish up whatever it is you're working on now, report to your nearest warehouse, and get to work. There is no room for cutting corners, and each book will need to be properly cataloged within our system so that we can be alerted once the books we're looking for turn up. Best of luck, and we'll see you on the other side."

Almost everyone around me started talking amongst themselves all at once, and it seemed like the excitement of Marissa's announcement had made those sitting closest to me forget who exactly I was. The conversations mostly seemed to be complaints, no one wanting to go back to the days of shelving and listing titles. And after seeing what Eliza was currently working through, I couldn't blame them. But I also wasn't going to sit around and wait for them to remember that I was at least one of the causes of their newest headache. I finished my sandwich and slipped out of the room as quickly as possible, already feeling a few people watching me go.

I got back to my room just as Marc made it back to his. "Hey. Where have you been?"

Marc shrugged and looked away. "I've been hiding mostly. I didn't want to deal with people today."

"I get that. But it sounds like there are going to be a whole lot more people here, and pretty soon."

Devon looked up from the book he was reading. "All

this excitement for little old us?"

I pursed my lips, not sure exactly how I felt. It was finally dawning on me that the end result of what was happening now, with white robed librarians rushing through every corner of the library, was awkward, but it could also result in finally getting my hands on the book that I'd come from. I hadn't thought about it much in the last few days, my plan to distract myself working a little too well. I'd been going under the assumption that maybe I'd stumble across it eventually. But I admitted to myself now that this more proactive plan was a lot more likely to get real results.

I could have that book in my hands by the next day. At least, if anyone would actually let me read it. I had to assume that there would be multiple librarians combing over it first, for any sign that I'd been lying about where I'd come from. But if that was the case, they'd probably know right away, and the end result would still be the same. I knew I hadn't seen magic for even a day in my life before coming to the After, and soon everyone else would know it too. And maybe Grayson would then stop looking at me like he thought I could be hiding something.

The guys and I didn't say much else to each other that night, all wanting the privacy of our own thoughts as we waited to see what exactly this new search order would mean for us. Already, the building seemed louder, both with the reverberation of frantic footsteps through the halls and with excited voices talking to one another, if never to us.

Whatever came next, I was going to need a good night's sleep first.

Devon was already awake by the time I left my room next morning. "He still in there?" I asked, looking over at Marc's door. I got up early that morning, unable to sleep a minute longer. I knew that no one would let me help look for my book. I shouldn't have even been helping Eliza before, and now with all eyes on me there was no way I'd be able to get anywhere near anything. But I wanted to be there the moment that it happened. The moment that someone held my origin story up in the air, with a shout of triumph like he'd found a golden ticket.

Devon nodded. He'd been a lot less chatty, a lot less happy ever since being locked away in his room. Not that I could blame him. But I had no idea what I could say to make what he was going through easier.

I knocked on Marc's door, and a second later he came and opened it. "You're going out there today?" he asked.

"Well, we've got to eat. And I kind of think that hiding out here is only going to make it look like we have something to, well, hide."

Marc thought about that for a second and then nodded. Soon, he was out the door.

"Is there anything we can bring you?" I asked, turning back to Devon one last time.

"No," Devon said with an over-exaggerated sigh. "They're still bringing me food. And more books than I've ever wanted to deal with. But I'm fine."

"Hey," Marc said. "They're going to find your story any day now, and then they'll know for sure that you weren't lying. You could go back to being a regular prisoner, rather than a super prisoner, any minute now."

Devon raised his chin a little, and while he didn't smile I could tell that Marc's words were having the desired effect on him. At least one of us had known what to say. "Okay, keep me posted."

Marc nodded, and I followed behind him like a hopeless puppy.

We'd only made it a few feet out of sight of our rooms before someone opened the door in front of us, almost bumping right into me as they moved into the hallway. It was a female librarian I didn't recognize, with long dark hair down to her waist. She gave Marc and I a quick look and then hurried down the hallway.

"I'd forgotten there were other rooms like ours," Marc said. "Ones that aren't being used as prison cells, that is."

"Do you think there are more librarians staying here now?" I asked. Marc didn't have an answer.

But my question was answered clearly enough as soon as we stepped out of the back rooms and out into the main library. Everywhere I looked were people in white robes, moving between the shelves either with carts of books or simply carrying around large piles in their hands. Each one wore a white robe with inky scribblings. They were all librarians. It was hard to wrap my mind around such a dramatic shift in numbers.

Marc and I kept mostly to the perimeter, well aware of how much we stood out in our jeans and T-shirts. But every single row of shelves we passed had at least one person standing in the aisle, all working away in near silence. Gone were the flurry of conversations from the day before. Now, the librarians meant business.

And when Marissa said all hands on deck, she clearly hadn't been kidding. Before that, I understood that most librarians didn't work within the stacks themselves. Some like Eliza had work to do shelving titles, or working with people who came into the building. But most had offices or workplaces tucked away from the bustle of daily operations.

But there were so many of them. I couldn't tell just from looking at them who was in what order, but in that moment, they were all working as one on one central task.

When we made it down to the lobby, not sure where else to go, I spotted Grayson talking to a few muscular looking women by the front desk. When he saw me, he quickly waved off the conversation and headed toward Marc and me.

"I'm not sure you should be here," Grayson said as soon as he reached us. "The last thing you want is anyone accusing you of getting in the way. Or tampering with the search." My eyes narrowed reflexively in response, more than a little sick of being under suspicion. "I don't think so," Grayson quickly clarified. "But it will be easier for everyone this way."

"And where exactly would you want us to go?" Marc asked. "Are we supposed to just hang out in our rooms all day?"

"That might not be the worst idea. Hopefully, it's just for one day and then you can go back to how things were before."

"Yeah, like that was so great. How things were before involved people staring at us and having absolutely nothing to do with our time. At least for a while there, you guys seemed intent on keeping us busy, at least while you could learn as much as you could about us. But now…"

"Stay if you want," Grayson said, "but do not touch any books today, and stay out of the way."

Grayson looked over at me. "It will be easier for you if you cooperate today."

In the end, Marc wasn't prepared to listen but I at least convinced him that we could get out of the library part of the building and go grab something to eat. Instead, he dragged me down the stairwell at the opposite end of the building toward the warehouse rather than to the cafeteria. "If nothing else, we can at least see how much progress they've made."

I didn't argue, my own curiosity getting the better of me.

We both did our best not to look at anyone directly as we passed crowds in the hallway, each of them pushing carts of books. There probably had to be an elevator somewhere we didn't know about, but I didn't let myself wonder about it for long. There was already enough to deal with, and I'd given up on ever really understanding how the Archive itself worked.

We pushed our way into the warehouse Eliza had shown us earlier at the first sign of an ebb in the crowd. I was more than ready to listen to Grayson's advice and stay out of people's way. Really, I didn't want anyone noticing me at all.

Inside, we found another massive group of librarians. They were pulling books from stacks, possibly at random, before entering information into various computers that had clearly been brought in overnight. I stood back in the corner and watched for a second, as each title moved from a stack, to a computer, to a cart to be shelved. Every time a new librarian came into the room, they brought back an empty cart and left with whichever one looked to be the fullest.

A few people noticed us, but nobody said anything, and that was all the permission that either Marc or I needed to stay put.

Already, the room seemed to hold far fewer books than it had the last time we visited. I didn't know whether or not librarians had been working through the night, but for having just started around dinnertime the day before they'd already made some serious progress. But there were still far more books than I could even guess at, and this was only one room. I didn't want to say it out loud, but I didn't think there was a chance in hell that this would all be finished in a matter of hours.

Still, as one of the newer arrivals, shouldn't my book—and Devon's and Marc's—have been at least somewhat easy to guess where it'd be?

"Do you want to stay here, or...?" I asked, once my legs started to get stiff from lack of movement. There was nowhere to sit in the warehouse that wasn't at the computer desk, and you couldn't have paid me to take up a spot there, even when the station was available.

"I just wish we could help," Marc said. "I know we'd probably just slow things down. And no one trusts us around these things anyway. But I hate not doing anything."

"Will you read your book? When they find it."

"Sure, I guess. I'm more interested in having my name cleared, but I'll take what I can get at this point. How about you?"

"Literally, the second that they let me. I just feel like that book is going to have some of the answers I'm looking for. I don't even know what the questions are, but finding that book, whatever it is, can only make things easier. At least I'll see what happened to everyone I know. And maybe figure out a few things I've been wondering about my life before." Like why Darren had picked Kelsey instead of me. It seemed far less important than it had a week ago, but I was still desperate for any taste of my life before. And I hoped that reading about them would help fill some of that void I'd been feeling, missing all the people I loved.

"Everything I want is here," Marc said. "In the After. All I really need my book for is to have someone here use it to help me figure out where it was I was supposed to start out in the After. Where Meg would be. I have to hope that she's still waiting for me."

"Of course she is. It hasn't been that long. I bet it takes a while to find everyone you knew before, even without all this nonsense." I waved my hands in the air, hoping the gesture would encompass everything we'd been through with the Archive and outside of it. "It will all work out."

"I hope so. But the longer we are here, the harder it gets. I think about that all the time."

The two of us stood in silence for a little longer, watching the flurry of motion around us, maybe imagining that the stacks we followed were getting smaller and smaller. I flinched a little every time a new book popped into existence, diverting my attention away from one that had been sitting there for who knew how long.

"We should get out of here," I said after a while. "This isn't getting us anywhere."

"There's nothing we can do here will help us or anyone else. This is as good as anything else."

"Yeah, yeah, Mr. Positivity. But getting some actual food may help keep me sane, at least a little longer. So why don't we do that for a while? We should probably bring Devon something soon, too, because I'm guessing with everything else going on they might have forgotten about him. And he's probably bored out of his skull."

Marc looked back over his shoulder before nodding. "How is it that you're always hungry?"

"I'm not. But if there's food available, I'm usually happy to eat it. Just in case." I licked my lips dramatically in response. "It's a trait I picked up from an old friend."

To my complete and total surprise, Marc actually smiled. "Meg is like that too. Somehow, guys get all the flack for our appetites, but it's the women in my life who seem to be more like bottomless pits. I had to stop to pick up snacks for her after every single one of my shifts."

"She sounds like my kind of girl."

Marc's smile disappeared slowly as he stared off at a nearby wall, lost in thought. "I just hope that wherever she is, she has enough to eat. Do you think they're feeding her?"

I didn't know who the they Marc was referencing was. And as much as I wanted to help, I didn't have the answer to his question. "I don't know," I said finally. "But I bet that wherever she is she's as worried about you as you are about her. So let's get something to eat and make sure that when you see her again, she can see you've been well taken care."

CHAPTER EIGHTEEN

Things didn't change much over the course of the next two days. No matter what time of day I decided to risk wandering out of my room to stretch my legs, there were always librarians around. My best guess was, there had to be at least a few hundred of them. It was more people than I'd imagined they had in their whole organization, and still there had to be more of them outside of the city who maybe couldn't show up at a day's notice, but already their numbers far surpassed anything I would've guessed.

On the third night, a knocking on my door woke me up only a few hours after I finally managed to get myself to sleep. I wondered briefly who I could talk to about getting an intercom system before my brain woke up enough to realize I was going to have to get out of bed and answer the annoyingly persistent rapping.

The sound came again, fiercer, and insistent. I was still pulling on my pants when I realized that this might not be a social call. Could my book have been found and somehow, someone didn't like what was inside? There might be armed guards waiting for me, prepared to disappear me to who knows where.

But what choice did I have, really?

Inhaling, I opened the door and braced myself for whatever came next.

Grayson stood there, hands behind his back. His dark hair looked more mussed than I'd ever seen it, the only testament how little he'd slept through all this.

He looked both formal and intense, but he wasn't pointing a gun at me just yet, so I reminded myself not to panic.

I had no idea what to say, or what reason he could have for showing up in the middle of the night, so I just stood there and waited. Hoping he'd offer an explanation before I had to say anything at all.

"They've finished." For a moment, I had no idea what he was talking about. "All the warehouses are empty, and every single book has been catalogued. It's going to save us a lot of work in the coming weeks and we have a chance of staying on top of the new arrivals now. But there's no sign of any book that features you Marc, or Devon as a character. We've even cross-referenced the list of names that you all gave us of other people your stories might've featured. But there's nothing."

I stood up a little straighter. "What does that mean? Did it get shelved already, and someone missed it? Or maybe I guessed the genre wrong and we were looking in the wrong place?"

"Unfortunately, no. We have more to go on than genre when looking up specific titles. We cross-reference character, setting, genre, and any other defining features of a story we can find. If nothing else, Emilio Croy, the serial killer Marc was working to find, should've been a sure thing."

"What does that mean?" I braced myself for bad news.

"Honestly, I don't know. There are already groups working on new theories, but mostly we're all just tired. Every bedroom in the building is full, and everyone else has gone home. But I know you were hoping for some answers, so I didn't want to keep you waiting."

I cocked my head a little, trying to find the meaning of what Grayson had just told me. After searching for days, he delayed going to sleep for longer than he'd had to so that he could tell me what was going on. Being on the receiving end of the common courtesy of being kept in the loop was something I'd become unused to. "Thank you. Should I be worried?"

"Yes and no." Grayson scratched at a day's worth of scruff on his jaw. "If you have nothing to hide…"

"I don't. I swear. I wish there was something I could do to show everyone that I am exactly who I say I am, which is completely boring and unremarkable."

"Well that much we know is a lie, but I'll let it slide, this time. Your arrival here in the After, along with the mark on your wrist, must mean something. We'd have had better luck if we were able to get to more of you on that first day. I've been looking at this as though each of you is a different piece of the puzzle, and the more we have, the more we know."

"Except, not one of us knows anything."

Grayson's gaze drifted over to Devon's room and I realized that my friend had probably caught everything that was being said. I wondered why Marc hadn't come out of his room already at the sound of voices to see what was going on.

"What do we do now?"

"First, I need to go meet with Marissa and the others. There is much we must discuss. After that, I think we all need to get some sleep."

"To be fair, I was already doing that."

The corner of Grayson's mouth ticked up the tiniest bit, and I smiled in response. "Don't worry, when it comes to sleep, I'm pretty sure it will more than even out. With all this hurry up and wait, I must have caught up on years' worth of naps by now. I'm the best rested person in the building."

"I don't know about that." Devon's voice came from

the room beside me. I chuckled, and even Grayson looked amused.

"Alright, well, I'll let you get back to sleep. Both of you."

"Who knows if tomorrow I'll manifest some sort of super awesome, bird power and we will have a little more to go on." I was joking, but the immediate shift in Grayson's expression made it clear that my attempt at being funny had been in poor taste. "Just kidding." I held up my hands to show I wasn't holding any weapons.

"I know, just tired. I'll see you in the morning?" He said the last part like a question and I nodded my head.

Hopefully, in the morning things would be a little clearer.

Once I closed the door behind me, securely back in my room, I let myself really absorb the fact that my book was missing. The answers I'd been looking forward to for days now weren't coming. I tried to believe that this didn't mean I'd never find them, but it was still a blow.

When I finally crawled back into bed, sleep didn't come quite as easy as I'd hoped. Instead I played back over the time I'd spent in the Archive, looking for any clues, or warning signs I might've missed. Something I could offer as proof that I wanted to help. That I wasn't the enemy.

But everything was just as confusing as it had always been. I wasn't going to be any help at all.

Apparently, Grayson's attitude the night before wasn't shared by the people he worked with. I left my room the next morning to find a female guard standing in the hallway posted at the juncture where our hallway met with a connecting stretch of bedrooms.

Another was seated in a chair by Devon's room, on duty to keep watch during the day even though Devon couldn't go anywhere. A petite woman stood at the end of the hallway, leaning against the wall beside Marc's door.

"Am I allowed to leave?" I asked, a hint of frustration in my voice.

"You can go wherever you like inside the building," the woman assigned to me said. "I just have to go with you."

"Any particular reason?"

"Orders." Okay, so this girl wasn't going to be all that chatty.

"Whose orders?" Devon asked from beside me.

Green eyes studied me, assessing for any danger or hidden agenda, but at least she answered. "Archivist Nyce. She thought it would be best if we could keep an eye on you. Suspicions are arising and she didn't want to take any chances."

"Wait, are you making sure I don't do anything?" I asked. "Or making sure someone isn't going to try to do something to me?"

My guard shrugged. "Basically, I'm here to make sure nothing interesting happens to you at all."

Nope, nope, nope. Nothing about this new development sat well with me. Marc, Devon, and I had been more than cooperative, if not always gracious. And now they had stuck us with guards?

The idea of a shadow watching me all day, every day, even more than up to now, wasn't going to fly. But throwing a tantrum about the whole thing wouldn't get me anywhere. What I needed, was to call in the closest thing to a favor I'd been offered so far.

"Well, then things are probably going to go pretty smoothly for you. I've got a long day of sitting around and waiting ahead of me." I did my best to smile, hoping my guard would realize that I wasn't directing my frustration at her. Not her specifically. Antagonizing the person I now had to spend the day with wouldn't get me anywhere. "What's your name?"

"Protectorate Bowman."

I nodded, assuming she already was aware of who I was.

"All right, Bowman. Can you help me? I'm guessing you don't want this to be part of your daily routine any more than I do, so is there any chance you could take me to Jonathan Credence?" Not that long ago, Jonathan *had* offered to be of assistance if he could. And I thought it was well past time for me to take him up on that offer.

It took Protectorate Bowman far too long to figure out whether I was allowed to be brought to any of the councilors, simply because I'd asked to be. It wasn't a privilege that most of the librarians got to enjoy according to her.

But in the end logic won out, or my guard just didn't care enough to argue with me, figuring someone else would tell me off later if needed. Though Bowman didn't end up leading me to the main offices like I'd expected. And I didn't miss how every few seconds she would look back as she led me through the building, to make sure I really was following her rather than trying to escape. Or she was making sure no one attacked me at random, but either way I wasn't exactly getting a warm and fuzzy vibe from my newest forced companion.

We found Jonathan in one of the newly emptied warehouses, poking around through a small stack of books that had accumulated since the night before. There were already a few hundred, and it was crazy to think about just how many books were created every minute.

And now, I knew that my book wasn't among the ones I was looking at. It was more than a little disheartening.

"Kadie, I've been told you wanted to speak with me."

He looked at the guard standing behind me and gave her a curt nod. A moment later, she disappeared back out into the hallway, giving us a moment to talk in private.

"I hope this is okay," I said. "Grayson told me yesterday that no one managed to find our books."

Jonathan picked up a stack of titles from the floor and placed them on a desk nearby. "Unfortunately, no. It's certainly an unexpected development." His voice didn't hold so much as a hint of surprise, but I suppose he had more time than I had to consider the repercussions of all this.

"Does this ever happen? Do people ever turn up and you just can't find their books?"

The young man in front of me gave me a sympathetic look. "Not really. Sometimes it can take a while, but that's usually because years have passed between a book's arrival and someone coming looking for it. And even then, everything turns up eventually. But I'm hoping your books will be no different. Sometimes it's just a matter of our not having all the right information in our catalogue. If the back cover doesn't mention you, it isn't always guaranteed that we will have your records."

"What's next then? I mean, as impressed as I am that you guys were able to get through that many titles in just a few days, I'm guessing reading all the books you guys shelved would be a different thing entirely."

"I think you underestimate just how much the people around here enjoy reading, but you do have a point. Still, we will come up with something. You don't need to worry about it."

I couldn't help it, I laughed out loud, surprised at how unconcerned the Head of the Archive seemed about all this. "I think that will be easier said than done." I paused for a second, the very beginnings of a plan forming in my mind. It wasn't a good one, but it was something. "What if I can help somehow? Me, or Marc. Even Devon. You know we all would be willing to do whatever we could to figure all this out."

"I have no doubts about that. But I'm not sure what any of you could do at this point that would make a difference. I know it's got to be frustrating for all of you, but I can assure you we're doing everything we can to sort out whatever's going on."

"What about the mercenaries? The people who tried to grab us when we first arrived? Are there still any of them in the city? Do you think they're still looking for us?"

"They are still in the city," Jonathan said slowly as though trying to figure out what it was I was getting at before admitting too much. "But they don't work for anyone in particular. They're hired muscle." I didn't interrupt to point out that I already knew what a mercenary was. "They may have given up the search after that first day."

"So why are we here at all?"

"It's not that simple. The politics of our world are… complicated."

"Try me."

"Think of it as a chess game. No, that's too cliché. Capture the flag, then. Except there are four flags. Each branch of the Archive of Ink and Soul. It is a common belief by those in the After that the Archive is the heart of our world. It holds all the knowledge that shapes our world, as well as so many of the people who populate it."

Jonathan rubbed his hands together as though for warmth as he continued. "For as long as there have been librarians, those of us dedicated to the protection and maintenance of the Archive, we have held control of the building and everything it holds. But as times change and the world grows, other groups vie for power. And there are those who would wish to wrest control of the Archive for themselves, believing it could help them shape a world more to their liking."

"The Literati?" I said.

"Among others, but yes. The Literati believe that by giving control of the Archive back to the people—more specifically, to themselves—that they can use it to create a better world. And their followers are growing. Many among the Keepers and the Protectorate believe it is only a matter of time before they make their move."

"So how do we fit in?" I asked. "Me, Devon, and Marc. And any others."

"That's the thing. We don't know, not for sure. But

your arrival here could signal a shift of some kind. Something that the Archive requires of us, or a change that we need to make.

I wanted to throw my hands in frustration but did my best to keep cool. "If you're so worried about the Literari making a move, then you should do something first. What we're doing now isn't getting us anywhere, and as much as I appreciate the desire to protect us—even if it's just so you can figure out how our existence affects you—maybe you aren't using all the tools at your disposal."

At last, Jonathan stopped moving and really looked at me. "I'm listening."

"Use me as bait," I said. And then backtracked because I realized I couldn't volunteer anyone else for what I was suggesting. "Just me. Let me go outside, follow me, track me or whatever and see what happens. If someone tries to grab me then we'll know that they're still looking for us. You can capture one of those mercenaries and get some real answers. Find out who hired them."

"We already have some pretty strong assumptions about who's paying the bills, but I appreciate your courage on this."

"Well, if you know who's funding all this, why aren't you doing anything about it?" Now, it was fair to say that I lost my cool. I took a step closer to him and let in a long breath. "Why won't you let me help? I want to figure this out as much as anyone."

"Until we understand more, I don't see that happening. I'm not saying no. But we can't risk your safety, not while there is even a chance that this is far bigger than we understand."

Huh. I tried not to let it show on my face that his response was far more promising than I'd prepared for. Still, it wasn't a yes, and I hoped I could use that.

"Okay, how about a compromise?"

Jonathan raised his blonde eyebrows, not speaking.

"Ditch the guards. Having them follow us around the

Archive is a waste of resources, and a waste of time. What exactly are you hoping for, having them tailing us?"

"Not me. Joanna. I voted against this, and I would again. We gain nothing by having the three of you followed. But I was outvoted."

Clenching my jaw, I tried to see my next step. I still didn't have a complete understanding of the Archive's hierarchy, but having three councilors intent on something didn't feel promising.

"Still," Jonathan said, without prompting, surprising me, "Joanna was the only one of us who felt sure this was necessary. If you could sway one of the others, the decision could be reversed. Perhaps someone who might be able to find more productive uses for the Protectorate."

"Grayson?" I asked.

"He would be the best place to start, yes. For now, I'll say that I'm not entirely opposed to the idea. And if Grayson will listen, then I'll back you up as best I can. But consensus will be key, in the end. Still, if you can get Grayson, as well as me then perhaps you'll get a chance."

Next step, it was Grayson's turn for an unexpected visit.

"No, no way. There is absolutely zero chance we'll consider using you, or anyone else, as bait," Grayson said, staring at me from the other side of his desk. His office was to the right of the central office where the entire group of councilors before questioned me before. It was a little smaller, and had a massive whiteboard on one side of the wall, plus more books than I could count. A treadmill stood in the far corner, but it didn't look like it had been used for a while as a pile of books was building up on the track. "I appreciate the offer, but Jonathan should have shut this idea down immediately."

I winced, feeling guilty under the intensity of Grayson's stare. "Technically," I said, "Jonathan said no too. I just wanted to float the idea, since this is more your thing than his. And there has to be more we can learn from those mercenaries."

Grayson shook his head, exasperated. "We've already tried questioning the mercenaries we could find, looking for the source of their orders. But not one of them remembers anything about who paid them in the first place. Even the man we saw that night, the one who took your friend, Harper. He doesn't remember anything about her, or what he did. So, putting you out there would be an unnecessary risk."

"Except, if no one is looking for us anymore, what's the risk at all?" I let out a huff. "Why bother holding us here?"

"Because memory work like this is no small feat. We cannot guarantee that they were the only ones looking for you, or that whoever did this hasn't put a different group on your retrieval now that they know we're on to them. Not only that, but now I'm starting to have some doubts about our working theories, and are certain what it all means, I'm not sure what we really have to gain by taking that kind of risk."

My heart sunk a little, I'd already suspected there was no way I was going to win him over to my idea. It was a good thing I hadn't bothered stopping in to see if Marc would be on board to help, as I know I would've gotten his hopes up and it would have been for nothing.

I knew I should have just walked away, right then. I had no way of knowing whether insisting on leaving the building would only do more to make me look suspicious. And if it would hurt Devon's and Marc's chances of earning some trust as well in the process.

"How long?" I asked. "How long do I have to wait before this just becomes a giant question mark in the history of the Archive rather than something that you're all still working on?"

"I'm not really one for quitting."

"Me neither," I said, even though a week ago, I wasn't sure that was something I would've said about myself. "I'm not willing to give up and just live here for the rest of my life."

"Give me one week," Grayson said after a minute. "After one week, I'll insist on a meeting between the councilors and moving forward with a new game plan. I can't guarantee that the action taken is going to be one you approve of, or something you like. But give me one more week and I promise something will have changed. We'll know more, or maybe you'll have displayed some sort of magical bird power and got yourself locked up."

I wanted to argue, but I saw a small smile touch the corner of Grayson's lips. "Did you make a joke?"

"I'm actually a pretty funny guy."

"Uhuh," I said with an exaggerated nod. "Sure you are."

"You've caught us all at a very weird time, Kadie. None of what is happening makes any sense. For every theory I have, another pops up and contradicts it. There's something I'm not seeing, that none of us can see. And already, with your arrival in the city being so unprecedented, it's clear that whatever is happening could have far-reaching repercussions. But we're all on the same side here, and if you can believe that, then I hope you can be patient just a little longer."

"And what about Devon?" I asked. "It's a lot harder for him to be patient."

Grayson nodded. "You're right. We've erred on the side of being overly cautious, in that case. That's not fair. But there's no denying he has access to magic that he shouldn't have. And even if that's somehow of no fault of his own, that can be undeniably dangerous."

"Well, all you people are magic. Can't you come up with some other way to help him control it other than keeping him locked up?" I couldn't believe that the extent of the ability to control magic all came down to lines drawn arbitrarily on the ground. There had to be more.

"I'll give it some thought, I promise," Grayson said. "If I can come up with something that mitigates the risk, I'll bring it to the others."

I smiled and nodded, grateful. My meeting with Grayson hadn't exactly gotten the result I was hoping for, but at least it had gotten me something. And hopefully this would result in a win for Devon as well.

"What about the guards you have following us around?"

"Joanna thought it would be in everyone's best interest."

"And you? Wouldn't you rather have all hands on deck instead of having some of your people wasting their time, walking me from office to office? And you know Marc isn't exactly going to be fun to work with."

Grayson sighed. "You really know how to push your luck." I grinned. "I'll see what I can do. But I'm not making any promises."

"Hey, I'll take what I can get."

CHAPTER NINETEEN

"Okay, seriously. This is getting ridiculous. Can you people come back at a reasonable hour?"

I sat up in bed, annoyed that once again someone was knocking on my door in the middle of the freaking night.

This time, they never bothered to knock a second time. But I was in the habit of getting up to open the door in my pajamas at this point, and I was already awake. Besides, I couldn't rule out the possibility that it would be good news waiting for me at the other side of the door.

Except, no one was waiting for me. There was an empty hallway, and that was it. When I took a step outside the threshold to get a better idea of what was going on, two things happened at once. The first was that the door slammed shut from the other end of the hallway. The second was that I nearly tripped over a book that was on the floor.

"Won't you people shut up." Devon shouted out from under his covers, his voice muffled. "I'm trying to sleep here."

Doing my best to keep quiet, I leaned down and picked up the book that had been left by my door, and slipped back inside my room. With a groan, I turned the overhead light on and gave my eyes a second to readjust.

First thing I noticed was a sticky note fastened to the front cover reading "from my personal collection." I removed the sticker and got a look at the cover of the book, getting less and less curious by the second as to why someone thought I needed to read this now. If someone had a book recommendation for me, it could've waited until the morning.

All In. The title of the book was *All In* and showed a beach scene stretching out over both the front cover and around to the back. But it wasn't the golden and red hues of a sunset over the water that caught my attention but a signpost and a bench on the far side of the image. I recognized this place, this stretch of beach. I'd visited it as a child, and while I hadn't been in years, I could distinctly remember a conversation I had with Darren about this exact spot.

My heart started skipping in my chest before I even realized what I was considering. I flipped the book back over and frantically read the perfectly aligned text on the back cover. I felt too frantic to concentrate on the blurb and didn't take much of it in. Instead, my eyes scanned for words that would jump out at me. They did.

Darren's name. Kelsey's. Several people I didn't recognize. No mention of me, but I was already certain about what I was looking at. This was my story, *All In.* This was the book I had come from, and for whatever reason somebody had hand-delivered it to my door not long after it was officially declared missing. I didn't have time to figure out what any of that meant. Like a magnet, I was already moving toward the armchair, suddenly wide awake.

It was here, my book. And I wasn't going to wait another second to read it.

At first, I tried merely flipping through and taking in random snippets, hoping to find the answers I was looking for, whatever they were, sooner rather than later. But there were so many characters, and places and plot lines going on that I couldn't follow any of what was happening. It wasn't a small book, and after fifteen minutes I hadn't found any mention of me whatsoever. Finally, it was clear that the only answer for me was to take my time with this. Not like, take my time, wait until morning when I had properly rested and had something to eat, take my time. But at least I owed myself and this book enough time that I had to start at the beginning, really read it, and go until I finished.

A quick glance at the clock showed that it was four in the morning. I knew I'd never get that night's sleep back, but the five hours I'd gotten would be more than enough to get me through this.

Almost holding my breath, I flipped back through to chapter one and started to read.

That's it? I wondered to myself as I read the final page of the book.

Rather than closing it I skimmed through the pages back to the beginning. I must have missed something.

I couldn't even bother lying to myself that deep down I'd been hoping this book would answer all the questions I had about who I was. That desire hadn't been deep down at all. I'd been expecting so much from this, and gotten so little.

All In had been one of those sweeping sagas about a group of people whose lives all interconnected in one way or another. There had been at least a dozen characters whose viewpoints were used by the author at one point or another. And their stories were all intricate in the way they meshed together by the end of the book. I was one of those characters, but just barely. I'd met Darren in the coffee shop that day. We had gone out on our first date. I'd seen our second date through Darren's eyes, which also happened to be the day he'd met Kelsey, and connected with her instantly. A woman named Margaret had spotted me doing yoga in the park one morning, but I hadn't noticed her and we'd never even talked. I was only a passing reference in chapter twenty-two. I showed up in a few more places, chatting to an old man in the checkout line at the grocery store, and on my fourth date with Darren passing by a girl walking a large pack of dogs as he and I whispered secrets to one another on the boardwalk. And all the while, Darren and Kelsey were falling deeper in love. Kelsey's sister had been that same girl on the boardwalk, and the one who would tip her sister off to the fact that Darren was dating someone else. But it hadn't been a secret, they weren't exclusive yet. At least not until that same night when Darren had decided to do the right thing and chose one of us over the other. Because his heart had already known exactly what the right decision was going to be.

And it wasn't me.

As I'd suspected, the last time the book focused in on me directly was when I'd gotten that phone call from him, that night in my bedroom. I didn't need to relive those moments to know exactly what happened, but I dreaded it anyway. It was like it was happening all over again, practically sending me right back to my bedroom. I was only reminded about what was happening when the splash of a tear hit the page I'd been reading.

My parents had never even featured in the book, only my mentioning in passing that I had dinners with them as often as I could. They didn't even have names, something that I'd never thought about before. But then, as I sat there in the chair trying to digest everything I'd just read, I tried to think of them and came up with nothing.

Who are they now if they hadn't had so much as names in the story?

I closed the book and let it sit there on my lap for second, just staring at the cover and the familiar landscape that I'd once loved. Darren and Kelsey had been the ones to visit the spot in the book, not me. I'd only mentioned once that I'd been there, and as far as the After was concerned, that was enough to form a memory for me once I'd arrived here in this new world.

It explained so much, and so little. And I felt more than a little sick.

I felt like a fake and a failure. I was a mess, and a mess without any real substance.

Hastily, I changed out of my pajamas and back into the clothing I'd been wearing the day before. I was out the door, book in hand, before I'd really come up with any sort of a plan. I just needed to move, to see the world around me and figure out what it meant.

"Hey, Kadie. Is everything okay?" Devon asked, voice still groggy. I winced a little, feeling guilty waking him up.

"I'm fine. I just need to get out of here for a bit. I'll talk to you later."

"But..." I was already around the corner, cutting off whatever it was Devon had wanted to say. It could wait until later.

It hit me then that Devon was my only real friend, since I hadn't had any in the book. I'd mentioned a best friend from before to Darren, but like my parents, she'd never even had a name. I searched my memories, but couldn't remember a single moment we'd ever spent together. Okay, I corrected myself, I do have more friends now, here in the After. But a big part of me mostly just wanted to feel bad for myself.

It was something I was turning out to be very good at.

I stepped out of the halls of the private rooms of the Archive and into the main library. It was open twenty-four hours a day, and seven days a week. But it was never all that busy in the middle of the night, and it didn't look like people had really gotten the memo yet that they were encouraged to come back into the building after the three-day hiatus.

I made my way down to the lobby. An older librarian I didn't recognize was sitting at the front desk. He looked up in surprise but didn't say anything when he noticed me walking by.

I just stood in the center of the lobby for a moment, staring at the glass doors that formed the entryway to the building. The rest of the world was right out there. People who had once been book characters like me, people who had been able to build lives for themselves, even if they'd been little more than minor characters in a past life.

And right now, I could be building a new life for myself. But instead I was stuck. No real past, no real future. Just stuck.

I took a step toward the front door, nothing happened. For a second, I almost considered it. Running. Just going out the front door and seeing what was waiting for me there.

But I never had the chance to figure out if it was something I would've done. Instead, Eliza came in through the same door I'd been watching, a few moments later. As though she'd appeared straight out of the darkness of the night. Her eyes widened in surprise as she noticed me standing there, staring right at her.

"Hey," she said once she was close enough. "What are you doing up this early?"

I didn't answer at first, and my eyes darted back to the door, to outside. To freedom.

"Kadie?" I felt Eliza's hand on my arm, but my vision was already starting to spiral, my breath quickening as panic filled my gut.

"Hey, Kadie. Stay with me. Tell me what's wrong?"

I wanted to tell Eliza every thought that was whirling through my head, but I didn't know where to start with any of it. How did you tell someone that your life had been barely a footnote in someone else's story? Especially someone like Eliza who would have been born to parents with names and histories of their own, and grown up in the After, with every possibility at her fingertips?

And I was just the rejected corner of a love triangle.

"What are you doing in so early?" I asked, doing my best to focus on Eliza's face, which contorted with concern for me. I couldn't be a crappy friend on top of everything else.

"Unfortunately, this is when my shift starts. I'm filing reports for Keeper Dorset today."

"Sounds like fun," I said.

"Okay, something is clearly going on with you. If you don't want to tell me, that's okay, but we should really get you some tea, or a cookie or something."

As soon as Eliza reached out to put her arm around my shoulder, something inside me cracked. I let out a shuddering breath, and a moment later burst into a sob. I didn't follow much of what happened as Eliza led me away, cooing reassurances as we walked, but soon she had me sitting in a chair, far away from the prying eyes of the man who had been working at the front desk. I only really zoned back into what was going on around me again when I felt her try to tug the book still clenched in my fists out of my hands. I squeezed harder and finally looked up at her.

We were in a corner of the library I didn't recognized, seated in two ragged armchairs sitting opposite from one another, a table placed at an angle in between us.

I wasn't sure what else to do, so I handed her the book. She raised her eyebrows for a second, but didn't question me. She studied the front cover for second, and then slowly flipped it over to the back of the book.

"I don't get it," she said, after a minute.

"That's my book. Where I came from."

For second, Eliza didn't say anything. Instead, she looked at me, and then back down at the book. "Where did you get this, Kadie?"

"It showed up at my door a few hours ago." I realized I was crying all over again and my words were barely understandable, but I still struggled to get them out.

"We need to tell someone about this."

I shook my head, frantically. I didn't want anyone else to know all this about me. Not that there was much to learn.

"Kadie, if you've been hiding this…"

"I haven't. It just showed up, with a sticker saying it was from someone's personal collection. I don't even know what that means."

Eliza moved to stand, but she sat back down as I started to fumble for the words to try to tell her everything. I'm not sure how much sense my mumbled synopsis of the story could have made, but Eliza didn't interrupt once. Instead, she just listened as I told her everything, including the storylines that had nothing to do with me other than a passing reference. I must've gone into excruciating detail on Darren and Kelsey's love life.

Once I finished, I'd run out of tears and barely had any steam left in me. I was desperate for a glass of water. "So, what does that all say about me? I didn't matter at all. You could take me right out of that story, and all that would've changed would be how long it took Kelsey and Darren to get together. My parents don't even have names! If I ever find them, are they even going to know who I am? Who they are?"

I was about to keep rambling on when I noticed an uncomfortable shift in Eliza's expression. I didn't know what it meant, but there was something Eliza knew that she didn't want to tell me.

"What is it? Just say it."

"We can talk with Protectorate Avos some other time," Eliza said, reaching out to put her hand on my knee. "Maybe you should get back to sleep for a little while. I can take this to the councilors."

"Tell me," I said, my voice hard. "Please."

Eliza sighed. "I'm not even sure how to explain this. If you'd shown up in any other part of the After, you would've seen it for yourself. But not every character in a book, makes it to the After. Sometimes, they just don't have enough substance to fully materialize in this world. It's not an exact science or anything, and without reading the book for myself, I can't even make a guess. It all depends on how real a character is in the context of a book. Are they just a passing detail, or would some reader somewhere fall in love with them? You'd probably be better off talking to one of the librarians who has dedicated themselves to studying this."

"So, you don't think my parents are here at all?" A new horror washed over me.

"I don't know anything. That was just the first thought that popped into my head. We should really talk to someone else. Let them know what's going on."

"How can I know for sure? What happens to characters who aren't strong enough to make it over here?"

"It's this thing with the bubbles. It's hard to explain without seeing it—" Eliza cut herself off abruptly, as though thinking better about whatever it was she'd been about to tell me.

But what she couldn't have known was that I had seen something with bubbles, on my very first hour here in the After. A screaming man, barely an outline hovering in the air. And then nothing, nothing except bubbles. Floating through the air. The lost remnants of someone who hadn't made it through.

Eliza must've seen the fresh look of horror on my face. "We don't know anything for sure. Can we please just go talk to one of the councilors?"

I sat there for second, trying to figure out if there was something I was missing. Something that might help. But she was right, we needed something more. Someone more. "Grayson," I said finally. "Would he be here already?"

Eliza nodded. "We'll go to his office, and wait for him if we have to."

We stood up together, and *All In* tumbled from my

189

lap to the floor. I hadn't even realized Eliza had given it back. When I leaned over to pick it up again, something fell out from between the final pages in the back cover. An envelope sat on the floor staring up at me. Taunting me.

CHAPTER TWENTY

"What's that?" Eliza asked.

My fingers wrapped around the thin, yellowed paper. "I have no idea."

Handing Eliza the book, I ripped open the envelope to get to its contents, dropping the discarded paper carcass to the floor.

Kadie Meyer,

We are sending this to you as a show of good faith, and to demonstrate to you just how far our reach goes, and what we can offer you.

Your time here in the After has been marked by intrigue thus far, and as a result, we do not wish to wait any longer to make your acquaintance. We have something you are looking for, something very close to you. Come to the harbor Reclamation Center as soon as possible. Show this note to no one.

You will not be harmed.

There was no signature.

Hands trembling, I turned the paper and showed it to Eliza. She read through it as quickly as I had.

"Okay, now we're absolutely going to Grayson."

"What if it's my parents?" I asked in a hopeful whisper, already falling behind Eliza as she moved quickly through the stacks. "What if they did make it here and someone has them to lure me out?"

"The sheer amount of information we don't have right now is astronomical, Kadie. But it's all going to be okay."

"You know, I keep hearing that and it's almost never true."

Eliza didn't answer, instead she continued leading me down the hallway to the offices of the councilors.

"Are they in?" Eliza asked the new girl who was manning the reception desk.

"The Heart and the Hand." Was her the response. "Scholar Credence already come and gone. Archivist Nyce will probably be a while yet."

"I hear that," Eliza said. "That woman couldn't wake up on time if the world depended on it."

I shot Eliza a harsh look, this wasn't the time for joking around with one of her colleagues.

"We need to see Protectorate Avos," she said shortly after.

The receptionist started to shake her head, but then looked at me a second later, realizing who I was. "Yeah, he's going to want to see her," Eliza said.

The receptionist didn't argue, and pressed a button on her desk. A second later, I noticed a flashing green light from around the same area. "Go on in."

I started talking as soon as I got through the door to Grayson's office, barely taking in his confused expression. A minute later, Eliza put her hand on my shoulder. "I've got this."

Eliza did do a far better job than I could've of explaining everything that happened that night, even though she hadn't been there for the whole time. Thankfully, she left out most of the pathetic details of my life before.

Finally, I handed Grayson both the letter and the book.

"What do you think it is? What do they have that I want?"

Grayson's eyes were still scanning the paper in front of him. "She thinks it's her parents," Eliza said. "But based on what she told me about their role in her book, I'm not sure it could be."

"Show me," Grayson said, handing the book back to me. "Find where they're mentioned. Whatever you've got, I need to see it."

It took me far longer than I would've liked to backtrack to the right spot in the story, as I got unwanted flashbacks of all the major plot points while I flipped through the pages. At last, I found the conversation between Darren and I where we talked about families. I handed the book to Grayson and braced myself.

"That's it?" he asked, after reading.

I nodded.

Grayson's already stern expression morphed into a frown. "I'm sorry. But there's no way that was enough to bring them here. Whatever it is that the person who had your book has, it's not them."

"But things were different for me. Isn't it possible somehow, whatever brought me here when I shouldn't be here, also brought them? What if someone made it happen?"

Grayson hesitated, which was enough to send hope swelling through me all over again. "I don't think so."

"But you can't know for sure?"

"Nothing is for sure in the After, we're always finding new people or places that challenge our expectations. But I'm confident in this. I can't imagine they'd have anything that would be of real value for you. My guess is they were just hoping you would read the letter and run out the door without stopping to think about it."

"Maybe I should've."

"That wouldn't have gotten you anywhere. Each door to the outside of the Archive has a spell to stop you, Marc, and Devon from leaving. You would've frozen in place until one of us could've come to collect you. So, whoever came up with this plan, clearly didn't think it through."

I slumped down into the chair I had been leaning against, all the wind knocked out of me. Now I knew both just how insignificant my life had been before the After, and that someone was officially trying to screw with me. I still didn't know who that someone was, or how I'd gotten sucked into their plotting in the first place.

"I'll have to keep these," Grayson said, placing my book and my letter on the desk in front of him. "You should get back to your room, get some rest." What he didn't say was that I certainly looked like a hot mess, and I was clearly worked up. But for very good reason, as far as I was concerned. "Eliza, will you take her?"

"No problem."

"No! Or... Yes, problem! We've been through this already. I don't want you keeping me in the dark anymore. Whatever you're going to do with those, I want to know about it. If you're going to talk to the councilors, I should be there. This is my life." My family, though I kept that thought to myself.

"I promise, as soon as we know anything for sure, I'll tell you. But all we have at this point is the fact that someone who knew where you were sleeping has had this book the whole time. This is our biggest concern. Something in the book itself may give us more to go on about where it has been. Jonathan might be able to magically backtrack its whereabouts. But for now, I'd like to know you're somewhere safe."

"Why? It's not like I can leave. Here or in my room, what does it matter?"

"It matters. Please... trust me on this." Grayson just looked at Eliza. It was all the nudging she needed to gently guide me by the elbow, back up out of my chair and out of the office. I cast one last look back over my shoulder at Grayson. His eyes locked onto mine right away and he gave me a small nod. I had to believe that meant that he'd do whatever he could for me. And at least that was something.

Still, I wasn't happy. I stormed back up to my room, so quickly that Eliza nearly had to jog to keep up with me for a change. Even though she hadn't been the one to do any of this to me, I was ready to slam the door in her face as soon as I reached my bedroom.

Instead, it was Devon who grabbed my attention. "Okay! Will someone please tell me what the hell is going on?"

I looked over at Devon who was standing right in the corner of his room, as close to the front of his cage as he could get. "Marc stormed out of here hours ago, and then you. And now you look like some asshole killed your puppy. What am I missing here?"

"It's been a super fun night," I said at the same time as Eliza caught up with me.

"What do you mean, Marc's gone?" she asked.

It was Eliza's question that Devon locked onto. "I don't know, he left in the middle of the night like a bat out of hell. I figure he just needed to stretch his legs. You know how he gets."

And for the first time, Eliza didn't comment on exactly what she thought of the way Marc could get.

"Was he holding anything when he left?" Eliza looked frantically between Devon and Marc's room. "A book, maybe?"

My heart dropped.

"I didn't notice."

"Okay," I said. "Stay with me here for a second. Did you see anything unusual tonight? While you're sleeping."

Devon gave me a look that made it quite clear just what he thought of my very stupid question. "I woke up tonight to the sound of someone knocking on my door. I got up and my book was there waiting for me."

"And then someone slammed... Marc. He slammed his door, right after you came out. I was barely awake." Devon elaborated. "But I think that's what happened."

"So, Marc got a book too. His book." I looked at Eliza, trying to figure out if her train of thought was the same as my own.

"Wait, you guys got your books? They found them?"

I shook my head. "Someone had them all along. They also came with ransom notes, trying to lure us out of the building." Too slowly my brain put the pieces together, along with what they would have meant for Marc.

"Meg," Devon and I said at once. I turned to face Eliza. "If someone has told Marc that they have his wife, he'll do anything he can to get to her.

"Well, he can't have gotten far." Eliza confirmed the one thought that was holding me back from an all-out panic.

"There was never any way we were leaving this building. Magic," I said, explaining to Devon.

"Then, where is he?" Devon asked. "It's been a long time."

"He's probably just working off steam, or something." Eliza didn't sound convinced.

"You don't think Marc would at least try to get out? Or go for help? Or something? He would not have gotten a message telling him his wife was in trouble and then get frustrated and pout about it for a few hours."

"I promise you guys, there is no way he left the Archive."

"Maybe check? Just to be sure?"

Eliza nodded, and disappeared soon after, leaving Devon and I alone in the hallway.

I used the time alone with my friend to fill him in on everything else that had happened. Specifically, everything I'd read and the note I'd gotten along with its ominous promises.

"I just feel so, empty," I said, finishing my story. "I mean, who even am I?"

To my surprise, instead of offering up some words of

sympathy or encouragement, Devon gave me a seriously unimpressed looked. "You're kidding, right?"

"What? This changes everything."

"How do you figure?"

"Am I even a real person?"

"I don't know, do you see me as a real person?" I didn't say anything, not sure what he was getting at. "We both know that I couldn't have been anything more than a side character in the story I came from. I mean evidently, I was fantastic and memorable, otherwise I guess I wouldn't have made it here. But I had nothing to do with the plot of that book. And I don't need some invisible asshole to drop my story on my doorstep for me to know that. But that doesn't change who I am to me, or I would hope who I am to you."

"No, of course not." Already, I felt like an idiot.

Devon leaned over against the rigid metal of his cage. "The way I see it, I am who I am. Or at least, who I was when I got here. But everything else is up to me to shape. God knows I've had more than enough excitement in the last little while to have some seriously confusing memories to look back on. And I've met people, made new relationships. What or who I was before this doesn't even really matter."

I did my best to hold Devon's gaze, considering the weight of his words. I wished they opened some sort of emotional floodgate for me, making it all better, but I wasn't quite ready to see it like that. And still, while my life before the After hadn't exactly been one of happily ever after, or riveting adventures, at least I'd had a life. I could still feel the love I held for my parents deep within myself. The love that a part of me still held for Darren. Those things at least, were all mine.

I opened my mouth to respond but at that same moment Eliza came back around the corner practically panting. "He's gone," she said. "Marc. He left the building hours ago, just walked right out the front door. Jace saw him—the guy working the desk tonight—but didn't think anything of it. Didn't even realize who he was until we asked. Nothing stopped him, he just left."

After that, all the guards we'd somehow convinced the councilors to get rid of turned up almost at once, searching Marc's room, my room, and everywhere nearby for any sign of my now missing friend. It didn't take long for them to determine that there was nothing there worth finding, and they were soon recalled back to Grayson's office to come up with a new plan. A plan that I couldn't help but worry was far too late to make a difference.

CHAPTER TWENTY-ONE

As much as it was unfair to Devon, I couldn't stay there in that hallway, just waiting.

I was so far beyond sick of waiting.

Instead, I made my way back out into the central library, doing my best not to catch anyone's attention. Already, quite a few other people had come in from the street to start perusing books, but it would be hard not to notice the librarians talking amongst themselves, whispering in hushed voices wherever I found them, doing the same thing I was in an attempt to keep a low profile.

Once again, I was back at the front door. The front door that I knew could no longer hold me, if it had ever been able to. A few people gave me cursory glances, but no one said anything as I took a few steps closer to the entryway. There were people everywhere.

Would anyone stop me if I walked out the door?

Maybe it would be a better plan to head for the back of the building and go out that way.

I slumped against the closest wall, with an exhausted huff. Why was I even considering going outside? What would it accomplish? I'd be better off staying where it was safe, and waiting for someone else to tell me what would happen next. But it had been over an hour since I'd talked to Grayson, and I hadn't heard anything at all. I was sure he would be involved in the search for Marc, both in the building and outside of it once it was clear he was missing. I was a footnote yet again.

They all had to be on their way to the Reclamation Center by now. Or they were already on their way back.

Which would mean I was about to lose my only shot of getting out of this building. I couldn't even say for sure how many days I'd been inside by then, but I didn't want my stay to last any longer.

And if going outside, right then meant there was even a chance I could somehow help Marc... Or find my parents... then I should take it.

But rather than turn for the back of the building where there were sure to be fewer people milling around, I started walking, doing my best not to look out of place or suspicious. But how did someone even walk suspiciously?

Right then, in the moment I made up my mind to go, someone appeared from the office behind the front desk, and I recognized Jonathan immediately. I saw him, and I saw him seeing me. There was no denying what I was doing, heading straight for the front door, but a second later, Jonathan looked away, and I was sure I'd spotted a conspiratorial glint in his eyes.

I didn't stop to question my good luck, and instead kept going, not even giving myself a chance to think or to change my mind.

I could taste the change in the air as I stepped out onto the front steps of the Archive, sunlight hitting my face. Real sunlight. My entire body breathed a sigh of relief.

I hurried down the steps, not making eye contact with anyone I passed until I hit the sidewalk. I was out, finally free of the looming presence of the Archive of Ink and Soul, and everyone who worked inside.

I promised myself I'd come back, not before anyone noticed I was missing, but as soon as I could. First, I'd head for the Reclamation Center just to see for myself what was there, *who* was there. I wouldn't get too close, but if there was a swarm of librarians already circling the building then maybe I'd take my chances.

The alternative was someone would find me before I had a shot to get anywhere at all. But at least they couldn't take this moment back from me, I thought, inhaling lungful after lungful of fresh, crisp air. I hadn't realized just how accustomed I'd gotten to being surrounded by the smell of books all the time, but the aroma of fresh air was unmistakable.

As quickly as I could, I merged with a passing crowd and shuffled along the sidewalk trying to look like I knew where I was going. The Archive still took up most of my peripheral vision from that side of the street. It was a little strange, seeing it from the outside again after spending so much time cooped up indoors. The building, it's purpose, its décor, none of it had been anything like I first imagined when I'd seen it, it was so much more. But for a few minutes, I'd certainly enjoy its absence.

How long did I have before somebody realized I was missing? Would they be able to find me right away? I walked a little faster, crossing the street with the group I'd adopted.

I just wanted to go a little further, be outside a little longer.

I looked down at my feet, trying to be inconspicuous. But that was when it hit me. My shoes. Jonathan had enchanted them a while ago, with the hope that it would give the councilors even more incentive to grant us a little freedom. Everything with Devon happened soon after that, and I'd never again thought about the changes he'd made. But if Jonathan thought of it, or if he'd already told the other councilors, then they could find me right away.

Or, they could find Marc.

I stopped walking at the first gap in the crowd, tucking myself between two buildings to give my thoughts a chance catch up with me.

Hopefully in all the insanity, no one had remembered the shoes either. But if there was any chance they would be able to find Marc; those same shoes could make all the difference.

I had to go back.

The Archive was still in sight, I could be there within minutes. I hoped the fact that I'd come back on my own would win me some points in the future, get me a little more time outside once I had this all sorted out.

Before I had a chance to even take a single step back toward where I'd come from, something sharp jabbed me in the side. Panicked, I looked down to see a tiny dart sticking out from my hip. I whirled around, trying to find where it had come from, but I was still alone. No one in the crowd was so much as looking at me.

As my vision began to blur, I tried to steady myself on the wall beside me, but I knew it was already too late. I was going down, and quickly. I opened my mouth to cry out for help, but couldn't make a sound.

The world around me faded away.

It took a long time for me to wake up. It felt like hours passed but I couldn't be sure if I was awake or dreaming. If I was dreaming, wherever I was would have to be a bizarre place to pass my sleeping hours, as every time I opened my eyes all I saw was a hazy half-darkness. My hands had been tied behind my back, and I felt like I was moving somehow. But before I could figure out any more than that, I was unconscious all over again. It was—or at least felt like— hours before I truly started to feel like my head was clear, like I could maintain a train of thought for more than a few seconds at a time.

I forced my eyes to open and take in the fading day around me. There was a window, or light source of some kind overhead but I couldn't move enough to figure out where it was.

I tried to force out a cry for help but the sound that came from my throat was rough and garbled. I coughed a little, clearing my throat and tried again. "Hello." I called out, now trying to keep my voice low. I knew I was as likely to attract the attention of my attacker as I was any kind of help, but I had to do something.

To my surprise, it was Marc's voice that answered me. "Kadie. What the hell are you doing here?"

"I could ask you the same question. Actually, I will. What the hell are you doing here? You ran out of the Archive without telling anyone. No one knew where you were."

"So, you decided to follow suit and make the same stupid mistake? They got me almost as soon as I left the building," he said. I tried to turn my head to see where he was, but only made out a fuzzy shape on the far side of the room. At least my vision seemed to be clearing up.

"Same here. I take it you got the letter, and your book?"

Marc didn't answer.

"Are you hurt?" I asked, changing my tactic.

"No. They shoved me in the back of a truck, as soon as they had me. I don't think I've moved, but I was out for a while. You got here a while ago, and I was getting worried you weren't going to wake up."

"Any idea who *they* are?"

"I didn't see anyone, not directly."

"Well, shit. Me neither. I was hoping that someone at the Archive would be able to track you, us I guess, by the shoes Jonathan enchanted. Hopefully he'll think of it sooner rather than later. But seriously, what the hell were you thinking?"

"Like you're in a position to judge."

"I was looking for *you*."

"And that's it?" Marc said.

"I don't know, maybe. I'm not sure if I'm hoping for

my parents to have been kidnapped by whoever is doing all this, but it beats the alternative. Both Grayson and Eliza seemed pretty sure that none of the people in my life other than the guy who dumped me would've actually arrived in the After."

"What you mean?"

I did my best to explain the same thing that Grayson had to me. "But that doesn't mean anything…" I hurried to explain, realizing Marc may take the news even harder than I had.

"How much of your book did you read?"

"Basically, none of it. I found the letter before I started reading, and it said they had my wife."

Well at least he'd been offered something a little more specific, but that no doubt had a lot to do with him making it pretty damn obvious exactly what to threaten him with.

"So, you just left? You didn't tell anyone where you were going?" I asked, indignant. I already knew the answer perfectly well.

Just then, the surface underneath us gave a rumble and my body jostled sideways a little before hitting the bed of the truck all over again. We were still moving, but it felt like the truck we were in had just taken a serious turn. I wanted to think it didn't mean anything, that the librarians could find us just as easily no matter where we ended up, but the fact that something was happening at all couldn't have been a good thing. They could have us through the Reclamation Center within minutes, as far as I knew. If Harper had been any indication. Was Grayson already coming for us? Or was it already too late?

Neither Marc nor I said much of anything as we moved through what I hoped were still the streets of Sanctum. Fortunately, or not, we weren't on the move for long before the truck we were in reversed directions, letting out a few loud beeps as it started to back up somewhere. I had to think that meant we'd reached wherever it was we were heading. Something was about to happen, I just couldn't say if it would be good news for either Marc or me. These could easily be my last moments in the After.

Knowing what I did about my book, I was more sure than ever that it wasn't a place I wanted to go back to.

At least in the After I'd have a chance to write a new story for myself, to create memories to replace the ones I'd never had, to build new relationships and, with luck, some actual friendships.

But back there, I'd never be anyone. I'd just get my heart broken in an endless loop.

Not something I could really look forward to.

"Any chance you've got a brilliant plan for when they come for us?" I asked Marc, hoping he'd used the extra time he'd had to plot a great escape.

"Not so much. I can barely move but if I get a chance to fight, I'm going to take it, I suggest you do the same. This is not the time for any passive, yoga nonsense."

"Oh, shut up. It might come as a surprise, but I've got a bit more fight in me than you think. I'm not going quietly."

My ears had gone into overdrive, listening for any clue in the world around me about who or what was coming for us. I did my best to brace myself for whatever was coming next. Whether I could claw my way out of my fate or talk my way out of it, I had to try. My life in the After hadn't been at all that I expected, but it was still a life I wanted.

A wall of light assaulted my senses as a shutter door I hadn't noticed at the back end of the vehicle rolled upward. For a second, I couldn't make out anything more than shapes, as my eyes adjusted. Then I saw what I thought was a man waiting outside of the door. His frame was slight, by the looks of him not even fully grown, but my brain still needed a moment to recognize who I was looking at.

Jonathan Credence.

CHAPTER TWENTY-TWO

They'd found us. I breathed a sigh of relief, relaxing against my bonds as Jonathan stepped into the truck.

"Good to see you both," Jonathan said. "I'm sorry to have had to arrange our meeting this way, but my colleagues left us little choice. Finally, the three of us will have a chance to catch up."

I looked over at Marc, not sure if I was understanding what I was hearing. He looked just as confused as I felt.

"Please," Jonathan said. "Let me explain. This isn't quite the rescue mission I'm sure you were hoping for. Grayson and his ilk may be scouring the city for you, but I've known where you were all along. This was my first opportunity to get out of the building. None of what happened to the two of you, or to Devon over the last few weeks had to happen. Unfortunately, you didn't arrive quite where I'd been anticipating. I've had to improvise a little. But now that you're here, I can assure you, we're all going to get quite a few more answers now."

Marc and I were only released from our bindings by the men Jonathan had with him long enough to be led out of the truck and into the desolate empty building we'd been brought to.

If I'd thought having Grayson hounding us after Devon's display of magic was intense—which, by the looks of it, had saved his life since he was still in a cage rather than here with us—that pressure was nothing compared to having one of Jonathan's flunkies breathing down my neck as he pushed and prodded me toward our destination.

Wherever we were, the walls were thin metal. One large window made up the top panel on the wall at the front of the building, though hanging bulbs illuminated the rest of the space. A few crates sat scattered around the space and a few support columns, placed systematically, reached from floor to ceiling.

I could still smell salty sea-air, which didn't guarantee anything but at least left me with a little hope that we were still in reach of the Archive.

"Put them there," Jonathan said, indicating two sets of chains welded into the back wall of the building. Gone was the kindly older man trapped in a younger body that I'd come to expect from Jonathan Credence. This version was all business. While they roughly dragged Marc and I from the door to the wall we were to be chained to, the councilor's expression didn't shift even a fraction toward sympathy. Whatever his plan was, it wasn't to force us back to our origin stories, at least not yet, but he wanted something from us, no question.

"Now, I'm going to ask you some questions, and I highly recommend that you be honest. Not only can this all be over quickly, but I suspect we are going to be on the same side."

"Where's Meg?" Marc asked. I could practically feel his body vibrating with anger beside me.

"Now, now. I'm the one asking the questions today, but get on my good side and you'll get the answers you're looking for," Jonathan said as he approached us.

"Go to hell." Marc spat at Jonathan's feet, missing the librarian's shoes by an inch. "If all you wanted was answers, you could have asked us at any time. Whatever you're after, it's not for all of us to be on the same side."

"You'll come to see that you are entirely wrong on that note. But until I know for sure what you're capable of, I'm not taking any chances. Now let's talk abilities…" Jonathan said, his voice quiet and smooth. "You aren't the prosaics you're pretending to be."

Marc snarled out something unintelligible so I tried to step in and calm the situation down. It might not be too late to get out alive. "We've answered this for you so many times already. I didn't come from anywhere with magic. I don't know what the hell happened with Devon."

"If it helps, I know exactly what happened to your friend. Now, since arriving in the After, have you exhibited any new abilities?" He looked from me then back to Marc.

"No," Marc said in a roar, shaking with frustration.

A moment later, with no warning, one of the guards that had been standing behind Jonathan, stepped forward and punched Marc in the stomach. I flinched where I was standing.

"You're lying," Jonathan sneered. "I *know* that each of you has some ability you didn't have before. I know, because I gave them to you."

I stopped breathing.

"I almost thought it hadn't worked, that you'd come through with nothing more than scars. But Devon went and proved me wrong. Or right, depending on how you look at it. But he's no good to me anymore. I need one of you so I can show the world what I've done. I'll ask you again, what are you capable of now that you weren't before?"

Marc shook his head, his jaw clenched. This time, Jonathan's guard didn't aim low, and didn't stop after one punch, hitting Marc's face three times in quick succession.

"You know what happens if you don't tell me." Jonathan turned and looked at me. "I can give Kadie here a try. Either she'll tell me what it is she's been hiding, or you'll tell me to protect her. This could work just as well either way."

"I'm in the same boat as he is," I said, keeping my voice as calm as I could while trying to quiet the panic that set a quiver into my voice. "I can't do anything. I've seen some stuff, sure, and I have the scar. But I'm not capable of anything magical. No more than I ever was."

"You don't understand yet. Those scars are everything. That scar proves not only that the channel I opened up to give you the potential for magic, but that the change remained once you came through."

"Came through where?" I asked. I wanted it to sound like there was a chance I would play along, if only to buy us more time. But I still didn't even know what it was I'd be playing along with. All I really wanted was to get Marc and I out of there alive. At least while I kept Jonathan talking, Marc had a chance to catch his breath.

"From the sounds of it, I'm guessing that you both missed the fairly massive red flag in your books. It was a risk, but people are nothing if not predictable."

I sat there in stunned silence, trying to figure out what he was getting at. I looked at Marc, but his expression remained unreadable.

"Let me ask a question," Jonathan said. Marc let out an annoyed grunt beside him.

"What?" I asked, before Jonathan could hone in on Marc all over again.

"What year is it?"

"Two thousand and two," I said right away. At least that was one question I knew the answer to.

"Nineteen ninety-nine," Marc said a second after.

The two of us looked at each other. Okay, that was weird. But it was more than possible that one of our authors had set their book a few years earlier or later than the other.

"You're both off by more than a decade," Jonathan said. He wasn't smiling, and yet I could still tell that he was

209

enjoying himself. "Based on the publishing dates we're seeing on the copyright pages of the latest titles coming into the Archive, we're only a few years off twenty-twenty. The turn of the millennium has come and gone a while ago."

When neither of us said anything, Jonathan continued. "Clearly, you don't see what this means yet."

"What I see, is that you're getting off on this. What year our books came from doesn't mean anything. An author can set a story at any time they want. I have no idea what you're getting at." The quiver in my voice was beginning to hint at both my fear and irritation. I wasn't exactly looking for him to go back to beating Marc, but I was sick of Jonathan's roundabout answers.

"The year you see in the copyright page isn't the year the book is set, it's the year the book was published. And since the Archive gets titles as they're published, they all come through at the same time. Exactly as they're supposed to. Incidentally, the years you both listed off, are the same years that your books entered the world officially through publication."

I furrowed my brow, trying to work it out before he opted to explain it to me.

Too late. "When you arrived in Sanctum that afternoon, that wasn't your first day in the After. It wasn't even your first year. You've been here before, you've done all this before. Not specifically in this city, but when your book finished you arrived just like you were supposed to."

"And we died," I said, finally getting up to speed. "When characters die in the After, they start over fresh as though their book had just finished."

I was still trying to work out the puzzle, but Marc looked positively sick.

"So, we had lives before this, jobs and houses and relationships. And our memories of all of that are gone now?"

"Right on target," Jonathan said, gleeful.

I could understand a little of what Marc was feeling. If I'd felt like a lackluster human before, just reading my story, that feeling amplified now. I'd had years to build myself up, and become someone new. I could've fallen in love, multiple times over the years. I could have kids. And now my memories of all that, gone forever.

"What happened to us?" I asked. Any second Jonathan could go back to insisting that he was the one asking the questions, but he seemed all too keen to share the details with us. He seemed to still think he could get us on his side somehow, even though he'd made it clear he had no problem hurting us if he didn't get what he wanted. I needed to keep his focus.

"It really isn't important," Jonathan said with a wave of his hand. "You need to start thinking big picture."

"No. You want us to cooperate, but it's time you started being honest. What happened to us? Why are we here?" Sure, everything he'd already told us was weird enough, but that didn't explain anything between our arrival in Sanctum right up to the marks on our wrists.

"After your first lives, you were both brought here to the After. What you did from there, I don't know. I found you both years later, prosaic, and boring. Your lives weren't anything special, I assure you. At least the little I saw of them." Jonathan turned back to look at Marc, but never truly turned his back to me, letting us both stand in his line of vision. "And I gave you *more*. I changed you at a level so deep that even the After had to acknowledge it. When you came back, the potential I had gifted you with came too. No more blank slate, no more drab nobodies with nothing to offer the world."

"You killed us," I said, my voice gravelly. Marc's head snapped up to look at me, but I knew I was right. "One after the other, for the entire length of time that we were appearing in Sanctum, that was you. Murdering us. How many people did you kill, Jonathan?"

"Enough. Not everyone made it through, but their

sacrifices were well worth it.

It was strange to think about the moment before I'd arrived in the After. At least, the time I could remember. But now I knew I had been standing on the cusp of the death of not one life but two. The truth of my origin story would follow me forever but another life that I knew I'd never remember would haunt my dreams.

"What about Meg?" Marc asked, all the anger sapped from his voice. Even his body seemed to have given up. "Where's my wife?"

"I don't know. But when I found you, you weren't wearing a wedding ring. You didn't mention Meg, or anyone else. I think part of you was even excited to get away from whatever life you'd created for yourself. You were in a prosaic city, working as a beat cop. The rest, I don't know. It wasn't important then, and it certainly isn't now."

It was then that Marc broke, almost roaring and sobbing at once as he let out a scream of frustration, like his beloved wife had been physically ripped from him and tossed away.

"And what do you want from us now?" I asked, trying to give Marc at least the semblance of privacy by keeping Jonathan's attention. "You've already taken enough from us."

"No, you don't understand. I've given you everything. You're capable of so much more than you ever could have been. All you must do is show me what you're capable of and together we can change everything. I just need proof that it worked."

"I swear," I said, "for the millionth time, I can't do anything else. Can you tell me what it is I'm supposed to be able to do?"

"Unfortunately, no. The procedure was anything but exact. All I did was open each of you up to the ability to connect with a magical source. Which one is anyone's guess. If I can see how each of your powers have manifested, I can make sure that the next batch goes more smoothly. And, with a little luck, I can ensure everyone wakes up again where they died moments before. No more hide and seek in the city. I'll do better next time. Soon, people will be lining up for the opportunity for a fresh start."

"I think you're overestimating how much people would be willing to give up to access magic." I looked over at Marc. There was no question in my mind that he would choose Meg over powers of any kind, every time. And me, I still hadn't seen any proof at all that Jonathan's experiment had worked as well on my body as it had on Devon's. For all I knew, I'd been perfectly happy before living my life. Getting older, and growing as a person. And now any progress I'd made was lost.

"Could be you're telling the truth," Jonathan said after his men had double checked we were secured. "But the human body is capable of incredible things when put to the test. Let's see what you both manifest after a day or so without any food or water. I'll need to be getting back to the Archive. I can only be gone for so long before the others start to suspect that I'm not out helping with your search and rescue effort after all. My boys here will take good care of you, I assure you. Well at least they won't do any direct harm. Not without me here to see the results. Stay put, and I'll see you both soon." Jonathan's voice rang with the false perkiness of a flight attendant or shop clerk.

So far, I wasn't loving the customer service.

Soon, Marc and I were alone, though I suspected Jonathan's guards were still close by. We were both sitting slumped against the wall, trying to rest.

"Weird day," Marc said. Instantly, my mind transported me back to sitting with Harper after our first day in the After. Back then, there had been no Archive, no previous lives to wonder about. Things hadn't been simple, but they'd been a lot easier than they were now. What ability had Harper received that she'd never had the chance to experience? Was it one that would've been able to save her?

And none of this answered the still looming question of who had been trying to do away with the new arrivals as they showed up in Sanctum. Clearly, Jonathan wanted to find us and hone our abilities, not get rid of us before he could see what we were capable of. At least as far as I understood any of this, which didn't seem to be that part well.

Marc stuck out his chin defiantly. "That guy is a bit of a bastard."

"I don't know about you," I said, "but I don't plan to be here when he gets back."

Marc shifted against his chains, wincing a little as he moved. "Well, I'm open to ideas."

"I've got nothing. But if you've been harboring any magical abilities, this is the time to tell me. The ability to melt through metal with your eyes would be particularly useful right now."

I was mostly joking, trying to lighten the mood. But as soon as I brought it up, Marc's expression shifted. There was no denying it, he looked guilty.

CHAPTER TWENTY-THREE

"Oh, you've got to be kidding me." I stared at Marc, trying to figure out what it was he was hiding from me. "You're seriously telling me you can change into a bird or something too?"

"Not that," Marc said with a shrug. "But not nothing either. It just happened. The day before everything went down with Devon. I was sitting in one of the reading nooks on the sixth floor, and there were a couple of university students at a table across from mine. This guy and his girlfriend, arguing over some essay or another. The girl mentioned she'd finished hers already, and somehow, I just knew she was lying. I can't explain it at all, and at first I thought it was just a weird gut feeling even though it was something she'd only said in passing."

"Okay," I said, drawing the word out when Marc didn't continue. At this point I was going to need everything spelled out for me.

"But it happened again that night. When the three of us were having dinner in the cafeteria and you said you weren't interested in Grayson like that, when Devon started pestering you about him. You were lying. Anyway, you'd done that before, but the feeling I had was so different from any other time the topic had come up, I had to think there was more to it." I flushed a little, but did my best not to break eye contact. Arguing now wouldn't get me anywhere, especially if he was telling me what I thought he was. "So, I started testing it out, and it became obvious pretty quickly that I can sense when someone's lying. Somehow."

"And I guess that counts as magic," I said.

"Well, it definitely isn't something I could do before this. Although it would've been damn useful at work. It took me a little while to trust what I was feeling, but once things happened with Devon, there was no way I was going to come clean. At least not until I saw how it played out."

I sighed, closed my eyes, and leaned back against the wall. "So, Jonathan is right then? Whatever he did to us worked, it changed us. At least you guys. Because I swear, I cannot do anything special. I mean, I'm flexible and know how to land a punch, but that's not magic."

"Perhaps whatever you have just hasn't manifested yet," Marc said, pointing out the obvious.

"Or maybe it didn't work for all of us."

"Jonathan seems pretty confident. He absolutely believes whatever he did to us worked."

I looked at Marc, measuring my words. "Why don't you just tell him what he wants to hear? He is obviously a monster, things can't get any worse than they are now."

"I don't think so. I couldn't work out the specifics while he was explaining his master plan to us, but he was lying. Mostly. Whatever is going on, I can't believe he has our best interest at heart. And even if he did…"

"Giving him what he wants probably means he kills more people to test his theories further."

"Exactly. I've dealt with guys like him, and power will come before anything. He wants to make an impact, to change the world. And he's willing to do whatever it takes to get there. I'm not exactly willing to be the catalyst that pushes that any further."

I flexed the muscles in my legs, trying to relieve a cramp in my thigh. "Where does that leave us?" I asked, not taking my eyes off my toes. "It's not like your new ability is going to help us get out of here. Can you get him to reveal something that might help? Or give us some leverage?" I knew I was fishing, and kept my eyes glued to my toes because I didn't want to see the resignation cross Marc's features, confirming what I already suspected, that we weren't getting out of this.

"The leverage we can use is exactly what we can't give him. Which leaves you. I should think that whatever Jonathan did, it worked the same for all three of us. But it's not like we can figure out how to make your ability work when we don't know what it is."

"Nothing has changed for me!" I said again.

"I feel the same as I did before too, but the evidence suggests that I have at least picked up one new ability. We just need to find a way out of here, out of the building. If we can get that far, then at least we have options."

"Neither you nor Devon could control when your ability first appeared. And if mine hasn't shown up yet, it seems to be a little more stubborn than what you guys got. Perhaps all I can do is sense the kind of sandwiches a person would most like to eat, or always tell you the exact right time." I searched my mind, trying to come up with any arbitrary information that seemed to appear in my head like magic. Nothing happened. "Not only is there almost no chance of me pulling this power out of thin air, but it's probably not even going to be useful."

"Alright, so what are our other options?" Marc barely waited for a response, since he knew as well as I did that I didn't have any. "Exactly. If nothing else, you have to try."

Hours passed and I attempted everything from meditating to searching deep within myself, to saying words I thought might be magical. Nothing happened. It was possible I had a bit of a nap during what was supposed to be my meditation session, but even as my stomach started to rumble, I still felt the same.

And our time was running out.

No, our time had run out. I heard the moment a car pulled back into the driveway outside of the building, far sooner than I'd expected and my heart beat twice as fast, while my breathing nearly stopped altogether.

"I'm sorry," I said to Marc. "I've got nothing."

"And unfortunately, I know you're telling the truth."

"That's it then?"

"Whatever happens next, I wouldn't bet on it being that much fun. But I don't think he's going to kill us."

"Why? If we're not being helpful, why bother keeping us around? We're a liability more than anything else."

"I'm going to choose to ignore the fact that you believe that to be true, because at this point I just need to believe there's some piece to the puzzle we don't understand. But…"

Marc never had the chance to finish his sentence, at that moment Jonathan returned with two new guards behind him. I wondered if these guys were secretly librarians as well, all betraying the thing they supposedly believed in most. And for what?

"Time for good news?" Jonathan said, striding into the room.

Standing, I drew my posture up as straight and high as I could, doing my best not to look like a target. Right away, I considered that I might have taken the other option and made myself seem small, pathetic, and not a threat. But there was no way Marc was going to make himself look like anything other than ready for a fight, and I knew we'd have a better chance of getting through whatever this was if we stuck together. For whatever came next.

Jonathan stopped walking and stood in front of both of us. I did my best not to squirm under his gaze.

"So, anything you'd like to share with the class?" Jonathan's face was barely hanging on to its expression of boyish charm and ambivalence. I didn't know why he was continuing to put on a show at all.

"Look," I said, before pausing to clear my throat. Not having had water in half a day had taken more of a toll than I'd realized when I'd been focusing inside myself rather than on my body. "We want to help you. Or more specifically, we just want to get out of this. If I had something to tell you, anything to share, I would."

"And maybe I believe you. This is new territory for all of us, and I'm more than willing to accept that whatever powers the After gifted to you may take a little more coaxing. An experience I'm sure neither one of us is looking forward to. I like you, Kadie. And I want to help."

Inadvertently, my gaze shifted from Jonathan's face to Marc's, right as my friend was rolling his eyes slightly. It was an expression that no one else would've noticed, but I chose to take it as meaning Jonathan was just as full of bullshit as I was imagining. This guy didn't care what happened to me. I was just another tool for him to use, with or without my permission.

"I don't know what to tell you. Let us go, and we can figure out a way through this. If you have done what you think you have, wouldn't the people you work with want to help you figure it out? With a little time and a team effort, we can get what we all want out of this."

Jonathan scoffed. "I'm sorry to say but you don't know my colleagues as well as I do. Those who are bound to the Archive, have a particular way of thinking. A way they all believe things should be done, and that way is exactly as the Archive dictates. How its will is interpreted, is left to those most stubborn and unwilling to change. So, you see where that gets me."

"But clearly," I said, "you don't see things that way. So, there could be others. You don't know."

"Don't try to lecture me, little girl. I have been here far longer then you will ever have the chance to be, no matter how today plays out. I know the people I work with. And I also know those who oppose them. There are so many possibilities we have yet to explore, but publicly allying myself with anyone other than my fellow librarians will only be met with scorn. They won't see that I am truly trying to benefit all of us, instead it will only be the betrayal that stays with me."

I wanted to point out that betrayal had that effect on people, but I kept my mouth shut. A minor miracle.

Jonathan shook his head, seemingly disappointed that I didn't have more to offer. At least I wasn't being quite as obstinate as Marc. I had tried to help, and I hoped that would count for something. Just not at Marc's expense.

I wasn't even sure what I was hoping for anymore. I just wanted to skip ahead to tomorrow and see where I landed.

Briefly, I closed my eyes and wished with everything I had to do exactly that. Could that be my power?

Nothing happened.

"Well, if that's all you have to say for yourself there is no more time to waste." Jonathan looked over his shoulder at the two men who seemed willing to obey his every command. "I suppose it's time to get started. Have we settled on a strategy for round two? Fenrix?"

The first man, tall with a trimmed grey beard studied both of us. "The girl," he said, and I swear he licked his lips a little as soon as he fixated on me. "With a little encouragement, perhaps we can convince her body to be somewhat more cooperative. And I have a few new strategies I've been dying to try out."

The second man shook his head. "As fun as that may be," he said, though he didn't look as enthused by the idea as his companion, "that's not going to be our best strategy. Our boy here is a fighter. Punch him, and he wants to punch back. As for the little lady, I suspect that seeing her friend hurt is going to do far more to encourage her along than harming her directly will."

Jonathan considered both their perspectives for a

moment and then finally nodded. "We'll go with Dash's plan. Let's start with Marc. If that doesn't work, then we'll call Kadie Plan B." His head slowly turned to face me. "Don't think for a second that this is going to save either one of you. I'm a man who gets what he's after, and I'm not a fan of those who would stand in my way."

"I believe you," I said, because clearly, he wanted me to say something. If I'd learned anything about Jonathan both during my time at the Archive and during this last day, it was that he enjoyed being the most important person in the room. The hero. Dropping off much-needed clothing. Being my ally, willing to listen to me when his colleagues wouldn't, though I had to suspect that there were other motivations behind his kindness.

Jonathan's men grabbed Marc first, unlocking him before man-handling him to the center of the room. All too quickly, he was taken over to one of the support beams, his hands fastened behind him so he was secured to the pole. Dash stayed with me, only a breath away as his hands stayed firm on my arms making sure I couldn't go anywhere as Fenrix disappeared back through the front door.

A moment later, he was back, wheeling a large chest behind him. "We're more than prepared to be creative. We've brought quite a few of our favorite toys to play with." And then the bastard winked at me. I shuddered a little, and looked over at Marc instead.

"You good?" he asked, I did my best to read the subtext under the question.

I shook my head. "I'm useless," I said, hoping my answer wouldn't be interpreted by Marc as anything other than literal. Which is, I suppose, how I meant it. I was useless. I hadn't been able to produce anything that could help. I squeezed my eyes shut, and tried to summon fire at random. It didn't come. Because of course it didn't. I wasn't a wizard, a witch, a shapeshifter, or anything else that could help anyone. I was just a useless girl from a useless town, who wasn't even wanted by the boy she loved. And now I was going to die, after watching some sick asshole beat my friend to death.

Marc held his own like a champ. They'd been going easy on him before, hoping they wouldn't need to do much in order to coax his powers out. But there were no holds barred now, and soon his face was bruised and bloodied.

But he never uttered a word. Sometimes, I could tell he was trying to keep himself from even crying out and not always succeeding. But he didn't crack, didn't share his secret. Watching him there like that had to be the most painful thing I'd ever experienced. But his ability wasn't mine to share, and it took everything I had to respect his wishes.

More than anything, I wanted to look away, but I made myself watch, made myself take in his pain and lock eyes with him whenever I had the chance. I didn't want to say anything out loud that might encourage Jonathan or his goons, but I tried to promise with my expression that Marc was not alone in this. That I was there with him. Finally, Jonathan caught the gaze between the two of us. For a second I thought he was going to let it go without comment, but instead his mouth twisted into a thoughtful grimace.

"This isn't working," he said aloud. Jonathan held up his hand, commanding everything around him to stop. "Maybe we've been overthinking this." Jonathan mumbled a phrase and a gun appeared in his right hand. Its lethal appearance was enough to leave me with a dry mouth and sweaty palms. "Now, this is one way to encourage you to cooperate, but really, it is only here to demonstrate just how serious I am about what comes next. He tucked the gun in the waistband of his pants.

Soon, he was muttering another spell and a long stick appeared in one of Jonathan's hands, silver with a pointed end that crackled with electricity. "I don't pretend to be an expert in torture, but I have to believe this will be most effective."

He reached out and, ever so gently, placed the end of the stick to Marc's throat. My friend cried out at once with a noise so animalistic I knew I'd remember it for the rest of my life.

"Three strikes from this device will kill any living creature. Animals die with only one touch. For prosaics, it takes only two…" He touched Marc at the shoulder with the device. This time, Marc's yell held far less power, but only because, by the sound of it, he had used up his voice after the first strike, and not because it hurt any less.

For the briefest of moments, I thought Marc had succumbed, but a second later he took in a gasp of air.

"Interesting," Jonathan said. "It would appear that whether or not you know it, there is more to you than meets the eye. And still, you are no good to me this way." He turned from Marc to me as his hand drew up again to strike Marc one last time.

Please, please, please. I begged myself to somehow become more. I should have magic! It had worked for Devon and for Marc, but I couldn't muster anything from the spark of a flame to a lightning bolt to destroy Jonathan.

He hit Marc again, and I cried out at the same time as my friend did.

We were all going to die here, but Marc was going to die first and I was going to have to watch it happen. Unless I could do *something*. But I couldn't wait a second longer, I couldn't stand by and watch Marc die. And I also didn't want him to give into Jonathan and confess his secret, proving to this maniac that what he'd done had gotten the results he'd been looking for. This had to end, and it had to end now.

I didn't have any secret magical abilities hidden in the depths my soul, but that didn't mean I had nothing.

Without thinking, I charged, screaming out with

everything I had, trying to draw attention to me and away from Marc. I couldn't see how the men around me were reacting as my vision narrowed in on my target, but I only felt the slightest touch of skin against my back as I surged forward, whoever had been looking to grab me had missed me by a millimeter.

I headed straight for Jonathan, hands behind my back. I knew it was hopeless, but I also knew it was worth trying.

At the last second, he put out his hand to try to deflect me, the stick he'd been using on Marc clattering to the ground, but my focus was laser sharp. I dodged sidestepping around Jonathan, spun back toward him and slammed my head into his chest, sending us both reeling onto the floor.

He was up before me, the advantage of his hands weighing the odds heavily in his favor. But I had at least one more person on my side. As I stared up at the ceiling, I saw Marc used his body weight to push against the pole behind him, throwing both of his feet at Jonathan in one strong kick. Marc managed to send him flying backwards again right as he had regained his balance, causing Jonathan to tumble into Dash at the same time.

From my position on the floor I used my feet, swinging out to trip Fenrix as he reached me. It gave me just enough time to pull myself upward.

Marc and I stared at each other for only an instant as they came for us, not sure what would come next. The element of surprise had played in my favor, but it wasn't going to be enough for the second round. These guys had weapons, an advantage in numbers, and the use of their hands. We were screwed, but we were going to go down swinging.

CHAPTER TWENTY FOUR

As the three men spread out across the room to make sure Marc and I were well and truly cornered, I knew I was going to die. But what really broke my heart was that I didn't have much of a life at all to flash before my eyes in my final moments. Try as I might, I couldn't even conjure up images of my parents to draw strength from. I had no one.

I was no one.

Jonathan rounded on us as he regained his composure, and I could tell from his expression that there would be no more speeches, no more explanations. He was finishing this, and he was going to do it as soon as possible. I didn't know what that would mean for his experimentation and quest for new ideas. But he still had Devon contained in the Archive, even if he would have to find a way to get him out of there. And Devon, he would already be far more useful than Marc or me. There was no denying Devon's abilities.

I tried to focus on what Devon would have to experience at the hands of this maniac, to let it fuel me. As Jonathan moved toward me, I watched for any sign of his next attack to at least attempt to get out of the way and give myself one more precious second.

Without warning, Jonathan swung for me, his fists flying out in front of him. The first blow barely grazed my shoulder, but when his knee swung up to hit me in the stomach, I couldn't avoid the impact. I crumbled over at once, rolling up toward the ceiling. A boot fastened itself over my throat as my eyes fixated on the large, lone window open to the hazy sunset through the skylight. I wouldn't let Jonathan's face be the last thing I saw.

It was over. I was done. Time seemed to freeze as the world moved on in slow motion around me. But I had at least given it everything I had.

An object, flying high above, caught my attention in the window, and I let myself fixate on that for the few moments it took for Jonathan to start mumbling over me. But the object in my vision was getting bigger. Closer and closer.

Was it a meteor come to end this all at once? The After sick of Jonathan's plotting. Wouldn't that be nice?

Except... it was a bird.

I recognized the seagull, only a second before I was sure it was going to slam right into the glass of the window. I'd watch the bird die right before my own life ended. And then I'd wake up right back where I'd started, only to be hunted by Jonathan all over again.

But the gull never smacked into the glass, instead it turned into a man, just long enough for the force of his body to shatter the window and come tumbling into the room, drawing absolutely everyone's attention and loosening Jonathan's grip ever so slightly. My baser instincts taking control, I rolled away, wincing in pain as my hands pinched in their shackles. But soon enough, I was on my feet again, quickly enough to take in the scene around me. One more body had been added to the fray. Grayson. Somehow, he'd found us. But that didn't mean the fight was over, only that we'd been granted a reprieve.

From the look of it, Jonathan's silver-bearded lackey

had felt the brunt of Grayson's body falling through the glass window. He lay on the floor, either unconscious or dead, I couldn't say which. Marc was currently taking on Dash, using only his powerful legs, while Jonathan had stepped back, watching with shocked interest. It couldn't be long before he threw himself back into the fight, and since Marc was still bound to the column, his life could be over in seconds.

I scrambled for the fallen man, hoping that he'd slipped the keys that would free Marc and I into his pocket. Once I was close to him it was clear he wouldn't be waking up anytime soon, or ever again. A small pool of blood was forming under the base of his skull. But I didn't have time to figure out how I felt about any of this as I maneuvered my hands into his pockets while still clasped behind my back. Once I had the keys, there was no way I could use them to free myself from the angle I had. But they might just be enough to help Marc. Keyring in hand, I moved toward my friend as quickly as I could.

By then, Jonathan had gotten himself into the fight, but the battle had moved just out of Marc's reach. I stopped for a second when I saw Grayson's two opponents had him cornered and it looked like him being outnumbered was going to be just too much. In the blink of an eye, Grayson transformed into a bird even smaller than Devon had become, flew upward and then shifted back into a man.

"Here, turn around." I rushed over to Marc, trying to get behind him.

Marc didn't ask any questions and instead did as I asked. It took precious seconds to free him, but soon his hands were his own again and he could free mine. But there was no time for self-congratulations, or anything else. Jonathan had gotten his hands on the gun, and pointed it at the clashing bodies on the floor as Grayson threw punch after punch at his opponent who was still able to kick, punch and throw his weight around but never quite gaining the upper hand. Jonathan was as likely to hit one man as the next.

I did my best to do as my self-defense instructor had once taught me and assessed the area around me and to find something that might work to my advantage. But Marc had no such hesitation, he was already moving toward Jonathan, at least attempting to be inconspicuous rather than merely yelling and charging. But I already knew it wouldn't be enough. He was no match against a gun, former cop or not. All it would take was one second, and his life would be over.

In slow motion, I saw the moment that it happened. I saw when Jonathan caught a flash of movement in his peripheral vision and assessed which of the two threats facing him was most pressing. And as I knew he would, he turned on Marc.

An instant was all I had, but I used it, bringing my newly freed fingers up to my mouth and letting out an ear-piercing whistle. It had the same effect as Grayson's dramatic entrance and drew the attention of everyone in the room. I heard the moment Grayson's fist collided with the other man's jaw, and then the distinctive crack of that man's neck. A second later, Jonathan's gun went off.

I gasped, unsure what had happened, my body was going into panic mode and was trying to search for any sign of injury. But Marc yelled out at that same moment, and I knew it wasn't me who had been hit. I turned to see Marc cradling his shoulder. He barely noticed as Jonathan swung his gun out toward me instead. Marc was still standing, hunched over in shock, but alive.

I, on the other hand, might not be for long.

"Shit, shit, shit." I dove toward the floor at the same time as the second bullet left the chamber of Jonathan's gun, and I could've sworn I heard it whizz over my head.

I was lying face down on the ground, perfectly aware of exactly how helpless I was. Once I flipped back over, using my arms to push myself off from the ground to standing again, Grayson had already tackled Jonathan, sending the much smaller man down to the ground. But it was still a less-than-perfect situation, as Grayson's back had somehow caught fire in the seconds I'd been looking away. I didn't know if the Hand of the Archive was capable of anything magical beyond shifting into the form of a bird, but we were all aware that Jonathan could do much more.

But Grayson was fighting through the pain all the same, and had managed to pin Jonathan's arms out at his sides. I ran toward the two of them as soon as I could, and even I could see that Jonathan was beginning to form the words for a spell to damage or even kill Grayson. Moments later, Grayson's head forcefully slammed into Jonathan's mouth, cutting off whatever he was going to say. I had nothing on hand, no water, no blanket, nothing to put out the fire, so I threw my own body down on top of Grayson's hoping it wouldn't distract him from what already had his full attention. "It's me," I grunted out as I flew downwards toward Grayson's flaming back, hoping my body would be enough to cut off the oxygen to the flame. Hoping that magical flames responded to oxygen. "You're okay, I promise."

Nothing about this felt like it was going to be okay, and for a second I felt the heat of fire sear through my clothing and tickle my skin. But a moment later, the heat and flame died out. But not before I'd cried out in agony.

I rolled off Grayson's back, as quickly as I'd landed there, and righted myself.

It was enough of a distraction for Jonathan to wriggle one of his hands free, and I could see him moving for the gun that had fallen only a few feet away. I grasped wildly, trying to pick it up before he had the chance, but I was too late.

Marc got there first, and held the cold black metal in his hands for only a second before pulling the trigger.

The third bullet going off was just as loud and disorienting as the first two, but this time, the gun's owner had been its target. And this time, the gun's wielder hadn't missed.

Jonathan didn't have so much as a chance to yell out before the bullet pierced his skull. He went limp instantly. Half a second later, Grayson stopped fighting against him, and slumped over.

From the way Grayson's eyes were already darting around the room, looking for the next threat, the next thing he had to attack, I knew he was at least not in any immediate danger of keeling over and dying himself.

Slowly, achingly, he stood up. The three of us stood there, alive but stunned.

We'd made it.

Between Marc's shoulder and the burns that both Grayson and I had, we were a sorry looking group, but at least we were in far better shape than Jonathan and his underlings.

It was strange to think I now had a life where people had minions, but I'd quickly come to accept it as part of my reality.

"You both okay?" Grayson said, once we'd all caught our breath.

I nodded and Marc grunted out a yes. "Took you long enough," I said, trying to keep my voice light, trying to relieve the tension. As if that was even possible.

"It was Jonathan's system for tracking you," Grayson explained. "Devon pointed it out, but it took way too long to figure out how to make it work. He didn't exactly share his idea with the group. And then, while we were inside the Archive, the spell he'd used should have shown you on a map. Except, it couldn't see past Devon. Probably deliberate. But it was Eliza who thought to try it again once we were outside, in the city. We'd been searching for hours already, and there was no sign of either of you no matter what spells we tried or methods we used. But there's a reason that Jonathan lead the Archive, there are few in the city more powerful than him. Once we tried the spell again, map in hand standing out in the street, it showed us exactly where you were. I don't know exactly how he set it up, but in the end, it doesn't matter. Reinforcements should be on their way, not that they'd be any use now. But flying here was the fastest way."

I gave a grateful nod. "Not sure what would've happened if you'd shown up a few seconds later." Even as I said the words out loud, I knew perfectly well what would've happened.

"What I want to know," Grayson said, "is what exactly I missed here. I can't make sense of any of this." He shifted around the room, taking it all in. "We suspected Jonathan was involved, or at least that he knew more than he was letting on when he kept disappearing. But I thought he'd come to help you, I didn't expect him to be the one to blame for all this. And I still can't put the pieces together."

I did my best to help Grayson along, explaining as much as I understood, with Marc filling in a few of the blanks. I still couldn't say I really understood what happened.

"I always knew Jonathan had some unconventional ideas, at least as far as librarians are concerned." Grayson lifted his hand to run his fingers over his jaw, scratching at an itch. "It was something I liked about him. For as long as I've known librarians, even before I was one of them, it was impossible to miss just how caught up in doctrine they can get. They do things their way. I mean, we do. And that's all there is to it. Jonathan had been one of the first I'd met who realized that things are changing around here, but I hadn't realized to what extent his mentality had shifted. I can't believe..." Grayson shook his head. "I can't believe any of this. It's far too bizarre.

Grayson turned away, giving me my first real view of his back. Both his jacket and shirt were burned away, and red, angry skin stared back at me.

"God," I said, mostly under my breath. "Are you okay?" I hoped to myself he had some supernatural healing ability, but the wound didn't seem to be getting any better, no matter how long I looked at it.

"Thanks to you I am," Grayson said as he turned back around. We both looked down toward my stomach at the same time. My shirt hung around my midsection in a few tattered scraps, but the burns themselves were far less severe than Grayson's, though still red and angry. I'd have scars for the rest of my life, but at least I'd have more of my life to enjoy.

"What do we do about these guys?" I asked, looking down at Jonathan and then the guy whose neck Grayson had broken. But as I turned to the third body, I couldn't find it. It had completely disappeared.

I turned around frantically, trying to remember where he'd been lying when I'd fished the keys out of his pocket. But that spot was empty. "What the hell? I think maybe one of them got away." My heart thudded in my chest. I couldn't take another fight, not now. Not ever.

But Grayson didn't look as alarmed as I felt. "It's okay, he's gone. The other two should disappear shortly, as soon as the After is ready to redeposit them back at the beginning of their journeys here."

My pulse settled, but only a little. "Not Jonathan," I said. "He wasn't a character from a book. So, he doesn't have a before to go back to."

"As with everything here, it depends. If I know Jonathan, and I'm not sure I do anymore, he'll have found a way to protect himself since he was able to control where and when your bodies reappeared in the After. We'll have to wait and see what happens to his corpse."

"No thanks," Marc said. "If it's all the same to you, I am done with this place. Never thought I'd say this, but I wouldn't mind getting back to the Archive, and back to my bed. At least if you have someone there who can see about this bullet wound."

"Doctor Maiz is on call for exactly this kind of thing, when we're not ready to share recent events with the city of Sanctum. If it will help the Archive, she'll come. But if you think I'm going to let you guys wander the city alone on your way back to the library, I wouldn't hold your breath. As soon as backup arrives, we will get out of here. But I'd much rather take a car then have to walk if it's all the same to you."

With perfect, almost paranormal timing, the front doors to the building swung open at once, revealing a white-haired girl, frantic and bow-wielding. "Hands up." Eliza yelled the words, arrow already nocked and pointed straight for Marc. A second later, a look of surprise crossed her face. "Oh. I guess I missed the excitement."

CHAPTER TWENTY-FIVE

Piling out of the van that had been sent for us, we returned to the Archive, exhausted and bloodied. Marc was still cradling his injured arm, and even Grayson walked a little slower, a bit more measured than I was used to seeing him walk.

At least Grayson knew several passageways through the city that would get us from where Jonathan had been keeping me and Marc, on the very outskirts of the westernmost quarter of the town, and back to the Archive.

Right as we reached the top of the stairs leading to the front door, my legs groaning in protest with every step, I felt a gentle tug at my wrist. I turned to see Grayson watching me, a strange mix of emotions across his features. Eliza and Marc continued inside, oblivious that the other half of their group had stopped.

"What's up?" I asked softly, trying to figure out what the Hand of the Archive could have to say to me that he didn't want to say in front of the others.

Grayson dropped my hand, but not my gaze. "I just... well... are you alright?"

I didn't answer right away; sure that the answer was obvious. I was a few notches down from alright. In fact, I was barely standing. But something in the way Grayson's eyes stayed locked on mine suggested there was something more to his question. Something that I was far too tired to even try to understand.

"I'll be better once I have something to eat." Grayson's mouth twitched a little at my answer, but he didn't respond. And he didn't head back inside. "Are you okay?"

To my surprise, Grayson shook his head. Despite the damage he'd taken in his fight against Jonathan, it was still hard for me to see Grayson as anything other than indestructible. "Today, realizing you were missing, that was terrifying. And then seeing you lying on the floor, gun to your head... if I'd been even a few seconds later..."

I reached over, taking Grayson's hand in mine before I could talk myself out of it, and gave his callused fingers a gentle squeeze. "But you did get there. I owe you my life, probably a few times over now."

"You don't owe me anything."

"Right," I said, still struggling to form a coherent thought. "Protecting people like me is kind of your job, right?"

Grayson's solemn expression finally faltered, and then, only for a second. "I would have done the same no matter... I'm just glad I made it on time."

"Me too."

"But we should probably get you looked over. You've been through more than enough already."

Something inside me wanted to stay out there on the steps with Grayson for a few moments longer, just holding his hand and enjoying the fact that I was still breathing, but the consequences of the last day were waiting for me, and I wasn't all that certain that I could stay standing for much longer.

Once we entered the lobby, I didn't bother waiting for instructions. I sat on the nearest armchair and flopped my legs over one side, letting out a loud groan. Marc sat on the chair beside me.

Eliza didn't bother going for a chair and instead star-fished out on the carpet. She had spent a solid hour running around and playing go-between once the rest of Grayson's protectorate had arrived, too late to help, but thankfully more than willing to assist with the aftermath.

Grayson had gone before I had even got to sit. I had to assume he had far more follow-up to deal with from all this than the rest of us. And that was saying something.

One of the councilors was dead. Maybe not dead in the usual sense, but for all intents and purposes. And for all we knew Jonathan was dead for good.

But that was too much to hope for.

For the first time since I arrived, the Archive closed their doors to patrons, only giving out a five-minute warning before closing and then kicking out anyone who was still inside. There weren't many people to guide outside, but every single one of them gave our little group a strange look on their way out. We must've made quite the scene.

I only stopped defiantly staring back at each of them and any librarians who stopped to gawk once Doctor Maiz arrived to see to our rooms, bandaging Marc's bullet wound right there in the lobby.

But the real change came once Grayson returned to collect me and Marc. This time, no escort to the councilors' offices to be interrogated, instead Marissa and Joanna met us in the cafeteria. To my surprise the Heart of the Archive put out a plate of grilled cheese sandwiches in front of us as we sat down. A peace offering, I was more than willing to take.

A second later, Devon appeared, unhindered and unescorted. Apparently, what happened that day was enough to get him off the hook, which probably hinted at just how much of our story Grayson had shared with both women.

Too tired to care what everyone would think of me, I shoved half a sandwich in my mouth and chewed greedily until the bread had softened enough for me to swallow it down. It only took me two bites to finish before I moved on to my second serving, and a glance to my left showed me that Marc was keeping pace.

The councilors all sat, no one bothering to interrupt us with questions as we ate our fill. I could tell Devon was less inclined to mind his own business, but the look of us must've been enough to have him keep his thoughts to himself for just a little bit longer.

"Well," Joanna said once everyone had stopped eating and had regained a little of their focus. "The good news is that all your names have been cleared." She nodded in turn at Marc, Devon, and I. "Grayson has assured us that you had nothing to do with your arrival here and, and that you were telling us the truth about your abilities before. And I am sorry to hear about what happened to you. It wasn't fair," she said finally. For the first time, I felt she was being entirely sincere, and finally seeing us as more than merely an inconvenience. Or a mystery.

The question remaining now that our mystery had been solved, was what to do with us.

"That means you'll let us go?" Marc asked right away.

The three remaining councilors all shared a long look that strongly suggested that that wasn't something they'd discussed during their meeting together.

"I don't know about that—" Joanna started to speak, but Grayson cut her off.

"You were never prisoners. You never have been. We kept you here for your safety, not because you were under suspicion."

Devon scoffed.

"Yeah, that's what I keep hearing," Marc said. "And yet, here we are."

"There's a lot to discuss," Joanna said. "But we're including you in the conversation."

"Well there's an idea," Devon said. "Why didn't anyone think of this sooner?"

Rather than chiming in that I wholeheartedly agreed with him, I shot Devon a look that I hoped suggested that this wasn't the best time to be antagonizing anyone. We still didn't know what they had discussed while we weren't around to hear it.

"What I still can't figure out," Grayson said after chugging down an entire glass of water in one long series of gulps, "is why either Jonathan or the Literati would have bothered hiring mercenaries to hide the evidence of what had happened, after the fact. It was to their benefit to keep you here, not to send you back to your original story."

I blanched a little, suddenly nauseous but grateful that no one was looking at me. I hadn't even considered that the threat wasn't over just because Jonathan was dead. He wouldn't have been the one to hire those mercenaries to attempt to get rid of anyone who had arrived here on the same day that I was.

"could be that the Literati were trying to cover up the mess he made in their name, after the fact?" Joanna said. While she had tied her black hair up in a messy knot at the top of her head and she wasn't wearing any makeup, she still managed to look far more elegant than anyone else in the room. That said, her eyes did look a little more worn around the edges, like she hadn't had enough sleep in far too many nights.

"Actually, that was me," Marissa said, her statement so matter-of-fact that it took me a few seconds to figure out what had just happened. Grayson must've gone through the same thought process that I had, because we all sat there in silence for second before he jumped out of his seat, and slammed his fist down on the table in front of him.

Marissa held up a hand. "You have nothing to fear from me now," Marissa said to me and my friends though she still directed her gaze at Grayson. "When reports of new arrivals started up around the city, I had to act at once. I knew there was no way that a change this big would occur naturally in the After, all at once. There had to be other forces behind it. And I can see now that I was right in my initial assumption. So maybe I acted a little hastily but with good intentions."

"Hastily," I said, my voice louder than I intended. "People died. Or..." I was too tired to make sense of the exact terminology. "We could have died."

"Marissa, what the hell were you thinking?" I was a little surprised at the tone Grayson was taking with the woman who had once been his mentor, but I shared every ounce of his outrage.

"I am the Heart of the Archive. It is my job to interpret its will, and I have been doing so for longer than you've been alive. And again, I remind you, I was not wrong."

Joanna put her hand on the other woman's shoulder. "Marissa, a decision like this was not yours to make alone."

"I had to act quickly. I had hoped I could do away with any evidence of what had happened, and then have time to get to the bottom of it before we were dealing with any consequences. Unfortunately, it didn't work out quite that cleanly."

"Thank God for that," Devon said. I looked over at him to find his usually friendly and open expression, which had shifted to distinctly pouty recently, had morphed into something far darker. It was hard to judge exactly who Jonathan's and Marissa's actions had hurt the most, but the way Devon had been treated right from when he'd showed his power, up until he'd been freed less than an hour before would've been enough to make anyone angry. It was enough to piss me off on his behalf. My behalf.

On Harper's behalf.

"And we can assume that you are also responsible for wiping the memories of those same mercenaries after you were done with them?" Grayson said, snapping out the words.

"The Order of Pheneus knew what they were getting into when they took the job. I paid very well to have them respond to the threat immediately. But after a couple of days, the leads dried up and I knew my chance of a complete erasure of the event was impossible. We already had these three in our care, and even I am not so heartless as to send them away after seeing their faces. After hearing their stories. And I'm glad now that my plan didn't work quite as well as I had intended, but my intentions were always to protect the Archive. You can't fault me for that."

"I sure can," Marc said under his breath but at a volume that absolutely everyone could hear.

I gave him what I thought was a sympathetic smile before he cleared his throat and continued. "So, we know that there won't be any other mercenaries coming for us," Marc said, talking slowly as if forming his opinions as they came out of his mouth. "Then you have absolutely no justification to keep us here any longer. We're as safe as anyone else in the city, and we have the right to make our own decisions."

After a long moment, where I wasn't even sure what kind of response I was hoping for, Grayson spoke. "You're right, of course. You'll be free to go." He looked over at Marissa, challenging her rather than waiting for her approval.

"I'll do you one better," the older woman said. "Because like it or not, the city isn't set up to take on new arrivals like yourselves. You're going to need places to live, jobs. And we can help, with at least a little bit of that. Long enough to get you settled, to offer you some of what should have been yours by right."

"But let me guess," Devon said, his tone matching Marc's, "we're going to have to stay here a little longer to make that happen. Just a few more days where you can watch over us, and make plans for us without letting any one of us weigh in on our futures."

"Only one day," Marissa said, "give us one day, and we'll show you what is available, and you can decide whether you want to take it, or if you want to set off on your own. Either way, we'll make sure you're taken care of, at least for a while."

Joanna chimed in. "But don't forget, just because you weren't brought here by the Archive after all, it doesn't mean that your presence isn't remarkable. There are still going to be people who want to control you."

Devon and I shared a look. A lot of those people were right here in this room with us in my opinion but it was one I thought it best not to share right then.

"We'll manage," I said, too tired to muster up any real snark.

"One day." Marc thought about it and finally agreed. "I'll stay here for one more day, but then I'm leaving."

Devon and I nodded in agreement. I wasn't sure I was looking forward to the opportunity to be out on my own, but at least I could trust my own judgement far enough that I knew I always had my best interests at heart.

"And at least now that we know you're not actually prosaic, you are fully capable of defending yourselves as well as any other citizen of the city."

"One," I said, holding up a finger, "it's not like there aren't any prosaics in Sanctum. You just choose not to see them. And two." I raised another finger, "I still don't have any ability to speak of. I'm the same as I always was, except for this." I held up my wrist.

"And we are still willing to do everything we can to help you find out what was done to you. Maybe it didn't work, maybe Jonathan's process wasn't a hundred percent effective. But you have a right to know either way."

I shrugged, not wanting to commit to one thing or another until I'd had some rest and a chance to clear my head. I didn't think that Joanna's offer was entirely altruistic. She was as curious as everyone else in the Archive about what Jonathan had been able to do, whether or not she approved of his motives.

"And now that you're willing to let me out of my cage," Devon said, "you'll be able to do more than poke and prod me in hopes of figuring out what it is I can do."

"I have a theory about that," Grayson said. "I was the closest magical person to you when your powers first manifested, and it can't be a coincidence that you used the same ability I was born with. While I'm sure there are other people with similar magics to what I inherited from my father, it's just too strange."

"You think I copied your power?"

Grayson nodded. "Whether permanently or not, I don't know. And it's entirely possible that you will be able to do the same to other people you meet, mimicking their powers if they're close enough to you. But at least now, we have a theory to work with."

Even Marissa looked a little impressed. "If that's the case, you may end up being far more powerful than the majority of people here who inherited or were given their abilities in a more natural way."

Devon didn't answer, but even I could see that he looked a little smug.

"What about me?" Marc wanted his turn. "Was I copying someone else's ability whenever I could sense lying?"

Marissa shook her head. "Since you've done it more than once, that's doubtful. From what you've told us, Jonathan's experimentation would have a different result every time."

As everyone continued to talk around me, I slumped back in my seat, bringing another grilled cheese sandwich up to my mouth as I tried to focus enough to keep up with everything around me. Both Joanna and Grayson seemed convinced that Marissa wouldn't act against us again, at least not without talking to them first.

And while I was convinced that I could trust Grayson at least far enough that he didn't want to see me dead, it still left me feeling uneasy. Along with absolutely everything else that had happened.

But I was damn well sick of being the victim of other

people's plays for power, or whatever justifications they told themselves to explain their actions. Especially now that it seemed I was the only one who didn't have an ability of their own.

Despite Doctor Maiz spending over an hour with Marc, Grayson and I, my stomach still burned, even as a magical salve worked into my skin doing whatever it was supposed to do. The doc hadn't been able to say whether I'd have a permanent scar, but I knew that whether this scar was internal or external, I'd carry that night with me for the rest of my life.

CHAPTER TWENTY-SIX

While I couldn't say much of anything for sure, I suspected that I fell asleep with my head on my arms at the table in the cafeteria more than once. But my power naps never lasted for more than twenty minutes at a time, even though no one ever purposefully tried to wake me.

Every time someone raised their voice, it startled me into consciousness again, but everyone was always right where I'd left them, still discussing the nuances of the night and all the revelations that had come with it.

I couldn't help but look over at Marissa. She'd been the one who had betrayed Harper, for no reason other than paranoia. She'd almost done the same to me, to Marc and to Devon. I wanted to ask exactly how many people like us she'd done away with before we had a chance to speak for ourselves, but I wasn't sure I was ready to know.

And did anyone know how many people Jonathan had brought through? We still didn't know if he'd been working alone, or if any among the Literati had known his plan. I liked to think that there were more people like us out there that had managed to get away, both from Marissa's hired hoodlums, and from the influence of the Archive.

But Grayson seemed to believe his old mentor when she said that now that everything was out in the open, she was content to let us be. I could tell that not one among the Archive's leading members liked the idea that Jonathan had blessed us with powers we were never supposed to have, but we were the victims in this scenario, and so for now, that would have to be enough to let us stay in the After.

I wasn't sure if they'd feel the same way if anyone started to wreak havoc with our newfound abilities, but at least they knew Marc and Devon and I well enough to at least give them the benefit of the doubt. After everything that the councilors had put us through, they owed us all that much. And of course, as always, I was a non-issue. I couldn't say it didn't sting that I hadn't come away from all this with any magical power to show for myself, but there wasn't exactly a good time to whine about it to my friends.

And because of our supposed abilities, and the fact that we were now at least well enough equipped to survive in the city on our own, assuming Marissa didn't send anyone after us again because there was no reason for the councilors to wait to follow through on Marc's request. Joanna had requested one day to get things organized for us, but then we could go. It wasn't as though they were tossing us out on our asses, and they'd promised they'd have details for us on somewhere we could stay, at least for a while, at least until we knew enough to make decisions for ourselves.

But I had one day left, living in the Archive and as the sun finally rose over the longest night of my life, it was weird to think I'd be saying goodbye to this strange and wonderful place by the same time the next day.

It was that thought, or maybe it was everything I'd been through, but beside a few impromptu naps in the cafeteria, my body had no interest in sleep. So, I decided to spend my last day in the Archive like I'd spent most of the calmer days before, reading.

Marc hadn't wanted to wait and had already gone out into the city, convincing Devon to go with him – whether for company or protection or just someone to talk to, I didn't know for sure. They'd both be back by nightfall, and then the three of us would set off together in the morning.

But I had had plenty of time to explore the city, and to be on my own. For one more day, I could find comfort in the familiar stacks of books in the Archive. I knew I'd be back, but it was the closest I had to a home in the After, and soon that too would change.

I ended up on the fourth floor, in a small sitting area with three loveseats surrounding a fireplace that despite giving off both warmth and light didn't produce any smoke. I wished I'd discovered the space sooner, because I could see it becoming one of my favorites.

The books I picked up had mostly come from the romance section, the one place I could be sure of a happily ever after, but no matter how many first chapters I read, I couldn't seem to focus enough to really fall into any one story.

After a few hours, I put down book number four and picked up the next one, a hardcover book with a sunset over water. It wasn't my book, not the book I'd come from. I didn't even know what had happened to my book, though I assumed it was still safely tucked away within the four walls of the Archive. But this book looked just a little bit like the one I had come from, just enough to leave me feeling restless and uncomfortable all over again.

I put the book down and slumped back into my chair. This was as good a place as any for a nap, assuming my body was willing to cooperate.

I swung my legs over one arm rest, and closed my eyes as I did my best to get comfortable, basking in the glow of the fire.

"I always find you doing the strangest things." A familiar voice interrupted me only seconds after I'd closed my eyes. "You know, this may not be the best place for a nap."

I opened my eyes to find Jamie watching me with a playful smile, leaning against the nearest bookcase.

With an unexpected yawn, I sat up, covering my mouth hastily. "Sorry, It's been a really weird day."

Jamie sat down in the loveseat beside mine, bracing his elbows against his knees as he looked at me. "I heard, actually."

"It's actually the reason I came here today, looking for you."

I sat up a little straighter. "How exactly did you hear? I..." His confession had me at a loss for words. Had the entire city heard about what happened? Was my picture plastered alongside Jonathan's in a citywide newspaper I didn't even know existed?

Jamie glanced away. And I finally remembered the conversation I'd had with Grayson, when he first warned me away from Jamie. Jamie, with the literati ties. Whatever that meant.

"I have to confess something," Jamie said. "I know who you are, what you are. I didn't that first day when we met, but after that..." he trailed off. After that, my mind filled in, when he'd tried to talk to me as I was shelving books with Eliza. When I'd cut him off and sent him away.

When Eliza had told me he was a vampire. This was something that should've concerned me more than him being a member of some secret society I didn't understand, and yet it left me more curious than anything.

"Look," I said, "I don't want to get involved in the political tug-of-war that seems to be going on in this place."

"There are a lot of people who are interested in you, Kadie. But I promise I didn't come here with any hidden motivation. I just wanted to see if you were okay. The people I work for, with, they had nothing to do with what happened to you. I can't deny that the possibilities you offer somewhat intrigue them, and would like to get to know both you and your friends better but in your own time, and only if you're interested. The Literati only works because we are a group of similarly minded people, working toward a common goal."

This was getting a little too philosophical for me. "And what exactly is that goal? Kidnapping helpless people and using them as pawns in your game against the librarians?"

"Not at all. I can see why you might've gotten the impression." He glanced up, looking around at the shelves that surround us. "But it's not like that at all. The people you would've talked to here are more than a little biased against us. But the Literati respect the power of the Archive, and what it represents. We just think there's room for a little more interpretation, for some of that power to belong to the people that the Archive represents."

"Honestly Jamie, this is not the day for this. I am too tired for any kind of sales pitch, and not super interested in getting involved one way or the other."

"You're right, I'm sorry. I really did just want to see that you're okay."

"I am as okay as can be expected," I said, not willing to commit to anything else. I wasn't sure how much Jamie had heard, or who he'd heard it from. If Jonathan really had done what he had to pledge to the Literati, I couldn't be sure that others in that organization hadn't known exactly what he had planned and had done nothing to stop it. I liked to think it wasn't Jamie directly, that he hadn't known, and really was just a guy who liked to read. But there were only so many people I felt I could trust implicitly, and they were the ones in the same position as I was, who weren't trying to push me in any one direction, toward anyone's agenda.

"So, are you really a vampire?" I asked in a desperate attempt to change the conversation.

Jamie laughed aloud. "Who told you that?"

"Does it matter?"

Jamie shook his head. "Guilty as charged."

"You don't look like a vampire. And how are you out during the day?"

"You and I are going to have a lot of fun together Kadie Meyer," Jamie said with a smile. "I think it's safe to say that you still have a lot to learn."

That night, I settled into my room in the Archive for the last time. But with the blankets tucked around me, reaching right up to my neck, I felt a sense of comfort that this place had rarely offered me. And tomorrow, it would all disappear. I was free to visit as often as I wanted, but I didn't know whether I'd be allowed back into the places usually reserved for librarians.

Instead I'd have an apartment of my own to decorate, in a building owned by the Archive, meant to house apprentice librarians. Eliza would be one of my neighbors, and both Devon and Marc would be in the building across the street. I wouldn't be truly alone, but I'd finally have some space, and some privacy.

It was exciting to think that I'd have the chance to decorate and make the space my own, but it was hard to get past the fact that I'd be starting completely from scratch. I wouldn't have any used furniture from my parent's house to fill the rooms, like I had in my first apartment in my life before.

I stared up at the ceiling for a long time, willing myself to sleep. Every time I wondered how much time had passed, or how much longer I had before morning came for me, I pushed the thought away and tried to clear my head.

It worked better in theory than in practice.

At least this time around, my fresh start was one I'd see coming. The last one—or the last two if I was counting my first life in the After, the one I'd never remember—had come like a punch in the gut, violent and jarring. A lot of good had come from it in the end, but I still had the scars to remind me of the cost, and I still felt the weight of Harper's absence every single day.

The two of us probably would have been roommates in my new apartment if things had gone even a little differently. Now, I had so little to remember her by, and every new thing I got to see or do would be one more thing she would never get to experience.

Not for the first time, I promised myself that I'd make the most of this chance, for her if not for me.

Which didn't make the prospect of falling asleep the next night, in a space that was entirely my own, any less daunting. I already had permission to take everything with me that I'd gained since coming to the Archive, not that it amounted to much. And really, most of what I did have was clothing given to me by Jonathan. I still couldn't decide if taking them with me would be an unwelcome reminder, or if I could make myself see taking what he'd given me as one small thread of a silver lining for everything that had happened. It wasn't as though I'd have much of an income with which to build my life. Grayson had bought us a little leeway, but I knew the rest of the librarians wouldn't want to support us for long, especially now that everyone knew that the After had never wanted us here in the first place. We should never have existed, and yet here we were. How well we could trust Marissa to keep her word not to try and do away with us again, I couldn't say.

But I couldn't think about that now, not if I wanted to have any chance at all of getting some sleep tonight. I'd already gone more than twenty-four hours without sleeping, and both my body and my mind needed rest more than anything.

And sleep would come. Part of me worried that if I closed my eyes for too long, something else would change or someone else would die. I didn't trust my reality to stay in one piece.

For the first time in what felt like years I longed for the ragged old teddy bear that I'd had since I was a child. I could remember looking at it that night, right as I answered the phone to get my fateful call from Darren. The idea of having something familiar tugged at me, filling my heart with yearning. Everything was changing so quickly, had been changing every day since I'd arrived in the After, and for who knows how long before then.

Even though that bear had only existed in that one line, in one sentence of one book, I wanted it, or something like it more than anything. I needed to have something familiar with me, something I could be sure wouldn't leave me.

And then I felt it. One moment, nothing, and the next a gentle weight against my feet at the bottom of my bed. At first, I froze in place, worried I was under attack all over again, worried I wasn't safe even in my room deep in the Archive. But nothing moved and eventually I had to open my eyes and sit up. As my feet shifted, I felt whatever had been sitting on them move too and fall away. As I reached for my night light to illuminate the space around me, I could see a lumpy shape sitting at the foot of my bed. In the light, a familiar grey fabric became perfectly clear.

It was Harper's backpack. The one she'd bought on our very first day in the After, the one we'd taken to the park with us to store our food and things we hadn't wanted to carry.

I stopped breathing and slowly pulled the covers away from me, worried that if I moved too quickly I'd wake myself since this was certainly a dream.

But despite how tired my body was, I knew I was still awake. As my fingers wrapped around the bag and pulled it close to me, I inhaled its scent. I didn't know how it had come to me, where it had been, but I was thrilled to have it with me then. Maybe because it was something familiar, exactly what I'd been asking for that moment, or maybe because I knew what I'd left inside.

Slowly, I pulled the zipper open and peered into the backpack. Blue fuzzy fabric waited for me, and in two pieces I pulled out the very same pajamas I'd been wearing when I'd first arrived in the After, just as dirty and worn now as when I'd last seen them.

I knew without a doubt that I'd left it and everything else that Harper and I had accumulated back under the tree where we'd been sleeping on the night she'd been taken.

And now they were back here, with me.

Did I do this? All I knew was I had been thinking about finding something familiar, and a second later the only thing that could have qualified in all the After had come to me, unbidden. Or... Bidden?

There was still be no sign of any magical power I could call my own, and yet I had been the only person who could've known what I was longing for in that moment.

I pulled the pajamas all the way out of the bag and found a few unused pairs of socks, just where I'd left them. Thankfully, the bloodied pair I'd taken off before going to sleep that night had not made a repeat appearance.

Not even caring that it was the coziest outfit I'd ever put on, I changed out of what I was wearing and pulled both the pajama top and bottoms on, feeling comforted all at once.

Tomorrow would be a new day, and one where I could find out for sure if I'd been the one to call the backpack to me. To find out if I had a magical ability after all.

But as it was, I felt better than I had in days, weeks even. And as soon as I crawled back into bed, I fell perfectly and completely asleep.

After the End

LEARN MORE AT
LIFEINTHEAFTER.COM

Printed in Great Britain
by Amazon